Gradiare

Book 1
Hannah Baribeau

This is a complete work of fiction. Brought forth out of the mind of the author for the enjoyment and entertainment of the readers.

Printed in the United States of America.

Cover by Sarah Burkey

Map by Hannah Baribeau

Formatting by Hannah Baribeau

Lovingly edited with the help of family and friends, couldn't have done it without you.

ISBN 979-8-9911903-0-5 (paperback)

ISBN 979-8-9911903-1-2 (hardcover)

ISBN 979-8-9911903-2-9 (e-book)

To my younger self.
Do you see what we did? That's ours!
You did it, kid.

Contents

1

Jewel

The sun rose and shone through the patchwork curtains of the small room, casting a beautiful array of colors that danced on the bare wooden walls of the bedroom. It was a small room, modest and handmade. In fact, the cabin was all handmade and old, but even still, the smell of wood filled the air, especially on a damp morning in spring.

Jewel opened her eyes and watched the blended colors of lights dance on the wall, breathing in deeply that beautiful smell of rain, wood, and even some dust. She burrowed deeper into her quilts, reveling in their warmth and being able to take it slow getting up. She liked this life. No getting up early, no bustling around from one meeting to another, no people crowding in on you saying you had a job to do. Alone, but not lonely, it was peaceful and perfect. At least, that was what she told herself.

Slowly, she sat up and let the quilts fall from her onto the bed. She shivered and quickly grabbed a long, flannel robe. Her long nightgown had kept her warm all night, but without the quilts the damp air chilled down to her bones.

Almost warm enough, she thought.

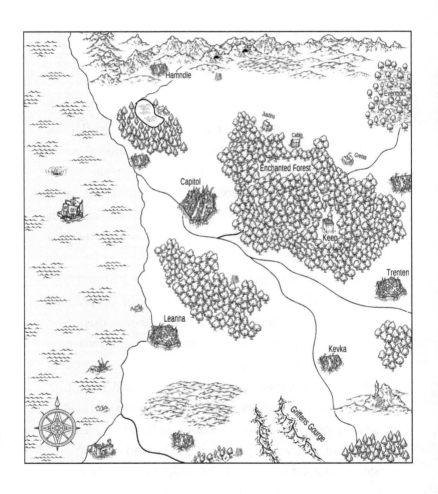

She put on her slippers and walked slowly into the kitchen to get some coffee. As she walked, she unbraided her hair. It had grown very long in the time since she'd moved to the cabin and was now well past her hips. She loved wearing it down, making her feel like a princess in one of the legends of old, something she'd never been able to do before the move. It had been important to keep it shorter and tied up before. Even in the cabin she still had to pin it up to keep it out of the way while doing chores.

It only took a few seconds for her to knot her hair into a bun, and a few minutes more to get her coffee percolating. She then stood staring at the fire, both mesmerized, and thinking of the hardest question she had to answer every day: what was breakfast? A relatively easy decision compared to some she'd made before the move, and yet one that still caused her some hesitation.

She blinked, coming back to the present, and decided a hearty breakfast was in order. Taking a bowl and walking down the narrow steps to her cellar, she collected some eggs and a stale loaf of bread, then searched through the canned goods for the last of her spiced pears. Turning to her meat hooks, she took down her last four link sausages.

Whatever I don't eat now I'll have at lunch, she mused. *I should go to Greta's farm tomorrow and restock some things. Oh I can't; Justin will be by tomorrow with my dairy.*

There was a hissing sound that brought her out of her thoughts and rushing back to the kitchen.

"No, my coffee," she groaned.

The percolator was sputtering and spitting coffee out onto the stovetop, sizzling, burning, and covering the top of the stove with coffee and grounds.

Jewel sighed and took it off the stove. "Well, there went that pot," she said to herself. She grabbed a rag, wet it, wrapped it around a pair of tongs, and started cleaning the burnt coffee and grounds off the stove.

It was a small wood burning cook stove, just big enough for her needs. It had the added benefit of being a source of heat in the winter. Jewel had learned by now that it wasn't nice to clean hot. Something she hadn't been expecting when she moved out on her own was how proud she'd be of little everyday things. The stove was one of those. She took extra care of it making sure the flue was cleaned and that the cast iron was always seasoned well. She couldn't tell if it was because it was the first time she was living on her own, or if it was because she'd hauled it into the cabin on her own.

There, She thought, throwing the rag in the sink. *Stoves clean, and now I'll make coffee and breakfast.*

After the second pot of coffee was brewed and her breakfast was in the oven, she took a mug of coffee with cream from her ice chest out to her front porch. This was the best part of spring; she could use her porch again. After a cold, brutal winter indoors, she relished shivering in the damp air and warming herself with her first cup of coffee.

She breathed deeply of that wet, spring-dirt-scented air. The trees at the edge of the woods were starting to bud with leaves and the grass was turning from brown to green. Out a little way from her porch, down the path, was an old, gnarled yew tree, its twisted branches holding up the large nest of a waren cat. She sipped her coffee and rocked in her rocking chair, watching the waren cat stalk a bird for its breakfast.

A loud crack broke the still morning air. It was followed by a second and a third. The waren cat ran for cover in the yew tree, and the birds flew off to their nests. Jewel set her coffee down and stood scanning the woods for what had made the noise.

Probably some deer, she thought, still scanning the woods for where it would exit.

To her surprise, a man came stumbling out of the trees on the far right side of the small clearing. He was clutching at his left arm, which was obviously wounded. He looked up at the house and collapsed to the ground.

Jewel kicked off her slippers and rushed out to him, inwardly swearing as her bare feet hit the ice cold dirt. It was too early in spring to be barefoot, but she couldn't run as fast in her slippers. She hated running in long skirts and had to hold the nightgown up as she ran to keep from tripping. She skittered to a stop in the wet grass and knelt next to the fallen man, flicking her loosed hair out of her way as she tried to examine him.

Maybe it's time for a haircut. Later. She'd have to think of that later.

He was a tall, well built man with dark hair. She couldn't see his face, as he was lying with it in the dirt, but his arm was what concerned her. She looked at the blood covered sleeve and decided that it had to go so she could get a better look. She ripped off the sleeve and was happy to see that the wound was not deep; long and oozing blood, but not deep. It looked more like a cut from a sword or knife than a wound from an animal. She used a clean spot of the blood-soaked sleeve to blot away some of the blood. It really wasn't too deep, but looked like it had been bleeding for a while. She absentmindedly stuffed the torn sleeve into one pocket of her robe, then reached into the other pocket and pulled out a long kerchief she sometimes used to tie her hair back. As she tied it around his bicep to stop the bleeding she looked around to see if anyone had followed him through the woods.

With the noise he was making, anyone tracking him would have been here by now, she thought. She checked to make sure the bleeding had stopped, then rolled him over and checked to make sure he didn't have a wound anywhere else.

"What idiot doesn't bandage his own wound? Unless you're left handed, you could easily have done what I just did." Jewel stood after wiping her hands on the grass. She groaned as she realized she would have to carry this man back to her cabin; it had to be at least 50 feet or so. She decided to take a better look at him since he was now on his back. His face was hard to decipher under the dirt and grass, but he was tanned and had a slight stubble. Or maybe that was more dirt. Jewel sized him up for a minute; he had to be at least a foot taller than her and was muscular. She sighed. Nothing for it but to carry him.

He's about the size of Ferga, guess it's just like old times.

"You better be a good guy. I'm not going to be happy if I nearly kill myself for one of the king's men." She stretched her arms and flexed her shoulders. Bracing herself, she grabbed his right arm and the left front of his shirt so she wouldn't hurt his arm more. She sat him up and, leaning forward, braced her shoulder into his stomach. Slowly, she leaned back and stood so he was lying over her shoulder. Taking two quick breaths, she readjusted him so she could stand up straight.

"Gah, why are men so heavy? You big idiot. You better not eat me out of house and home," she groaned, taking a few stumbling steps forward. Even at her full height and with him half over her shoulders he almost touched the ground. "Good nightgauls, sir, what did your mother feed you?"

Jewel slowly walked back to the cabin. Her feet tingled, numb from the cold; her legs shook and ached from the effort of lifting the man. It had been a long time since she'd done anything even remotely like this.

Well, she thought, *breakfast should be ready when we get in the house.*

"Oh," she sighed audibly, "I won't have leftovers for lunch now. I hope you're grateful whoever you are."

It took a good 10 minutes or so for Jewel to make it to her porch. She stared at the two steps in front of her. Two options faced her: carry him up them and hurt her back and legs more, or skip the stairs and lay him on the porch. *Second*, she thought. She eased him off her shoulders onto the porch, laying him out flat and checking his bandage to make sure it was still secured.

Groaning as she stood back up and stretched, she heard her back pop and crack.

"Oh, I'm too old for this." She wasn't really, but she felt old.

She climbed the steps to her porch and walked neatly around the man to get to her coffee. She finished it in a few gulps and sighed again. Staring off into space again, she saw the waren cat sitting under the yew tree licking its paw, its red eyes looking her in the eyes. She shivered at both the little cat's gaze and the cold.

The man groaned in his sleep, bringing her back to the task at hand. She looked at him with a baleful grimace. Somehow she had to get him into the house and next to the fire to warm him.

That wound needs better dressing too, maybe some stitches just to be safe.

An idea came to her. She pulled her slippers back on and took her empty cup into the kitchen. She then went to her bedroom and rolled up the big woven rug on the floor. She brought it back to where the man was and unrolled it, laying it next to him. She then rolled him onto the rug, trying to keep his arm safe as best she could in the process, then began dragging the rug back into the cabin and into the kitchen.

The kitchen wasn't the biggest room, but it was the warmest. It was ideal for cleaning the wound since there was a sink and open floor space for the rug.

Jewel sighed. She hadn't done this much heavy lifting since she'd installed the stove. She poured herself more coffee with cream and sipped it. Then she remembered

breakfast. She quickly washed the remaining blood off her hands, then pulled out two pans. One a beautiful oven bread custard with spiced pear, the other a sausage bake. She set them on the countertop to cool, breathing deeply the wonderful spicy and savory smell.

Focus, Jewel. There's some stranger bleeding out on your kitchen floor, she reprimanded herself. *No, it's fine, he's not bleeding out and I can't waste food to burn. Ok, that's out, now focus on this guy.*

She set a kettle of water on the stove and went to the bedroom for her medical kit. While she was in her room she quickly got dressed and hurriedly braided her hair. She picked out a simple green dress with short sleeves, and a nice brown wool sweater. She braided her hair and pinned it in a crown around her head so it would be out of her way. Her last step was pulling on thick socks and her warm, short boots. They had the double benefit of keeping her feet warm, and her hem from brushing the floor so much.

Her medical bag wasn't too big, but it was full of all the essentials she could need. She always made sure it was well stocked and ready for any injury, especially with her tendency for them.

The kettle was boiling when she got back to the kitchen. She took out a clay baking pan and poured the boiling water into it. Then dumped it into the sink and filled it again. She set the medical bag on the table and pulled out some needles and suture thread. She found her sealed wax packet of gauze and another one of bandaging. Then pulled out her surgical pliers and shears and put all the metal items into the boiling water. Then she rolled up the sleeves of her sweater, washed her hands thoroughly, and grabbed a bottle of strong alcohol that she kept for just such an occasion.

"I'm very sorry, but this will hurt. I really hope you stay asleep for this part."

It didn't take her long to sew up the wound and put a new bandage on it, making sure to cover it with a special ointment that Greta had given to her. She'd said it would keep away infection, and while Jewel knew how to clean and dress a wound she was always nervous she'd missed a step and infection would set in.

She sat at the table sipping her coffee and staring at the man laying on her kitchen floor. He had stayed asleep while she cleaned his wound and stitched it up, but now she wondered if he would wake up at all.

She had cleaned his face of dirt and grass, and while she had never been a boy-crazy girl, she had sisters who were. Tall, dark, and handsome. That would have been how they would have described the man. He was tan and had slightly rugged features, and it had turned out to be stubble. His hair was black and curling. When she had checked his eyes to see if he might have a concussion (he didn't), she had discovered his eyes to be a nice, comforting brown.

But really looks don't matter, she thought. *He could be the most handsome man in the world but if his character is ugly he'll always look ugly.*

She stood and started to plate herself some of the breakfast. "If you lay there all day there'll be no breakfast left for you." She had been talking to him like this the whole time but this time when she turned around to glance at him she nearly jumped out of her skin. His eyes were open and he was staring directly at her, looking slightly confused.

"Heavens above!" Jewel shouted, "Say something next time, don't just stare at someone."

The man gave a tired and crooked smile. He groaned as he sat up. "I wasn't staring for long; just opened my eyes." He looked down at his wounded arm and made a face. "Did you bandage my arm?" He then looked around at the kitchen and at Jewel. "How did I get in here?"

"I carried you, you giant. And yes, I bandaged and stitched you up."

"Where am I? Last I remember I was running through a woods," he groaned again and leaned against the wall.

"Yes, you came crashing out of the woods disturbing my peace and then passed out."

He furrowed his brow and looked at her with a questioning glance. "Wait, you carried me? You and all 90 pounds?" he scoffed. "Sorry, I don't doubt that you're strong, but I'm at least a foot taller than you and you look like a child could lift you." He gave a chuckle at the thought of her carrying him.

Jewel glared at him while he laughed at the idea of her carrying him. "You done yet? Because I can just kick you out to whoever you were running from. I'm being nice by taking care of you but I don't have to."

"Sorry," the man said, clearing his throat. "I'm very grateful for the help. I'm Pendry," he said, holding out his right hand.

"Jewel," she said, handing him a plate of food rather than shaking his hand. She poured a cup of coffee and cream and gave it to him. She then filled a plate for herself and took it to her spot at the table.

"Now, Pendry, before you take a bite I need to know: good or bad? What side of the law are you on? And don't lie because I hate when people lie to me, and I know when someone is." She fingered the butter knife that was on the table, debating if she would need to kill him.

Pendry slowly stood and set his food and coffee at the table and pulled the only other chair up to the table. "Well, that's not an easy question to answer. I'm a peace officer, so I'm on the side of the law, but I found out something I shouldn't have and now I'm running from the law. Is that an ok answer?"

Jewel nodded slowly, letting go of the knife, "Nuanced answer to an nuanced question. I'm satisfied with that answer. You can eat."

Jewel pulled her sweater around her as she sipped her coffee and watched Pendry eat.

A *peace officer, and wanted by the law. This could be interesting.*

2

Pendry

P endry ate. He tried to not eat like a ravenous animal, but he also felt as if he'd never eaten food this good. It was warm and comforting and filling. He glanced across the table at the woman sitting across from him. She was a slight woman with pale skin. *She's cute*, Pendry thought. He liked her freckles and dark green eyes. Her hair was obviously long as it was wrapped around her head in a braided crown; it was brown with reddish hues that shown through. He couldn't picture this small forest girl carrying him. If this was the house he had seen before passing out, then she had carried him a ways.

No, she doesn't look like she could lift me let alone carry me any distance, there has to be someone else here.

He kept expecting someone else to come into the kitchen, but no one did. She had to be telling the truth. Although he was having a hard time wrapping his head around the idea of it, there seemed no other explanation.

He finished his food, sighed contentedly, and leaned back in his chair. "That was unlike anything I've ever had," he said pointing to his empty plate.

"I find that when one is tired they tend to feel that way, and it helps that you're suffering from blood loss and fatigue," Jewel said, finishing off her own plate of food. "But thank you nonetheless. Now that you've eaten, I need to know this story of a law man running from the law. We can talk more in the parlor."

"Ok," Pendry said hesitantly, giving her a quizzical look. *Did she just say that my blood loss helped her food taste better?*

They moved to the parlor and sat in some of the biggest and comfiest chairs that Pendry had ever seen or sat in. He had to fight the urge to take a nap right there. He was exhausted after his run through the woods.

That's not something I want to do again, He thought as he remembered the experience.

"Now," Jewel said, sitting in an equally comfy large chair. He couldn't tell if she made the chair look bigger or if it made her smaller. She set her coffee on a nearby table and, from a basket below it, pulled out some knitting. "Begin at the beginning. I don't need in-depth detail, but I do like knowing enough background information to have a solid base."

Pendry raised an eyebrow. She had an air about her that contradicted the way she dressed. *Who is she?* he thought. Her attitude was very commanding as if she was used to giving orders and having them followed, and yet her casual knitting had the effect of telling your grandma about your adventures in the neighbor's yard.

"Right, well," he leaned back in his chair and thought of where to start. *What's the beginning of this? Probably when I became a peace officer.* "I became a peace officer about eight years ago, after finishing my training in two years. I loved the job; always believed in keeping the peace and helping those in need. And I didn't mind the attention that the uniform brought," he said, smirking at Jewel, who stared blank-faced back at him until he continued. *Ok, not that kind of girl.* "Ehm. I made Sargeant three years after that, number 5729 of the 10th ward. I'm not sure if you're from the capital, but there are 11 wards and the higher the number, the closer to the castle you are. That is to say, my rank and position were good. And to top it off, a number starting with 5 is in good favor with the chief of officers. Anyway, I'm on my path to rise in the ranks, ready to become captain of the 10th. There's a get together party thing for the higher ups, and I get invited. I think they wanted to see if I really was captain material." He stopped at that, looking down at his feet. *Why am I telling her this? She's not someone who can help. Could be someone who could hurt. No, doesn't seem like it. What do I have to lose?* He sighed and continued, "That's when everything went wrong. It was a fortnight ago. It started well, but then the captain of the 11th came to me and said to meet him outside next to the dock by the river a little after midnight. Well I didn't realize that the clock in the hall was fast, so I went out a little before midnight and walked in on the murder, and subsequently the coverup, of the captain of the 11th."

Jewel put her knitting down. "Who did it?"

"The King's Guard, they're the elite soldiers close to the King,"

"I know who they are," she said quickly, waving off the comment.

Pendry raised an eyebrow, *so not a lowly hermit.* "Well they saw me and even though I ran, I woke the next morning to being at the top of the most wanted list and was thus captured by noon," he sighed. *Not one of my finest moments.*

"So you ran and let them kill him, and then you were arrested anyway?" she asked with a very accusing tone.

He was quiet for a moment, not entirely sure how to respond to that. He tried to fathom how this slight girl (or more woman) had the audacity to accuse him in such a way of being a coward and a fool. "He was already dead when I got there, I watched them pull the knife out of his chest and dump him into the river. I also was seen because I took too long to run, so that's how I was taken. And I don't take kindly to your tone; I'm no coward, and what would you know of it? You're what, eighteen, live in the woods, and have nothing of a peace officer about you. You know nothing of our training. We have a code of honor you know."

"I've lived in this cabin for two years, and before that I lived in the capital. I know more than you of that pithole of a city, and even more about the corruption of the peace officers and King's Guard," She said, sitting back in her chair eyeing Pendry with disdain. "I may be young, not eighteen years young, but I've lived more life than you can imagine."

The air felt heavy. There was a tension about Jewel that made Pendry feel she was trying to decide whether or not he was worth keeping alive. "Look, I'm sorry. You have shown me great hospitality and I thank you for that, but I don't think you qualify for giving advice on my situation." He said hesitantly, wondering why he was even telling her his situation. "If you don't mind me sleeping here one night, I'll be on my way tomorrow. I'm heading south to Leanna and I should make it in two days."

Jewel started chuckling. "Oh, you are an idiot. You went north east, and Leanna is south west; it would take you a week to get to that town." She rested her head on her hand, giving him a smirk and a condescending look. "You are a city boy through and through."

Pendry didn't like being called an idiot, or a boy, but something about this woman intrigued him. He'd never been laughed at and called an idiot by a woman, let alone one so much smaller than him.

"In any case, yes, you can sleep here tonight. You'll have to help with the chores and you'll be sleeping in here. I don't have a spare room." She stood up, picked up her empty mug, and handed it to Pendry. "You can start with the dishes."

"Has anyone ever told you you're bossy?" he asked, taking the mug.

"All the time. Come on, I'll show you where the soap and rags are."

Pendry had finally finished the dishes. It had taken him a while to locate where everything went. He was just drying his hands on a dish towel and looking around to find Jewel. She wasn't in the parlor or on the porch. That's where he stopped.

There, standing on the porch, was a small cat. It was a dark gray with brown mottled coloring on it. It had red, jewel-toned eyes that stared at him as its tail flicked back and forth. It was no bigger than a normal house cat from nose to tail tip, but its body was small like that of an older kitten or a young adult cat. Its tail was longer than a house cats' and was bushy.

As Pendry looked at it, he felt transfixed by its eyes; they glittered and shone, a chill went down his spine, and his legs felt heavy and immovable. A low moaning growl escaped from the animal's mouth. It started to stalk closer to him, tail flicking head low. He tried to move but couldn't.

What is this thing?

A stick came flying from the right side of the house and startled the cat so it ran away into the bushes near the cabin.

"Don't look a waren cat in the eyes when they're that close. Did your parents teach you nothing of nature?"

Pendry turned to see Jewel standing at a chopping block with an ax buried into the stump. She wiped sweat from her brow, pulled the ax out, and put another log on the chopping block. She'd taken off her sweater, which was laying on the ground behind her.

"Waren cat? What is a waren cat?" Pendry asked as he walked down from the porch to talk to her better.

"That is a waren cat. They're little wild cats that live and hunt in trees. They have a venomous bite and can hypnotize their prey so they can't move." She swung the ax down, splitting the log. "They're ambitious creatures; think they can take on anything, so you have to be careful when they look you in the eye. If they think you're scared, they can transfix you and bite you."

"I'm sorry, did you say that thing is venomous?" He looked over his shoulder trying to find the small cat, but it was well hidden in the bushes. *Where did it go?*

"Yes," Jewel said, putting another log on the block.

"That can't be real. I mean, I've heard of the legends of magical and strange creatures, but those are only legends." He gave a nervous laugh and looked back at Jewel. She didn't look like she was joking. *Does she always just stare blankly at people?*

She swung the ax and split the log. "Believe what you will, but if one bites you you have one hour to live unless you get the antidote."

She bent down, picked up another log and placed it on the chopping block. Pendry watched, more interested in how she was able to split every log with one swing than he was in some legendary cat. She was very small; muscular but slight. Now that he was standing, he could see that she was more than a foot shorter than him, around 5'2". With her hair being braided up, he could see about four small hoops that hung from her ear. Her face was soft in shape, like she was meant to be smiling and kind, but so far she'd only glared or scowled at him. As she lifted the ax, his eye caught something on her arm.

A tattoo, or maybe a scar? No, scars aren't black. Didn't think her the type.

He tried to look at it closer, but it was hard when she was moving. There was something about it that seemed familiar to him. She brought the ax down again and split another log. He stepped in close and caught hold of her arm.

"What do you think you're doing?" she asked, pulling slightly.

"Ah," he said, holding up his index finger. He put the towel that was still in his hand over his shoulder and pulled up her sleeve. "Now what is this? A tattoo?" he said in a mock shocked voice. "I should have known you weren't the gentle forest girl you pretend to be."

"Pretend? When did I ever say I was a gentle forest girl?" She started to pull harder to free her arm.

Pendry tightened his grip. "Ah ah, not so fast; I know this tattoo. Give me a minute to place it."

The tattoo was of a dagger with a ribbon tied in a bow, with three loops around the handle. Tied to the handle were two flowers, one a dandelion in bloom and the other a dandelion at seed.

"That's long enough," Jewel said, pulling her arm free with a strength that was uncanny for her small frame. "If you've seen it before, it's because I used to live in the capital. And you never said why you thought I was a gentle forest girl. Explain yourself."

Pendry straightened, still trying to place the tattoo. "Hmm, oh, well you dress like a gentle forest girl, I mean look at you. Long dress, apron, wool sweater, and your hair is braided into a crown thing. Who wouldn't think you're a gentle forest girl?"

"Really, simply I dress the part I should play the part? Wow. You're an idiot and a pig," she scoffed as she bent to pick up the chopped wood.

"I'm not a pig, I'm simply saying that at first glance I took you for a gentle forest girl. But now that I saw that tattoo." He froze. Jewel was glaring at him, he had made the mistake of bending down to help and was now face to face with her and she had murder in her green eyes. "I'm sorry if I misjudged you. But really why do you dress like a quiet forest creature if you aren't?"

"Quiet forest creature!" Jewel said with a venomous tone, she stopped and rubbed the bridge of her nose. She reminded Pendry of one of his school teachers from when he was a kid, eyes closed deep breathing, did they all have to look like they were using so much restraint. She took a deep breath and opened her eyes, they had softened slightly, "You're forgiven, but only of misjudging."

Why did I call her a creature? I never do that... that tattoo made me think of creatures. Monsters? Or—"The Gradiare!" It came to him so suddenly that he said it without thinking. He stood up slowly, heart pounding at the realization. "That tattoo is the signet of the gang the Gradiare. That means you're an ex-gang member." He gaped at his own realization.

This isn't good; we're supposed to be enemies, but this... she... no. She can't be one of them.

He stared at Jewel trying to picture her as one of the gang members he'd fought, her attitude towards him suddenly making sense. They were enemies—she shouldn't have even bandaged him. Or at least, they would have been if he was still a peace officer, and if she was still a member of the Gradiare.

"I thought once you were in that gang you were in for life. How did you get out?" he asked quietly.

"I simply said I was done," Jewel said in an even voice. "Now, If you're done gawking at me, you can help me stack this fire wood."

"I wasn't gawking, I'm just processing." He stumbled over his words. The Gradiare had the best fighters, especially those in the capital. His heart raced as he remembered stories of the Lion of the Gradiare, and the nightmare-inducing fights he'd heard of. Thankfully, he was dead.

"Well, whatever it was, you can stop it and help stack the wood. Two are faster than one, even if one is injured and seems a bit slow." She stood up with her arms full of wood, still with a look of annoyance and frustration as she went to stack the wood. Before Pendry could respond, she had walked away.

"I'm not slow," he muttered to himself, "I'm just not seeing it." They had been taught to never face someone of the Gradiare without backup, but he still couldn't see Jewel as one of those fighters.

Maybe she'd worked in the kitchens. Do gangs have kitchens? He continued to think about the situation and try to work out the logistics of it. *She could have been one of their smugglers. Small enough for it.*

They stacked the fire wood in silence for a few hours. Once it was done, Jewel went inside. Pendry stared at the door, rubbing the bandage on his left bicep. He wanted to ask more about why she was there and who she was, but the look she'd given him when he started to ask anything told him that if he wanted to live then he shouldn't talk.

She definitely seems more like a gang member than a forest girl, he thought. *She's feisty and doesn't put up with nonsense, or at least what she thinks is nonsense, and she has secrets. What's not to like? Oh, that's right, she wants to kill me,* he thought sarcastically. *Two years of living out here in the cabin, so she served under the Lion.* He straightened his shoulders and winced at the pain in his left arm. His thoughts continued. *She's a good cook, and can do a field dressing. She chopped this wood and knows about wildlife.* None of that told him who she could be or what role she'd had as a gang member. He slowly walked towards the door, pausing before entering. *Yes,* he thought, *well I'm intrigued. This girl is fascinating. A complete mystery.*

He walked in and took a moment for his eyes to adjust to the dark of the cabin. He heard Jewel in the kitchen stoking up the stove.

He decided to take this time to look around the small cabin. To the left of the entry was the parlor, with the two large, comfy chairs, a small potbelly stove, and a massive bookcase on the wall across from it. In front of him was a small hall that led to the kitchen, and a second door that he assumed was the bathroom. To the right of him was the bedroom, the door slightly open. He peeked in and saw a simple bed and a nightstand full of books.

So she likes books. Maybe she was in information? He walked over to the bookcase to see what books she was interested in. There were an assortment of books, from trapping, gardening and foraging to history, legends and myth. *Ok*, he thought, *she just likes books*. As he scanned the shelf, something caught his eye. Just to the right of the bookcase was a small table with a beautiful gramophone. It was a newer model, and it was well taken care of and maintained. The horn was a dark, black metal, which was why he didn't notice until he was so close to it.

"That was a gift from my family," Jewel said, walking up behind Pendry and holding out a glass of cold fruit juice to him.

He thanked her and took it. "It's beautiful. One of the newest models, right?"

"I think so. I'm not big on technology, but I was missing music out here so my family brought it on their last visit," Jewel said as she watched Pendry take a sip of his juice.

He nodded, "I think that would be the first thing I would miss about the city: the sounds. The smell I can do without, but the sounds are something I just grew up hearing. How did you manage to sleep without the sounds?"

"Oh I grew up going to the seaside and the country for holidays when we needed time away from the city, so it wasn't hard. It's not necessarily quiet outside the city. Besides, I lived on the side of the city that had solid walls." She sipped her juice, staring at him with a stony expression.

Pendry spluttered slightly at her last remark, it was a jab at the fact that the Gradiare was notorious for being well hidden, and when outposts were discovered they were basically fortresses. On the raid two years ago they'd only discovered a small portion of what had appeared to be a well armed fortress. They had never been able to locate the actual headquarters. They didn't even know where it was possible to be. Most likely it was in the capitol, but that hadn't been proven.

"Sorry," Pendry said, wiping his mouth on his only remaining sleeve.

Jewel eyed him closely for a second, then turned and said over her shoulder, "If you're staying the night you should clean yourself up. I have some men's clothes in a chest around here from my dad, and there's some bandage covers in the cupboard in the bathroom, down the hall to the right."

"Um, yes, but I doubt that you have pants long enough for me, I'm not the average height you know," Pendry said, following her to her bedroom door. He stopped and looked inside.

She was kneeling at a chest, pulling out clothes, and looking them over. "My dad was tall and broad; I think you'd be lucky to fit his clothes. They said he was part giant, but I think that was just a rumor." She pulled out a pair of pants that were definitely tall enough for him. Maybe even a bit too tall. She stood and handed him the pile of clothes, including a sweater and socks. "Here. It gets cold at night in this cabin."

The shower was just what he needed. He had been surprised to see running hot water for the dishes, but was very thankful for it with the shower. He kept thinking of the little snippets of information she'd given. She had a family and had grown up going from the city to the country. And what was that about her dad being part giant? There was so much to take in, and he was still trying to gauge if he could trust her.

The clothes were a bit big, but they were clean and warm. He found Jewel sitting on her porch staring out into the woods, sipping on a cup of hot tea. She had a far away sad look in her eyes.

She seems a little young to have that look, he thought as he stood in the doorway. "Thank you for the clothes, and the food and the shower. Still not sure how you managed that all the way out here."

He'd had to roll up the legs of the pants and the sleeves of the shirt. *Her dad really had been a giant of a man*, Pendry thought. He was tall, about 6'5", but this man must have been 7' easily. *How does someone so small have a dad that was so tall?*

He walked out onto the porch and sat in the second rocking chair. *Two, there's room for two everywhere in this cabin but only one person, was there some tragedy, is that why she is so snappy with me and has that far away look?*

"I have to ask," he said, getting up his courage, "why is there two of everything? Two rocking chairs here, two big chairs in the parlor, and your bed is big enough for two. Did you lose someone?" He hesitated, realizing it might be a sensitive subject.

Jewel gave a little laugh, "No, and you should know better than to judge based on what you see." She sighed, "It's a family cabin. My parents had it furnished for them to come to and get away from the capitol when they needed time alone. It was boarded up after my dad died.

That's why some of his clothes are still here. My mom said I could have everything that was in it. That's why there's two of everything."

"I'm sorry. When did your dad die?" Pendry asked, genuinely sad and curious.

"I was fourteen," she said sadly.

"I was eighteen when my dad died," Pendry said. "He was a peace officer. He died protecting the King. That's why my number started with a 5; the King was grateful for my dad's sacrifice and service." He felt a small lump forming in his throat at the memory of his dad.

"Sorry for your loss," she said softly.

Somehow the day had passed and it was already sunset. The birds were singing their goodnight calls and the waren cat was back in its nest in the yew tree, its red eyes glittering in the dusk.

"Are you hungry? It's about time we had some supper," Jewel said, standing up suddenly and walking into the house.

Pendry sat for a minute more watching the sunset. He'd never seen such a beautiful sunset; the capital was so full of tall buildings that blocked the setting and rising sun. He stared in wonder at the beautiful pink and purple of the sun hitting the clouds, a beautiful watercolor of pinks and purples mottled the sky. The sun was tucked behind some clouds and it made for a picturesque scene.

It's not so bad out here. He could see how someone could decide they didn't want to go back to the city. Then he remembered he couldn't go back to the city. He sighed and stood, taking one last look around before going into the cabin.

Supper was just as good as breakfast, if not better since Pendry was able to slow down to eat and enjoy the flavors better.

"Well," said Jewel, standing and putting her plate in the sink, "if you push together those chairs in the parlor you should have a nice cozy bed, and there are some blankets in the chest next to the stove in there. Don't open the front door for anything. I sleep with a knife under my pillow, and I know how to use it." She said it all so sweetly, but with slight contempt dripping from her voice.

"Wait, when you say don't open the door for anything, don't you mean anyone?" He suddenly felt nervous being out in the middle of the woods.

"No, I mean anything. If you thought waren cats were legends then you wouldn't like to know what else isn't a legend." She turned and walked out. "Goodnight," she called over her shoulder.

Pendry heard her lock the front door and then close and lock her bedroom door. He was alone. Alone in a house with an ex gang member, in the woods where legends were real and magical creatures might try and come in. Part of him felt like he should leave and risk it with whatever lived out in the woods, then he remembered some of the legends he'd read as a kid and the strange noises and feeling he'd heard and felt running through the woods the night before. Suddenly the house felt safer.

He went into the parlor and pushed the chairs together, found the chest, and pulled out two big blankets. After wedging himself down in between the two chairs, he waited for sleep to overtake him.

It wasn't long before he fell asleep; the last time he's been this tired he'd been in peace officer training.

What was that saying, run them to the bed or you run them to the grave? No, that's not it. He fell asleep before he could remember the full saying. It was a nice, deep, dreamless sleep.

A scream rang out in the darkness. Pendry woke with a start. It was so dark he couldn't see anything at first. The scream rang out again sounding like someone was being tortured. *Jewel,* He jumped out of the makeshift bed and stumbled to her bedroom door. He knocked fast and hard.

"What?" Came the muffled reply.

"There was a scream," he said, looking around for signs of entrance. "Are you hurt?"

"No, that is the 'anything' that you don't open the door for."

"What in all creation is that?" he asked as another scream rang out.

"Seriously?" There was a light thud and the door of the room swung open and Jewel stood there in her night-gown, her braid hanging over one shoulder. "I thought you said you'd read the legends. That would be the grawn wrathe. They do whatever they can to make you open the door to your house so they can come in. They're completely harmless; they just want to get warm. But once they're in they won't leave, ok? Can you sleep now city boy? They're in cities too. Everyone just assumes it's a person and moves on."

Pendry stared at her. He had never seen hair as long as hers, and for some reason that realization made the whole situation a little more fantastical. "Right," he said, pulling his view from her hair to her face, "So what do you do about the noise?"

"They scream four times, then they leave. It happens most nights when the weather is cold. Now go to sleep." She closed the door.

Pendry stood blinking in the darkness, she'd had a small lamp in her room, or something, and his eyes seemed like they didn't want to adjust to the thick blackness that filled the room. Slowly, he shuffled and felt his way back to the makeshift bed. *Well,* he thought, *that's two legends that are real. Wonder how many more there are?*

3

Jewel

J ewel lay in her bed staring at the ceiling, her knife clutched in her hand. She hadn't slept with a knife in a year, so she knew it wasn't a dream. There really was a strange man in her cabin, and he was a peace officer wanted by the law. That would just be her luck. She sighed, *Guess I'll get dressed.*

She fell back into dressing how she had before her cabin years, lightweight pants and short boots. A loose short sleeved blouse and oversized wool sweater. She stepped out of her room, still fiddling with her hair when she heard a groan come from the parlor.

Guess the chairs aren't as comfortable as I thought they'd be.

"Ugh," Pendry groaned, sitting up, "I don't think that thing stopped screaming last night," he said glowering at the door, "How do you sleep with all that noise?"

"Simple. I don't listen to it," she said, tying her hair in a knot and pinning it securely to the back of her head. In truth, she'd only just gotten used to the noises, but she wasn't going to tell him that.

She walked into the kitchen, coffee on her mind, and wondered what food she could make to eat. She was low on most of her supplies; still had some eggs and potatoes, maybe some cheese. She knelt at the stove and started rekindling the fire from last night.

"I wanted to apologize for yesterday," Pendry said, following her into the kitchen. "I wasn't feeling my best after my run through the woods and I was not thinking well after the blood loss. I should not have judged you so harshly." He leaned against the door frame of the kitchen.

"Thank you. You are forgiven," Jewel said as she stoked the small fire. *I hate when people try to talk to me so early, and especially before coffee,* she thought as she blew on the embers. *Especially people who annoy me.*

"I will say, I don't think I fought any beautiful women when I fought the Gradiare," Pendry said, seeming like he was studying her. "I've never seen hair as long on any of the gang members either."

"Are you trying to flirt with me?" Jewel said, giving him a slightly disgusted look.

"Um..." he started, looking confused.

"Because you can stop that this minute. I'm not some hormonal teen that swoons the moment someone calls them beautiful." She slammed the stove door closed and stood up.

Can I just get my coffee?

"I'm really not good in the morning, again I'm sorry," Pendry said, raising his hands slightly in a sign of surrender. "Is it such a bad thing though to be told that? I've never had someone get so violent from a comment like that."

The disgusted look on Jewel's face was more apparent. "Oh my, evnton wrathes take me away. You really are an idiot," she said, her grip on the poker tightening. "You know nothing about me and yet you think that I'd like a comment like that? You must've lost more blood than I realized." She walked towards him, poker still in hand. "Good thing you leave tonight. Watch out for faie and goblins, and don't eat the candy red apples." She glared up at him, now only a foot or so away.

"Whoa, hang on." He stepped back, until his back was against the opposite wall of the small hallway.

She kept walking towards him as she talked, "You know what? There's the door, and I'd recommend taking it before your mouth gets away from you again."

"Wait, you're kicking me out now? I haven't eaten or packed food or anything," Pendry said, eyeing the poker warily. "I wasn't trying to be rude or anything. I honestly don't understand why you're so angry."

Don't, she thought, you just need food, you just need coffee. Take a breath and take it easy, it's not like it's "him." You're fine.

"Too bad," she heard herself say, "you won't take no and shut up for an answer, and men like you are on the list for why I moved out to this cabin."

"When did you say shut up? When did you say no?" he asked nervously. "I was just making conversation. I'm sorry, can we try this again where I don't talk?"

Jewel ground her teeth and glared at Pendry, who stood frozen with his back against the wall.

Breathe, she thought, *coffee, food. Maybe he just talks unending when he wakes up, just like you get angry when people talk to you first thing in the morning.*

"I'll shut up," He said cautiously, "I'm sorry if I offended you. Most of the women I know like hearing they're beautiful. Now I know you don't like that."

Jewel took a step back lowering the poker. She glared at him, "They teach you to generalize and categorize everyone and everything when you join the peace officers. That's the first thing you need to stop; people don't fit in your neat boxes. You probably got away with a lot of saying the wrong thing just because of that uniform."

"Ok," Pendry said lowering his hands, "again, I'm sorry. I will control my words better."

"Thank you," she said, turning back to start some coffee.

"Can I stay for breakfast and take some provisions for the road? I'm not sure what a candy red apple is but I'd probably eat it if I saw it."

"Fine," Jewel snapped over her shoulder. "And a candy red apple is an apple that is so red it looks fake. It's poisonous, and will put you in a coma for a week before you die from organ failure."

Pendry looked at the front door of the cabin in horror of the world outside. "Good to know," he muttered.

There was a knock at the door and he jumped slightly.

She smirked at him. "You aren't scared of a knock are you?" she teased, then stood from the cupboard and went to answer the door. Pendry stayed where he was.

She opened the door to see an older man. "Good morning Justin," she smiled. *Maybe I'm just snappy because I don't trust Pendry.* "I wasn't expecting you until noon."

"I'm not here with your dairy," Justin gasped, clearly out of breath like he had been running.

"What's wrong?" Jewel suddenly felt a panic rising.

"King's Guard, they came to the farm yesterday," Justin panted out. "They were asking about a man, said he was wanted dead or alive."

It's him. They wanted him, are they hurting people because of him? Jewel thought, trying not to give away anything. She didn't move or change her expression, her grip on the door tightened as she restrained the anger that rose in her.

"They raided my cellar and destroyed half my field. They said if I was hiding him they'd find him and they'd kill us both on the spot." Justin's voice was quavery. "Jewel, they said they were going to the next farm over, that's Greta and the boys. She's been through enough already. I can't make it there on my little wagon but you're still young. I need help."

Justin didn't even finish what he was saying before Jewel turned and was in her room. *Not on my watch. No one hurts her, not again.*

She heard Justin talking to Pendry. "You! You're the man they're looking for aren't you? If I was any younger I'd beat the living daylight out of you and make you pay for the damage they did to my farm."

She came back out holding two packs stuffed with supplies. In her hands she held four short swords. The blades were slightly longer than a man's forearm and twice as thick as a rapier. The hilts were thinner than the blade and made of a bronze colored metal wrapped in a dark red brown leather. They had small, round, ornate hand guards.

"He's wanted by them for a reason, Justin. He may as well be one of us," Jewel said, handing Pendry a pack and two of the swords. "We'll go to Greta's, rest here until you've caught your breath, Justin. When you go, put out the fire and lock up." She strapped the belt with two of the swords around her hips, adjusting them to either side. "I have a feeling these King's Guards won't stop until this man is dead, so I'll be gone for a few days. Please keep an eye on the cabin like you always do and check in every now and then."

"Wait, are you handing me over to the King's Guard?" Pendry asked, slipping the pack onto his back. "And how did you pack these so fast?"

"I always keep a few go bags ready, and your katshme go on your sides, not your back," she said, pointing to the swords that Pendry had just put on the back of his belt. "No, I'm not handing you over to the King's Guard."

Justin smiled dryly at Pendry, "Boy you're in for a treat; Jewel isn't some simple backwoods girl. She's a Gradiare finest, she—" but Justin stopped and cleared his throat when he saw Jewel glaring at him with a look that could scare even the bravest of men. "Thank you Jewel, I will take care of the cabin."

"Come on peace officer, let's see how fast you can run," Jewel said, starting down the front steps and turning down to the left. She started a slow even run into the woods, all thought of food and coffee long gone. Behind her she heard Justin talking to Pendry.

"Peace officer," Justin said, eyeing Pendry up and down. "What foolish thing did you do to warrant a dead or alive wanted?"

Pendry smirked at the old man and started after Jewel, "Sorry, I'd love to stay and tell you everything, but it seems I have to run to catch the wild woman that isn't what she seems."

They ran at a steady pace for about 20 minutes. Jewel in the lead, and Pendry not far behind. She didn't bother to make sure he was keeping up; as long as he was following she didn't care. They jumped over logs and dodged around trees. One moment they were running up a hill, and the next sliding down the other side.

She'd spent her childhood running in these woods as well as running through the Gradiare tunnels. This was nothing new for her. She'd made sure to practice this run for just such an emergency.

She restrained herself to keep an even, steady pace, although she was tempted to bolt the last of the distance. She wasn't sure how used to running Pendry was so she stayed at a slower, easier pace for him to follow.

Can't let her down, Jewel thought, *can't let her do it alone.*

The thoughts of what the King's Guard could do to hurt Greta suddenly filled Jewel with rage; she couldn't hold back any longer and sped up. They broke through the woods and came to a farm. It wasn't a big farm but it was a nice, quaint farm.

Jewel was now sprinting towards the farm. Her hair had come undone from all the running and was streaming out behind her. She ran straight to the small farmhouse. Not stopping to knock, she burst through the door and ran in. Pendry followed close behind.

"Greta!" Jewel called as she started searching room to room, one hand on the hilt of a katshme. "Greta are you here?" She could hear the fear in her own voice as she called out again. "Greta!"

"Jewel, is everything ok? I'm here in the kitchen."

Jewel ran to the back of the house into the large, steamy kitchen. She sighed and dropped her pack to the floor, then ran forward and hugged Greta.

Greta was a big woman, round and tall. She had on a kerchief and was covered in flour.

"Oh Jewel sweet, is everything ok? I haven't seen you like this since late winter when you trekked out here after that blizzard because you thought we would be snowed in and dead." Greta had a big voice, one that carried well but was still comforting. She stroked Jewel's hair as she hugged her. "There there, I don't know what's scared you this much, we're all good here."

"Where are your boys?" Jewel said, pushing Greta back gently but firmly.

"They're out doing the chores, you know how it is, the yaksme are calving and the liontons need to be put out to graze." Greta looked up, seeing Pendry for the first time. "Who's your friend?"

"He's not my friend." Jewel waved off the question like she was shooing a fly. She looked her friend in the eye, "Do you have an alarm to sound for the boys to come in?"

"Yes, but we only use that when there's an emergency or danger," Greta said, suddenly concerned. "Why what's wrong? You're scaring me."

"Sound the alarm for them; King's Guards are on the way and I don't want them to find your boys in the field or your animals." Jewel turned and headed for the door.

Greta ran to a second door in the back, there was a loud bell-like sound that rang out. It went on for a good minute.

When it stopped, Greta came back into the kitchen. She eyed Pendry up and down warily. "You wouldn't have anything to do with what's scaring Jewel would you?" She said, crossing her arms.

"I'm afraid I might be partially involved, not because I was trying to get people hurt or in trouble."

"Who's been hurt?" Greta asked, she looked ready to fight and help all at once.

"No one, at least not that I'm aware of," he said, hands raised trying to calm her.

Jewel came back into the kitchen, pinning her hair up again. "They aren't here, and I see the boys bringing the animals in. We'll head down the road and make sure they don't make it here. And you," she pointed at Pendry, "we're taking you back to the capital. You can either face the peace officers and King's Guard alone, or you can go to the Gradiare and put whatever you know to good use."

Pendry blinked at her. He seemed to be thinking for a minute, then he sighed, "Let's go to the Gradiare."

"Good, get your pack. We leave now," Jewel said, picking up her pack.

"Not without some food for the road," Greta said, snatching the pack from Jewel's hand. "Let me get you some food. Sit and eat some breakfast before you go." She indicated a table full of scones, breads and a pot of what smelled like a savory porridge.

Jewel reluctantly sat down and grabbed a scone. "Fine, but only if it takes less than 5 minutes."

"Deal," said Greta, taking the pack from Pendry. She set them on her counter, grabbed a full loaf of bread and several scones, and stuffed them into a small bag. She then went into a different room with two more small bags.

"Sit and eat fast," Jewel said to Pendry, pushing over a bowl that she'd just filled with some of the savory porridge.

No point in arguing with Greta, and I was in need of something, Jewel thought, though she wasn't going to let her friend see just how much she'd wanted food.

It took them a little over 5 minutes to eat, and for Greta to give their packs back, topped off with food and some flasks of water.

Jewel gave Greta a long hug as they were about to leave. "Stay in the house until noon at least. Don't leave the farm for the next few days, you or the boys," she said to her friend.

"Ok, you stay safe. When you get back, come visit and tell me all about it," Greta said, squeezing Jewel's hands one more time before they headed out and down the road.

Jewel looked back once to make sure the boys were back at the house.

They were safe, that was what mattered to Jewel. She turned back down the road and started that same run heading to the woods, Pendry doing his best to keep pace with her.

4

Pendry

"Ok, I'm calling it. Can we please stop and rest?" Pendry said, gasping for breath.

Jewel stopped, breathing heavy but not gasping like Pendry. "Fine, but only until you catch your breath, then we keep going."

"I'm sorry, I'm not some machine that can go with minimal rest and refuel," Pendry said, hands on his knees panting and gulping for air. "Just what or who are you that you can run like that half the day?"

Jewel squinted at the sky, "It's not even 10 yet."

"Not the point," Pendry said, pulling his pack off and opening it, his hands shaking, all of him was shaking. "Did Greta say she put some flasks of water in here? Ah, there." He pulled out a water skin, pulled the cork out and gulped down about half of it before he resumed panting for air.

I think I have a cramp somewhere, no, just spasms.

Jewel eyed him with a confused look, "I thought you were a peace officer, don't you train? You look like you train."

"Now who's judging who by their looks?" Pendry said as he breathed deeply, he grimaced. "Yes I train, but not in running for hours on end through rough terrain. There's different kinds of training."

I feel like jelly, he thought. *I don't think I've run long distances since I was a kid, and even then it was never this much.*

"Yes, there's also a difference between judging someone on how they dress and judging someone on what their job is and what that would require," she sighed, "but you're right, I won't assume you're strong and capable simply because you have muscles."

Was that an insult, should I say something about it?

She took her pack off and removed her sweater, folded it neatly and put it in her pack then pulled it back onto her back.

"I guess that would be ridiculous to assume I'm not strong when it's very apparent that I am," he said, still gulping air. He followed Jewel's lead, removing his sweater and putting it into his pack. "Aren't you thirsty?" he asked, noticing she hadn't drank anything.

"No, I put my water skin on the outside of my pack and I've been sipping it from time to time so I don't get a cramp."

Pendry stood processing what she'd just said to him. "You've been drinking water this whole time and didn't say anything?"

"Well yeah, why didn't you say you needed a water break sooner?"

"Because," he stopped, how could he say that he was too proud to tell a woman to stop so he could rest and drink. "I didn't know you were drinking this whole time. I thought you'd stop sooner or later."

"Well," said Jewel, smiling dryly at him, "have you fully learned your lesson on judging others?"

"I sure hope so," He pulled his pack back on. "Ok let's continue, but could we please walk instead of run?"

"Yes," Jewel said, turning and leading the way.

Pendry sped up to walk next to her. "Ok, you know my story, so now you tell me your story. How did a young woman join one of the most notorious gangs in all the kingdom and then retire young and go off to live in the woods?" He was now walking backwards in front of her, still trying to catch his breath but trying not to make it too obvious.

Didn't think she could run like that. She isn't even that winded.

Jewel rolled her eyes at him, "I'm not that young and I'm out here to get away from my past not to relive it by telling it to some strange man I just met."

Pendry chuckled, "Well I'm assuming it's a long walk to the capital so you may as well tell me to pass the time."

There was a crack followed by the thudding of hooves. Pendry stopped suddenly, he spun around and blocked Jewel from whoever was coming towards them. From down the path, the sound of horse hooves grew louder coming towards them. Round the bend came the King's Guard. Their long orange cloaks trailing behind them. They stopped as soon as they noticed Pendry. The leader dismounted and strode forward a few steps, he had a smug look on his face.

Ugh, it had to be him.

"Pendry," he said in a mock jovial voice. "I thought you were arrested and sent to the Keep. Did you escape them?" he laughed and looked back at his two companions who had dismounted and were standing close behind.

"Who, me?" Pendry asked in a casual jesting voice. "No, I was sent to the Keep and they decided I wasn't arrested and let me go, all a misunderstanding."

The King's Guards drew their swords, "Misunderstanding, ha, you must think I'm a fool."

"What? I'd never take you for a fool Monty," Pendry said, his voice changing to a dark serious drip. "Only a fool would think you're a fool."

Monty stepped forward sword pointing at Pendry, "Who's your friend? Someone special? How special is she if you're hiding her away from everyone?"

He said it in such a cruel way that Pendry was sure that he meant to do harm to Jewel simply for associating with him. He wasn't going to let that happen. *I can't take them all and win with these little swords, but maybe Jewel can get away.*

With that Monty lunged forward, Pendry reached back for the katshme but felt himself getting shoved to the side. He heard metal hit metal, a gasp, then he hit the ground with a thud. He rolled over to see Jewel standing with his katshme interlocked with Monty's sword.

Monty, stared at her with fear in his eyes, he had been the one to gasp. "What? How? You're dead," Monty stammered out, backing away. There was a fear in Monty's voice that Pendry hadn't heard before or expected from the captain of the King's Guard.

Jewel strode forward tossing her pack to the ground next to Pendry. There was that air about her again, and a glint in her eye. "You're dead." The words Monty had said didn't quite make sense to Pendry.

Jewel started swinging the katshme in her hands. They spun in a circle, slowly at first then faster and faster. All three of the guards' faces had gone white. Like they not only saw a ghost but as if they were facing death itself. The knives were now a blur in Jewel's hands and from somewhere in her throat a growl had started. It was inhuman and otherworldly. It grew louder and louder until she was roaring. She leapt forward, katshme blurring, roar ripping through the air. Monty ran, sword still in hand, practically diving onto his horse leaving behind the other two guards. One guard was already fighting for his life.

Jewel fought in a way that almost seemed like a dance. She used her whole body, kicking and slashing, hitting with knife and shin. And all the while that roar continued, never wavering, never ceasing.

Monty had ridden away down the path, not once looking back to see if his companions were following. They weren't. The first fell, he barely had time to defend against the first blow. She had struck at him with a whirling katshme and when it was stopped by the blade she whirled her body kicking him in the back and bringing the other whirling knife down cutting his neck. He hit the ground gurgling and sputtering, watching his captain ride away. The second didn't last much longer.

Pendry realized the way she fought was with the knives spinning always. If they stopped, her body spun instead. He'd never seen a fighting style like it. And yet something gnawed at the back of his mind, something they'd been taught in the peace officers' training.

The second of the guards fell. He had two wounds, one in his throat and one in his leg. Jewel stood still. The knives stopped spinning. The roar was gone. There was a sad look in her eyes as if she was disappointed in something.

Pendry stood and stared at her. The thought leaped to the front of his mind; he did know who she was and he did know why they were so scared. He felt the blood drain from his face at the realization of who she was. The tattoo, that beautiful tattoo of a dagger with a ribbon tying the two dandelions one in bloom and one at seed, that tattoo that everyone in the Gradiare had. The Gradiare, the biggest gang in the kingdom, the very one they had been working to overthrow.

"They said you were dead; they, he said he killed you," Pendry said slowly, taking a step towards Jewel. "That noise, the way you fought," he stopped looking her in the eye. He felt the sadness from her green eyes, "You're the Lion of the Gradiare aren't you? I remember when we went on that raid and they said you were dead, they said a whole wall collapsed on you." *How does someone survive something like that?*

Jewel didn't move for a moment. She watched him flounder and wrestle with himself. She sighed and bent to clean the knives. "Don't bend your brain trying to work out how the King paints me as the villain but I'm not a bad person." She stood and gave the katshme back to Pendry. "The King says that anyone who isn't singing his praises is his enemy. It's what all the kings have done for a century so my family has been their number one enemy from the beginning simply because we oppose what they say."

Pendry looked down at Jewel, this slight, short woman, who couldn't have been much younger than him at twenty-eight, was the leader of the Gradiare? This girl, who he'd found living in the woods, was the Lion of the Gradiare?

"I'm having a harder time grasping that you, a woman of twenty-five?" He hesitated at the age, "That you are the renowned leader of the Gradiare and that you somehow survived an arrow through the heart and a wall falling on you? I mean I already know the King is corrupt and evil, so the fact of you being an actually decent person isn't hard to face. I was also under the impression that the Lion of the Gradiare was a man."

"I'm twenty-seven actually and I gave up the position of Commander of the Gradiare two years ago when everyone thought I was dead. Now we can keep talking about this as we walk, or ride," Jewel said, pointing to the two horses from the guards she had killed, "or we can stand here spilling every secret to each other until Monty comes back with more of his men to attack us?"

"Oh he won't be back. Monty talks big but he's the biggest coward I've ever seen. Did you see how he ditched his men the moment you got ready to fight?" Pendry said, stowing his katshme into their sheaths and picking up his pack that fell when he was pushed aside. "But I do agree that we should keep moving and I'm grateful for the horses."

"By the way, that's one reason you put your katshme on the side, that and you can't ride a horse with them on your back." Jewel slipped her pack on and slowly approached the horse nearest her. "You do know how to ride?" she asked over her shoulder.

"Mmmm, yes, I was one of the top students in the mounted officer training, it's required if you plan to be captain some day," Pendry said, moving his katshme to his sides. He eyed the horse hesitantly, "The beasts never seemed to like me." *Although I don't really like them after that one bit me when I was a kid.*

"Wonder why," Jewel said, hoisting herself into the saddle. "Come on mounty, show me your skill, or are you all talk?" she said with a slight teasing air about her.

Pendry shot her a confused look, *Did she just tease me?* he thought. *I think I prefer not knowing how dangerous she is.*

"Ehm," Pendry cleared his throat and reached out to the horse. It backed away. Every step he took forward it took a step backwards. Until in desperation he lunged forward trying to grab the reins before it could back up. It bucked, startled at the sudden movement, ears back it turned and bolted back down the path.

Great, forgot to never do that.

Jewel raised an eyebrow at him, "All talk."

He sighed. At this rate he'd be lucky if he had a shred of dignity left by the time they reach the Gradiare head-quarters. "Guess we're riding together," he said, trying for a smile. "Do you prefer front or back?" His smile felt forced and pointless. *You can't butter up someone who doesn't like butter*, he thought.

"You can ride in back since the horses don't like you. Also I don't trust your navigational skills since you thought you were heading to Leanna and were going the exact opposite direction," she said leaning on the horn of the saddle.

Pendry's smile faded as he realized he would have to sit squished on the edge of the saddle between it and her pack. "Umm, do you think the packs can be lashed to the saddle somehow?"

"No. Get on or walk, I'm not picky." She scooched forward in the saddle as far as she could.

Pendry slowly and painstakingly eased himself into the saddle. He took a moment to figure out where to hold on. He almost grabbed her waist then decided after the fight he'd seen that he wanted to keep his hands. He settled with holding her pack hoping it would be safe.

He only just grabbed on when Jewel snapped the reins and they took off. It was a painful, excruciating ride for Pendry, unlike what he remembered from his training. He kept having to readjust how he was sitting, trying to keep some space between himself and Jewel while also maintaining his balance. They rode like that in silence until it was well into the afternoon.

Pendry couldn't stand it any longer. "Stop, please, for the love of all things good please stop."

Jewel pulled on the reins stopping the horse abruptly. "Are you hurt? Was it a run-along?"

"What is that?" he squeaked out as he all but fell from the horse. "We've been riding for hours and I've been sitting on that darn lump in the saddle and trying not to bump you or sit too close because I'm absolutely sure you'd stab me with one of these obnoxious knives, which have been digging into my hips because I had to angle them onto the back of the horse so they wouldn't stab the horse." He took a deep breath, "and my ankles and feet hurt like I've been stabbed with needles, something I don't remember from my mounted training."

"That," said Jewel sliding gracefully down from the horse. "would be the run-along bite. It stings like pins and needles but is completely harmless."

"What is a run-along?" Pendry asked, looking around for the new mythical creature that he'd never heard of.

"A run-along is a creature that runs beside fast moving objects. They're in the city too but people assume it's their mind playing tricks on them. You can only see a run-along when you're moving fast and out of the corner of your eye." Jewel slid her pack off and let it fall next to Pendry. "They can nip at you when you're on horseback, but people usually think their foot fell asleep."

Pendry stared, open mouthed, "Why am I not surprised?" He rubbed his boot then moved to stand only to realize he couldn't. "Gah," he cried out. He rubbed his rear end rolling onto his side. "Next time I sit in front. Oh, I can't. I think the run-along should have just eaten me whole instead of nipping, then I would be out of my misery."

"Do you really have to be so dramatic?" Jewel said, looking around. "There," she pointed to a huge tree, its roots stuck out of the ground like small walls, with the base of the tree creating a small triangular shelter. "Make it to the base of that tree and we can camp here for the night."

"Give me a minute to actually feel my thighs," Pendry groaned, still rubbing his rear.

I'm not being dramatic, is it dramatic to express pain and frustration? This isn't anything I'm used to.

Jewel led the horse over to the tree carrying both packs. She tied the horse to a low branch overhanging the roots and set the packs down.

She then disappeared into the woods. Pendry hardly noticed. He ached everywhere.

Maybe death would be better. Maybe I should have stayed captured by the King's Guard. Maybe... But there were no other maybes. He was so exhausted from running and riding and not sleeping because of the screaming wrathe that he fell asleep lying on the side of the road.

He half woke to the sound of a fire crackling and some-one moving him. He felt himself being lifted and carried over someone's shoulder, then set down next to a warm fire. His eyes flickered open and he saw Jewel putting a blanket on him. *Funny how she can be so cruel and sharp with her words and so caring a moment later*, he thought, then passed out again sleeping through the pain and aches.

5

Pendry

P endry was startled awake, the sound of howls and screams echoing through the woods. There was one sound that rang out louder than the rest, a howling wail that invoked a feeling of dread and panic.

It was pitch black out. Only the glow of the fire casting a light in the small circle allowed him to see what was nearby. Jewel sat with her back to the root of the giant tree sipping on a steaming cup of something. Her eyes were roaming the forest, one hand rested on a katshme that lay beside her. She was humming softly to herself in between sips of her drink.

Pendry groaned, slowly sitting up. "What is that noise?"

"Shush," Jewel hissed at him. "If you talk too loudly it will come here and I'm not about to try explaining what you're hearing. It's the stuff of nightmares so trust me and shush." She whispered only barely loud enough for him to hear.

Pendry slowly scooted closer to the fire, partly because it was cold this early in spring. And partly because he heard a twig crack just behind the root he was leaning against.

I hate the woods at night.

Jewel handed him a steaming cup of whatever she was drinking. He sniffed it, and was surprised it smelled sweet. He blew on it and took a tentative sip. Whatever it was, it was incredible. He felt warmth seep all through his body, suddenly feeling alert and stronger, like it had opened a deep store of energy. The drink was thick and creamy with a sweet caramel-like flavor. But at the end there was a sour almost tart taste that lasted only a moment before disappearing.

Pendry's eyes widened and he stared at the steamy cup. "What magical kitchen witch gave you this incredible drink?" He whispered.

Jewel let out a little snort like she was containing a chuckle. "That would be Greta. She makes a powdered drink for her boys when they're out on hunting trips." She stopped, gripped the katshme tighter and set her cup down. There was a scream from behind them and then a long howling wail. Suddenly the horse let out a long braying noise and disappeared into the darkness, or more the darkness consumed it. The horse hadn't moved, the darkness had simply wrapped around it and it disappeared.

Pendry froze. He hadn't seen what took the horse but it had to be big. There were no drag marks and no noise. It had simply vanished.

"Wha- what was that?" He stuttered in a hoarse whisper, glancing around for something to fight with.

"That would be the evnton wrathe that you've been hearing." Jewel said, speaking in her normal voice. "Anyway, to answer your question, this is crestym, a drink mix that Greta invented to keep her boys awake and aware when hunting or out in the fields on late nights, and it has the added benefit of keeping you warm."

Pendry stared at Jewel mouth half open. "Are you just going to ignore the fact that the horse just disappeared? Shouldn't we go after it?"

"No." She sipped her crestym. "The horse was dead the moment it left our sight. Evnton wrathes travel between space, it's thought that they go to other worlds but no one has ever lived or returned from being taken by one."

Pendry shivered and pulled the blanket around himself. "I think I liked traveling through the woods when I thought all those creatures were legends." *Probably helped that I passed out several times from exhaustion.*

"It takes some getting used to but you learn the sight, sounds and feel of a magical creature nearby. It helps if you don't sleep."

"I don't think that will be a problem. Just keep the crestym coming." Pendry said, sipping on his cup.

"Here."

He turned to see Jewel handing him one of the scones that Greta had packed for them. "Thank you." He took it, suddenly very aware that he needed food. "If we're going to be awake for the night I think it's only fair that I learn a little bit more about you. You said you're twenty-seven and you faked your death two years ago so you were twenty-five. But I know that the Lion of the Gradiare was the leader for the last eleven years, but that can't be right. That would have made you fourteen when you became the leader." He looked her in the eye. She blinked and sipped her crestym. "You were fourteen?" Pendry said, almost shouting it.

"Shh. It's not that big a deal and if you shout you'll draw attention to us again." She put her cup down next to her. "Yes. I was fourteen when I took over the Gradiare. My dad died and the right of succession isn't always straight forward. My four older siblings passed on being the Commander. I could have passed but that would have passed it on to my younger brother who was twelve and I decided not to be selfish and took on the role of Commander."

"What kind of messed up right of succession leaves a fourteen year old trying to decide between being a teen or being the leader of the country's most notorious gang? And you thought it would be selfish to pass." Pendry was indignant. Who were these people to rip the childhood away from someone? "Why did your older siblings pass?"

Jewel smiled sadly, "My oldest sister passed because she was newly married and didn't want the responsibility, or the added stress. She was never much of a fighter either. She chose a quiet life in Leanna and I'm very happy for her." She stoked the fire and added more wood. "My second oldest sister passed for similar reasons, she didn't want the burden of it and wanted to pursue marriage, although she hasn't married yet. She's an excellent fighter but likes her freedom. My older brother, he claimed he couldn't lead, but really he wanted to join the spy ring. I'll admit he does make the perfect spy. And the sister just older than me wanted to be a medic, and she was born for that job, couldn't have pursued that if she was Commander. Mostly my sisters were concerned with finding husbands and not wanting to be in such a masculine role as they put it. And so the role was passed on to me." She sighed, "Honestly none of us were really ready for the role. But I did my best, took over the entire western side of the outer ring and established smaller bases in Leanna and Trenton for training and building our army."

"Army?" Pendry said, suddenly realizing why they had never been able to weed out the Gradiare. "You're not just a gang, you're an army with spies and training bases?" He paused to think, "Why start an army? Why pretend to be a gang?"

"We aren't pretending. We just aren't showing our full hand," Jewel said, sipping her crestym. "We've been more of an army since the time of my Grandfather's Command."

"Why are you telling me this?" he asked, eyeing the katshme, wondering if she was planning to kill him.

She breathed deeply, "Because you can't go back to being a peace officer. Not only would they not take you with the dead or alive warrant on you but you would not be able to serve the same way after seeing the corruption you witnessed," she sighed. "No, there's no harm in telling you what we tell all new recruits.You may as well be a new recruit."

The fire crackled and they sat in silence for a while, each dwelling on their own thoughts.

She commanded an army at fourteen. I think I broke my arm trying to jump out my bedroom window at fourteen.

Pendry looked down at his empty cup, realizing he'd been sipping it the whole time. "Do you happen to have more of that crestym?" He asked sheepishly.

Jewel smiled at him and pointed to a small kettle next to the fire. "I made a whole pot, help yourself."

Pendry grinned like a kid who'd been given a candy jar. He poured himself a full cup being careful not to spill any of it.

"So," he asked, blowing on the steaming cup, "Why did you fake your death? I mean you were causing real damage in the capital and to the King but then you let everyone think you died even after they thought you couldn't since you took that arrow to the heart the year before." He stopped and thought for a moment, "Hang on, how did you survive that, and how did you survive a full wall falling on you?"

"Oh I almost didn't," she said, perking up at this new information to share. "So I'm what is referred to in those old legends and myths as a dragon's blood or gold vein. Its hereditary and at least half of the Gradiare are gold vein."

"I'm sorry, what? The beings who can heal rapidly and are hard to kill? They're real and that's you?" He eyed Jewel warily, "No I'm sorry I've had too many weird things happened today, prove it."

"What?"

"Prove you're a gold vein or I'm just going to accept you're a witch and I'm back in your cabin half dead and none of the odd creatures you keep saying are real are."

He turned to face her squarely, he felt like he was about to have a nervous breakdown.

Maybe none of this is real. She might have poisoned me while I was passed out. What do I do if this isn't real?

Jewel calmly set her cup down, pulled her katshme out of the sheath and pricked her finger on it, then held it out for him to examine.

A bright red drop of blood formed on the tip of her finger, in the blood was gold scale like flecks. Pendry took her hand and looked at the blood closely. He watched as it slowly dropped from her fingertip to the ground between them, But no more blood came out. That was it, the spot where she'd pricked her finger was healed. There was a pink scar but nothing else.

He looked from her fingertip to her green eyes then back, "There's still a scar," he said quietly. "Do you still have scars from your other incidents?"

Jewel pulled her hand back slowly, "Yes." She straightened her sweater.

"But I don't see any scars."

"That's because they're all easy to cover, also the smaller the wound the faster it heals." She eyed him warily.

Arrow to the heart, chest, ok makes sense not to see that. But a whole wall falling on her?

He noticed her hand tightening on the hilt of her katshme. He had been staring at her chest thinking about the arrow that had pierced it and not about where he was looking. He swallowed. The memory of the fight he'd witnessed during the day coming back to him. "Sorry, I was thinking and not noticing where I was looking." He quickly looked away.

Have to be careful, she definitely can kill me and probably wouldn't hesitate to.

Out of the corner of his eye he saw her relax, release her katshme and pick up her cup. "Now," she said, taking a deep breath. "You know more about me so now it's your turn. Do you have siblings?"

Pendry gazed into the fire, he sighed, "No, I was my parents first child and unfortunately my mom died giving birth. So it was just me and dad along with his peace officer buddies." He stared deep into the fire, letting the flickering and dancing flames cast their meditation spell on him.

"I'm sorry. Really I am," he heard her say gently. "Not only did you lose your job and goals but you lost all your family. I can only imagine the pain that must be causing you."

He blinked, no longer mesmerized by the fire. He groaned, "Really, ugh, I didn't think of that. Seriously. Here I am thinking I still have some friends I can turn to, and then you smack me with the biggest reality wake up call ever." He rubbed his forehead, "Why on earth were they planning to make me a captain? Here I thought I was clever and not this dense."

Am I really this dumb?

"I'm sorry. I thought you realized," Jewel said grimacing. "Do you need a minute?"

"Yes please," He said, pinching the bridge of his nose.

He sat for a good while contemplating life and the fact that he had nothing left of his life. Not even friends because they would be told he was a criminal. Then a thought occurred to him suddenly. "They're going to pin that murder on me aren't they?"

"Oh absolutely. They probably already have and that's why they want you dead or alive. They'd probably prefer dead. No court hearing or you trying to tell people the truth. They were taking you to the Keep so I'm assuming they really don't want you talking to anyone."

Pendry flopped back onto the ground and stared at the sky. The trees were so tight and close that no light from stars or the moon shown through.

All I wanted was a nice quiet life, now I get this insanity. Why wouldn't they want me to talk to anyone? It's not like I know anything.

"Greta wouldn't have happened to pack any mood lifting food or drink would she?"

"Um, let me check," Jewel said, digging through the packs.

He'd said it sarcastically but now was interested in the idea that there was something that could help his mood.

She pulled out a small purple pouch, "Here we are. She makes these little sucking candies for when life is just too much. Her son Fin says they taste like sunshine and thunder. He's seven so take that how you will." Jewel held out the pouch and he took one and popped it in his mouth as he sat up.

He sucked on it for a minute nodding, "Sunshine and thunder, I'd say Fin got it right. Whew, a little lightning thrown in there too."

Jewel smiled, moving closer to the fire and pouring herself another cup of crestym.

"How's the arm?" she asked, sipping her cup.

Pendry lifted his left arm and flexed it. *That's odd.* he thought. *I didn't even remember it had been injured.* "A little stiff, sore, almost like a bruise, how did you?" He didn't finish the thought, "Is that just magic or something?"

"Not really, just good medicine and sanitizing." She blew on her crestym, "Actually the plants in the medicine are magical and the sutures are from Greta so I do think there's some magic but none that I did. How's the candy? Feeling any better?"

Pendry blinked, "Whoa, I think that just knocked all the negativity out of me. What and who is Greta that she can make these things and why is she living out in the middle of nowhere?"

"Hmm, that's a long story and not my story to tell. But you did have it right. She is a kitchen witch of a kind. She's part elf. They're very emotional beings and because of that they have developed a magic to treat and care for the emotional and physical well being of themselves and those around them." She smiled and leaned back against the tree root, "As for why she's out here, that is her story and even I don't know all of it."

Pendry nodded, finishing off the last of the candy and sipping on his crestym to wash down the last of it. He shivered, then asked, "I overheard that guy Justin say that she'd been through enough this last year. What did he mean by that?"

Jewel raised an eyebrow at him, "Prying a little into other people's lives?"

Why does she keep doing that, what is the big deal with asking about things? Isn't that how you have a conversation?

"Oh, I'm sorry. It's just, we can't sleep and need to do something to keep us awake." Pendry fumbled over his words, "Although, you could share more of your life story." He smiled smugly at her.

Jewel made a face, something between a glare and a grimace. "Her husband died last spring. I won't go into detail, but it was very traumatic for Greta and the boys. Justin and I have been doing all we can to make sure she's ok and taken care of." She took a deep breath, "As for my life, It's mostly boring, full of politics and paperwork. There were some fun times and sad times and some adventures. But really, I'm trying to move past it all."

"Wow, that told me absolutely nothing about you. I'm very sorry for Greta and her boys. But wow you really are terrible at letting anyone in aren't you?"

"I made that mistake one too many times. I prefer now to take my time with letting people in," she said, nestling back against the tree and sipping at her crestym.

"Fine, but I do have a few questions about that fight yesterday," he said, prodding the fire.

"Such as?"

"What was that? I mean I've never seen knives like these and I've never seen someone fight like that. And what was that roaring thing? How do you do that and fight without passing out?"

She chuckled, "Ok, first, the fighting style was developed by my great great grandma or something, family style only taught to family and high ups in the Gradiare. Second, the katshme was specially designed for the fighting style, we call it Katsa. And third, the roar is a part of the fighting style, it's breath work. Different people do it in their own way. It was supposed to be done quietly, but I could never do that. It's kinda how I got that nickname of the Lion, but it was never supposed to be loud." She finished her crestym and set her cup down. "I haven't been in a real fight since the wall, although I still do my training."

Pendry sat in silence thinking over what he'd just been told. "Ok then. I was never in one of the actual fights with the upper ranks of the Gradiare, but I'd hear stories of them defying gravity and sounding like monsters. I just thought they were made up by scared recruits."

"Well now you've seen it, do you think the description is true?"

"Yes, and I can see why everyone would be scared of you after fighting or seeing you fight." He turned back to her. "Is that why they always said you were a man?"

"Probably, I never heard rumors of me being a man, but I wouldn't put it past Monty to say he lost to a man and not a girl." She shrugged.

"Hold on, he lost to you and lived?"

"Yeah, that was a mistake I made when I was younger. There was a very short time when I thought it would be better to show mercy. He was the last one I let live when they lost." Jewel pulled out a blanket from her pack. She sighed, "Now, since you've had your sleep, I'm going to get some of my own. Keep the fire nice and bright. Most creatures out here hate light," she said, snuggling down and pulling the blanket over herself. "If anything comes close, wake me and don't talk to anyone or anything. Singing is good but only do it softly. There's more crestym mix if you need, and all the flasks are filled with water. Wake me when you can't handle the fear or being awake alone anymore. Night." It sounded almost like she was mocking him as she said the last word in a singsong fashion.

"Night," Pendry whispered back hoarsely. *What have I gotten myself into now?* He thought, sipping his crestym and reaching to make sure one of the katshme was nearby. He looked out into the darkness and saw red eyes looking back at him. A chill went down his spine. *I'm ready to go home.* He thought, then remembered he didn't have a home. His room in the barracks was probably already given to someone else. His belongings were probably locked away until claimed or given away.

This was his new life, this strange world filled with chaos and monsters. It was the same world he'd always lived in and yet it felt new and terrifying. *They live in the city too.* Jewel had said that about at least two creatures. How many more of the legends were real?

He shuddered and scooted closer to the fire. The dark had an odd feeling to it, almost a drawing in. Every time he looked out into the dark woods he had a pulling feeling. He quickly realized that looking into the fire was the only thing that made that feeling dissipate.

She said the fire and singing help. Pendry had never been much of a singer but he no longer cared about that. He started humming a song; he wasn't even sure he could remember the words but even the humming seemed to help. He relaxed a little and thought about everything that had happened that day, and about what Jewel had told him about herself.

She said her dad died, but if her dad was the previous leader of the Gradiare then he was executed.

Pendry remembered that day. It had been a public execution. He had been too far back to see much, hidden with some of his friends who had snuck out to see the execution of the leader of the Gradiare. Even from that distance he could see that the man was huge, if he remembered they'd nicknamed him Dragonsbane. He glanced over at Jewel who was sleeping soundly.

Fourteen, she was fourteen when she started leading. He hadn't actually watched the execution, but he knew it was a grizzly scene. Some of his friends still had nightmares about it. *It was probably better for her to pretend she had died rather than get caught and face the executioner.*

He prodded the fire, listening to a bird singing, hoping it was a harmless creature.

6

Pendry

The morning came, and as the dim light grew and pushed away the darkness, the eerie noises and glowing eyes slowly diminished. In their place was a picturesque forest with dappled light and vibrant colors.

Pendry had watched the light go from pitch black to a dusty orange to a warm dappled light. He caught himself staring at the spot where the horse had stood, half expecting to see evidence that it had been there once. But there was nothing, not even a bent blade of grass.

Jewel stirred in her sleep. He expected some violent, sudden jolt from her, or for her to be holding her katshme when she woke up. She didn't do either of those things. Instead she started talking to him before her eyes were even open.

"If you're so bored that you feel like staring at me, then you can busy yourself with breakfast."

He looked away, wondering if her being a gold vein meant she had eyes buried somewhere under all her hair, or maybe being a leader of a notorious gang meant just really heightened sense. Probably the latter, but with all the weird stuff that had happened the day before, he couldn't be sure.

He turned slowly and deliberately to the packs and started digging through to find something to eat for breakfast. He took his time examining each wax packet, looking, smelling and even breaking off a crumb and tasting it, but he still had no idea or clue what any of it was or what to do with it.

I can't tell what's medical supplies and what's food. Really should have paid more attention during the emergency medic training. Should I ask? Could get hurt. Better to ask than act an idiot.

He worked up his courage and turned to ask Jewel what all of it was. She was sitting crossed legged, eyes closed and fingers entwined in her hair. A comb lay on one knee, a ribbon and a stick were in the other.

He watched, trying to figure out what she was doing and how she knew what to do. He'd never seen a girl do their hair and was fascinated by it, the way she had the hair wrapped around her fingers and then flicked them out every so often. He watched as she stopped and picked up the ribbon and added it into what he could only assume was referred to as a braid. She got to the end and tied the two ends of the ribbon in a bow. She then twisted it up and stuck the stick through the loop of braid pinning it to the back of her head.

She sighed and flexed her fingers, then stretched her arms first forward then up. When she opened her eyes she stared at the fire for a moment.

"I thought you were going to get some food going?" she asked, turning to Pendry.

"Oh, I was," he said, pointing to the open packs. "But I was distracted, by um your hair floppy thing."

"My hair floppy what?" She asked, looking like she was trying not to smile. She pursed her lips like she was fighting back a laugh.

"Um," Pendry said, floundering for words, feeling like he might lose a hand or an arm if he upset her. "I don't know, just, um, the thing you were doing with your hair was a little, or a lot distracting and I don't even know what to call it. Maybe braid or bunning?"

Jewel sucked in her cheeks slightly, closed her eyes and tilted her head. She blinked a few times, frowned and then cleared her throat. "I'm sorry, my hair is distracting you from getting food out? Have you never seen someone braid their hair or pin it up?"

"Well I'm an only child and I didn't have a mom growing up, so... no," he said, slightly confused.

"Yes but you went to school with girls and you've worked with women. Right? So somehow you've never seen anyone do what I just did," she said, indicating her hair.

"Um, no..." Pendry said, thinking for a moment. "I think most of the girls and women I knew kept their hair shorter. Not sure why."

"Ok," Jewel said, picking up her comb and slipping it into her pocket. "Moving on. Grab some scones and the two yellow wax packets and we'll break camp."

Why was that funny? He thought as he got the food she'd said.

The yellow packs were some dried meat, and the scones had both cheese and dried fruit. The crestym and the food helped to energize Pendry and made him feel like he could hike the whole day, maybe not run like yesterday, but hiking should be ok.

It didn't take long for them to break camp, merely rinse cups and kettle in a nearby stream that Jewel had found the night before while Pendry slept. Repacking the packs, making sure the fire was well doused, and they were off.

"How long do you think it will take to get to the capital?" he asked as they hiked along. Part of him missed the horse, then he remembered the pain he'd been in the night before and decided walking wasn't so bad.

They were no longer on the main path, but instead following the river, climbing over and around rocks and large tree roots. It was nice to take it slow after a day of rushing.

"About one more day. We could make it there sooner if this forest lost leaves in winter, but these are enchanted trees," Jewel said, caressing another of the gigantic tree roots, similar to the ones of the tree they'd slept under the night before. "It's harder to navigate in this part of the woods."

Pendry looked up at the leaf covered canopy. It hadn't occurred to him before, but it was early spring and there shouldn't be full leaves on the trees yet. "Wait, what trees are these?" he asked, then stopped. "Hang on, I'm getting a little tired of feeling like I know nothing of the world I live in. I'm not dumb. I went to school, I learned things, and yet in the last two days that I've known you, you've said wrathes are real, and I've heard them and seen what they do. But really?" He ran his hand through his tangled hair, "Why don't I know these things? How do you know these things? How is your friend a half elf and you're a gold vein? Just how?" He started to move forward when Jewel grabbed his arm.

"Whatever you do, don't move, don't take a step or anything out of the circle." She was looking down at the ground. All the blood had drained from her face and she looked like she was going to be sick. She kept looking down, then at the river. She was tense and looked like she'd run or fight any second.

"What?" Pendry asked, looking at the ground. "All I see are red and purple mushrooms."

"Yes, in a ring, a ring that you are standing in. It's a faie circle. It's a trap and you are in it," she said, her tone growing more anxious as she talked.

"Mushrooms? Mushrooms are what scare you, Miss Leader-of-the-Biggest-Gang?"

Jewel ignored him, circling around him and carefully examining the mushrooms.

"Seals and serpents," she muttered.

"Really," Pendry said as she stopped, throwing his hands up exasperated. "You're a gang leader but you can't swear?"

"Swearing is for the non-creative normals. Also, most swear words are blasphemy," she said, still staring at the ground. "You're standing in one of the best or possible the worst faie circles I've ever seen."

"So you're a gang leader who's religious and believes in magical creatures."

"I am a magical creature," she snapped, taking her pack off slowly and setting it gently on the ground. She pulled a small pouch out of it and gently untied it, still examining the mushrooms.

"Right, but it's not the same. You're a gold vein that's completely different from a faie. Wait, you've seen one of these before?" Pendry said, watching her move slowly around the small circle of mushrooms for a second time. Fear started to rise, twisting his stomach and making the hair on the back of his neck begin to prickle.

"Would you have said that two days ago? That a gold vein is different from faie?"

"Ok fine, but just what are faie? Because stories vary and you're making me extremely nervous with this slow moving that you're doing. You're also shaking and sound scared out of your mind." He didn't know what to expect but anything that made someone like her scared had to be terrifying.

She stopped circling him and bent down staring at the mushroom in front of her. "There," she whispered. Pulling some odd powder from the pouch, she sprinkled it on the mushroom, her hand trembling. The powder was green and smelled of watermelon and a summer breeze, but as it hit the mushroom it turned purple and had an acrid smell of mold.

Pendry blanched at the purple smelly dust, "Oh gods what is that?"

"Ok, if we're talking about religion, then you should know, of course I'm religious. Only an idiot thinks every-thing in its complexity was created from nothing," she said, standing and retying the pouch and putting it back in her pack before dusting her hands on her pants. She looked Pendry in the eye, "And only a fool would think a being of that power would share that title and space with anyone. I believe in one God, unlike what that chapel the kings invented that teaches of the twelve or so made up gods." She tilted her head to the side, still looking Pendry in the eye, "Are you a fool, Pendry? Or are you an idiot? Either way, it's not looking good for you."

"I feel like you're avoiding the question that I have asked twice now." He didn't like being called a fool or an idiot but wasn't in the mood for some religious debate. "What are faie and why are you of all people so scared of them?"

"You'll soon see, and I have a lot of fears. I just learned early on that a good leader hides them well." She took a deep breath, "I've also only ever seen a faie once and that was with my dad, so…" she cleared her throat. Turned to face the river, spreading her legs slightly to brace herself, she took another deep breath. "Ok, so what I did was make it so the faie wouldn't know who stood in the trap, but it will still be coming. I will deal with it and you need to stand behind me and not move at all. They don't see the same way we do and rely on their traps to follow their prey." She looked Pendry in the eye. "Am I understood?"

He was confused, scared and intrigued all at once. Her green eyes reminded him of a venomous green snake he'd seen in a traveling show when he was a kid. They were just as green and just as deadly. Her tone invoked obedience, as any commanding officer's did.

"I don't like the idea of hiding behind someone, and I don't think I could hide behind you, but I understand." His instinct was to protect someone smaller, especially a woman, but in this case it seemed wiser to push down those feelings.

"Right, when I say jump, jump, and stay behind. Both feet need to leave the trap and hit the ground outside. This will come in fast and you will freeze," Jewel said, wiping her shaking hands on her pants again, and slowly pulling her pack back on. She took a shaky deep breath, squared her shoulders and straightened to her full height. "Ok, now."

Pendry jumped, and felt the air crackle with electricity and heat. He felt the presence of the faie before he saw it. But when he saw it his blood ran cold. He knew why Jewel was so scared.

The faie was tall, a behemoth of a creature. It stood as tall as a house. It was human-like in form but that was where the likeness stopped. Its skin was like ancient paper and its eyes were black. No pupil or white, simply gaping black voids that all light seemed to be sucked into. Its body was wispy and solid. You could see it and see through it. It had hair like spun gold that gave it the sickly appearance of being on fire. It looked right at them and opened its mouth. The mouth alone would give Pendry nightmares for years, a cavernous maw filled with jagged pointed teeth. Its tongue was a bloody and bright red. It leered forward moving what must have been an arm out towards them. Its slender finger-like appendages reached out and almost touched Jewel.

Jewel hadn't moved. She stood there trembling but firm in her stance, staring the creature down. Pendry could see how scared she was, and yet she didn't move. She stood between him and a creature that should only exist in nightmares. There was something to admire in the steadfast courage she displayed, but at the moment he was a little preoccupied by his own fear of the creature.

Then the faie spoke. It spoke in a growling gurgling splutter. No distinguishing words could be heard and yet, to Pendry's amazement and utter horror, Jewel spoke back.

She made the growling noises and pointed in the direction they had come from. The creature pulled its hand back and looked in that direction. After a moment it moved down the river in the direction Jewel had pointed. The way it ran was so disturbing and horrific that Pendry blocked it out of his mind, but the speed that it moved was added to his nightmares.

Jewel grabbed his hand and started running, dragging him along with her leading him into the river then out again, running back to the main road and off again in a looping zigzag pattern that he'd heard was used to throw off predators.

They ended up on a smaller slightly overgrown path leading back in the direction they had been traveling. Jewel stopped running and let go of his hand.

"We're good, It's safe now." She gasped out.

Pendry was shaking now, gasping for breath and wiping sweat from his face. "I have never and hope to never see one of that thing again," he gasped, "Oh, I'm going to see that face every time I close my eyes. Ugh." He started pacing in a circle, hands on his head. He stopped and turned to Jewel. "You spoke to it. You said last time you saw one your dad was with you, but your dad died when you were fourteen. How have you slept a full night since?"

She spoke to it, how did she speak to it? He felt slightly disgusted that she had spoken to it and at the same time in awe of her for both speaking to it and having seen one as a kid.

Jewel shrugged. She was still shaking and sweating almost as much as Pendry. "I've faced worse, and yes, I learned one phrase just for incidents like that, I basically told it that its prey went that way," she said, slumping to the ground. "But yeah, I still have nightmares of them and do my best to avoid spots where they're common. River side is usually safe, so that was unexpected."

"Oh, right, they have preferences," Pendry said sarcastically as he plopped down on the road.

"No need for sarcasm. We're still alive. I think that was a young male. The female ones have antlers. They get bigger," she shuddered.

Pendry stared mouth agape, "Bigger?" He almost squeaked the word out. "That massive giant thing was small? What nightmarish thing did you see as a kid? And antlers, really? Your God just said you know what, I know what will make it better. Let's slap on some antlers!" He was practically yelling. His shaking was almost violent and he felt like he might throw up.

Suddenly Jewel started laughing, hysterical, gut wrenching laughter. "Oh, you were saying you went to school and knew things and that they were only legends," she cackled, "and then one appears and you just about peed your pants."

Pendry started laughing, "I think you almost peed yourself just from seeing the mushrooms." Her laugh was infectious, it wasn't the small girlish laugh or giggle he was used to hearing. Instead it was hearty and warm. He wasn't used to hearing someone cackle either. That alone made him laugh.

They laughed for a good minute, then wiped the tears from their eyes and sat in silence. He felt better and worse staring into nothing and feeling drained.

"It's part of why I left," Jewel said softly, "the corruption, the utter embedded corruption of the people. It's not as bad in other cities and it's even less in towns, but who teaches their people that creatures like that aren't real? What's the point, other than thinking you can sway them over to fully trusting you?" She sighed and put her head in her hands. "I couldn't take it anymore, being the bad guy in a world so corrupted by such wickedness that good isn't seen as good anymore."

Pendry watched her for a moment, "Are all magical creatures bad? I mean I know you're one, but are they all like wrathes and faie?"

"No," she said, looking up and smiling. "Elves are pretty great, and the most harm a goblin will do is pickpocket

you unless there's a lot of them." She thought for a moment. "Pixies are nice, a little thick and dumb but it can be
fun to watch them play and dance. And the first time I saw
a phoenix," she sighed dreamily, "that was breathtaking."

He smiled trying to picture what the creatures she was
talking about might look like. "You said earlier that these
trees and this forest are enchanted. Is it the only place to
see all these creatures?"

"No," she said, standing up and dusting off her pants.
"There are lots of places. The ocean alone is teaming
with magical creatures. Caves and mountains are almost
always magical. It's just a matter of getting out of the
capital. There are stories of other countries full of their
own magical creatures."

Pendry stayed sitting and thinking for a moment, "So
this is just something that the king has hidden from his
people? Why?"

Jewel looked sad for a moment, "That is something I
have yet to fully understand. I've asked older members of
the Gradiare and even they don't know, it's one of those
ongoing questions that we've never known the answer
to..." Her voice trailed off and she stared down the road.

He followed her gaze and they both looked down the
path for a moment, trying to prepare themselves for what
they might find down it.

"Right," she said, clapping her hands. "This path will
take us to the capital, but we still won't get there until
late tomorrow. Let's get going. Night is dangerous and I'd
rather not spend more time out here than necessary," she
was looking up at the canopy of leaves.

He followed her lead and looked up. "How can you tell if it's getting late?"

She helped him up and they started walking as Jewel replied, "Like I said, the trees are enchanted; there are some that glitter gold in the sunlight— that's how light comes through during the day. They turn a copper color as the sun sets, once they're copper we have one hour before it's completely dark in here."

Pendry looked up at the leaves above them, stopping for a moment to focus on them better. It was hard to distinguish from so far away, but it appeared that there were indeed some gold blotches, but it wasn't gold like autumn, more like sunlight shining through a fine gold fabric. He had noticed how thick the canopy was, but hadn't fully thought about how they were able to still see.

"How do you know so much about this forest and the strange creatures? I've never even heard of them except in legends and myths, and that was usually a vague description." He looked closely at the bark of one of the trees, realizing for the first time that even the bark glinted and reflected light.

Jewel had stopped and was watching him. "I had good teachers and books. You went to the schools, right? The King's schools. They teach what the King wants you to know and how he wants you to perceive the world."

Pendry was suddenly acutely aware of the beauty of the world around him. The glittering bark of the trees and the glowing leaves were only the beginning. The rocks on the path seemed to emit a light of their own as well, adding to the bright daylight under the full canopy.

"How have I not even noticed the beauty and magic of this wood?" He knelt and picked up a rock to look closer at it. "I was out here on my own before I met you and we spent yesterday out here too."

She sighed, "Don't be hard on yourself. It's hard to stop and look around when you're running for your life."

He chuckled, "Right, I think I'm still rattled from the faie." He put the rock he was looking at into his pocket and stood. "Shall we keep going?"

"Yes," Jewel said, eyeing the pocket he'd placed the rock in. "Before we do, what color was that rock you just pocketed?"

"Green. Why?" He suddenly froze to the spot. Inwardly cursing at what demonic or monstrous thing was now sitting in his pocket.

"You're good, green are good rocks." She turned quickly and started to walk away.

Pendry looked at the ground and saw green, blue and red glowing rocks. "What's wrong with the others?"

He heard an odd noise, almost a snort. He looked around trying to figure out what new creature he was in for meeting. He heard it again, and realized it was Jewel trying not to laugh.

"Are you messing with me?" He said in a whispering yell. "It's not funny, I don't know what's safe and what's not safe."

She was full on laughing again, almost cackling at him. "No but it is funny. It's just a rock, nothing special about it except when light hits it they glow." She snorted again, "They aren't even special to these woods. You can find them all over, but you live in the city where they make brick roads."

"Are you kidding me? You had me shaking! I thought some creature was going to climb out of my pocket and try to eat me!" Pendry yelled. He stood for a while, hands on his hips and breathing deeply to calm himself. Jewel was doubled over laughing, it slowly morphed into a cackle. He couldn't help but laugh with her. "I don't get you. You seem serious one second then cackling the next. Do you have a middle ground?"

Jewel took a long deep breath. "I don't cackle," she said, straightening up and dusting herself off. She wiped tears from her eyes, still chuckling and smiling.

"Yes you do. You sound like a rooster or a chicken," he said as he started to walk down the path.

She glared at him as he walked up to her. "I don't think anyone has ever been brave enough to tell me I cackle, and the only people who have seen me laugh have never made me laugh that hard."

"Does that mean you're going to kill me, Miss Lion?" Pendry asked, smirking down at her.

"No. You still have valuable information. Maybe after you've met your use..." She glared at him then turned and they both headed down the path.

After a few minutes of silence, Pendry started to chuckle. "Wow! You really got me with the rock. I was so shaken and so in awe of this new magical world that I was ready to believe anything. Nice delivery too."

Jewel smiled smugly, "Oh, it helps to have some truth to it. These rocks are all safe but if you ever see the orange glowing boulders, I'd suggest running."

He glared at her. "Are you messing with me again?"

Jewel turned to look at him, smiling and looking angel-ic. Then she picked up her pace and walked on ahead of him.

"That's not funny!" Pendry yelled after her. He looked around, then sped up to stay close to his guide.

7

Pendry

The second night was uneventful and felt shorter than the last. Possibly because there were less ominous noises or because Pendry felt less nervous that Jewel was going to kill him. In either case, the night was quieter and passed without event. In the morning, they had a quick breakfast and it was decided that they would reach the city by dusk.

"Doesn't that mean we'd get there after curfew?" Pendry asked as they started down the path.

"Not unless they changed the curfew since the last time I was there," Jewel said as she finished pinning her hair up.

"So," Pendry started, then stopped, wondering if it would be intrusive to ask. "Just curious, when was the last time you were in the city?"

Jewel took a deep breath, "Not entirely sure, I haven't been back since I moved to the cabin two years ago, but I wasn't completely present and keeping up with the laws before that."

"Ok, yeah, they changed the curfew, at least the gate curfew. It's now a few minutes after dusk and the gates are closed, then an hour until the bells and that's the house curfew and another two hours and that's the lights out curfew." He almost walked into Jewel who'd stopped and was staring at him with a look of disgust and disbelief. "What?"

"Why? Why is the king like that? Why do you people put up with it? Why do you serve someone who would take every freedom from his people including their time?" She had that same dangerous look in her eyes and an edge to her voice.

"Um."

I thought we were past this.

"What do you do in winter? Has the morning curfew changed too? Was no one there to say no? Did Ferga do nothing to fight it?" She was yelling now and almost looked like she was going to fight him.

"I'm not the one to fight on this." He took a step back, putting his hands up slightly to show there wasn't any need to feel threatened.

"But you were a peace officer, right? And you enforced those laws. How many people did you imprison for leaving a light on or for getting home a few minutes late?" She took a step toward him.

He had to admit for someone as small as she was she had a way of making herself bigger and intimidating.

"No. Look," he was tired of her treating him like some dumb enemy. "Just because I was a peace officer doesn't mean I agreed with and upheld every law. In fact, most people have taken to using blackout curtains and none of the peace officers would arrest someone for not follow-ing that dumb law." He wanted her to stop being so angry at him, maybe even be friends since he now had none. "I did escort people home after the bell so the King's Guards wouldn't arrest them and I did knock on some doors to let them know their curtains weren't closed enough." He paused to let his words settle. "I'm not a monster. I became a peace officer because I wanted to uphold what was right, and those laws weren't right."

She took a step back, eyeing him like she wasn't sure if what he was saying was true or if he was just trying to avoid a fight.

"If you cared so much about the people and what they were going through, why did you leave?" It came out a little harsher than he'd meant it to, but Jewel didn't seem angry about it. Her eyes seemed to soften and look a little sad.

"As you pointed out the other day, I should be dead. I spent about two years fully recovering in that cabin, and that was after a few months of recovery in the Gradiare sickbay. I don't know how long it took in total, but I didn't leave because I stopped caring, if anything, I cared too much." She clenched her fist and glared at the ground. "I spent most of my life caring for and leading people. The first time I didn't have to do that was because a wall fell on me." She sighed, turned and started down the path. "Come on, we can't spend all day standing here talking about the past."

They walked on in silence for a while. Pendry felt bad. All those stories he'd heard were of her. No wonder she wanted out and took so long to recover. The number of battles and fights he'd heard of were more than he could remember, and those were the ones people had survived. How many battles had she actually fought? How many times had she lost people? He'd seen fights. He'd been in the attack on what they thought was the Gradiare hideout. It wasn't something a kid should see.

"I'm sorry, I wasn't meaning to be offensive again," Pendry said softly.

"Yeah, I'm sorry too. Most of my experiences with peace officers has been them arresting someone for breaking one of those dumb laws. We had some join, but even they used to enforce those laws." Jewel was fiddling with the straps of her pack. "I also was having trouble handling the stress of everything," she chuckled nervously, "I was starting to have some health issues. I actually had some family members telling me it might be time for me to hand off some responsibilities to others. I wasn't planning to, but then I took that arrow to the chest and I kinda had no choice. Then I had a wall fall on me and I decided I needed more than just less responsibility."

Well yeah, you had responsibilities of a commander since you were fourteen. Pendry thought, suddenly understanding a little bit better why she would randomly lose her temper and why she was quick to fight. "How did you get people to listen to you and respect you as Commander when you were fourteen?"

"I didn't at first," she said, sighing, "I had a lot of respect to earn and I had a lot of challengers to fight. I think it was two ish years before all the other higher ups respected me."

"Ok, that's rough. No wonder you're so angry all the time."

"I'm not angry all the time," she said indignantly.

"Well you've spent the entire time I've known you yelling at me or threatening me. I wouldn't call that nice," Pendry said, straightening his sweater.

"Ah," Jewel squeaked.

Pendry looked back at her. She'd stopped walking and looked a little hurt and sad. "Sorry, am I being judgemental and offensive again?"

"No," She said slowly, walking up next to him, "I just didn't realize I was being so rude. I'm sorry. You kinda interrupted my peace and dragged me back into this stressful life that I didn't want to go back to at all, let alone be dragged into." She rubbed her forehead, "I guess I was jumping ahead and taking on all the stress that I used to have."

Pendry watched her walk past him. She seemed sad. He had dragged her back into the life she'd left, and he had quite literally crashed into her peace.

She took a slow deep breath, still rubbing her forehead, "I'm sorry. You're a new recruit and I've been treating you like an enemy."

He took a deep breath as well, "Well let's try again." He held his hand out, "I'm Pendry, I'd like to join the Gradiare."

She smiled slightly and shook his hand, "Nice to meet you, I'm Jewel."

"There, is that better?" He asked as they started back down the path.

"Sure, I'll try to remember you're friend not foe," she said, still smiling softly.

"Oh friend, do you really want to call me that?" He smirked.

"I call all the Gradiare friend, it's either that or family and that's not going to happen."

Friend it is then, he thought, feeling a little better about his situation.

They walked on for a few hours. Every once in a while Pendry would ask about the different things or sounds that surrounded them. It was a peaceful walk. They didn't run into any more creatures and more importantly, they didn't see the King's Guard.

"I've noticed we haven't seen as many creatures today," Pendry said when they'd stopped for a rest and some food.

"That's because we're getting close to the edge of the enchanted woods. Most of the creatures in here prefer the dense center of the woods." She handed Pendry some more dried meat and some dried fruit.

"But we haven't run into the King's Guard either."

"No," she said sitting back, "They stay on the main road. They have outposts that they stop and sleep at. The King doesn't want anyone to know these creatures are real, not even his own guards."

Pendry nodded, he'd stayed at one of those outposts when they were taking him to the Keep. "So they only use the main road?"

"Yes, that's why I wanted to walk by the river. But that didn't turn out." She rolled her eyes at the memory of the faie.

"Yesterday you said faie don't normally set traps by the river or something like that." He pulled out his water flask and drank the remaining water.

"Right, they prefer swampy areas or places where the water isn't so clean. Don't ask me why, I don't know. Not many people try asking them." She finished her dried meat and folded up the empty package.

"Ok then, and I'm guessing you learned that from reading?" He watched her slowly fold up the empty packages and place them neatly into her pack.

She seems to like things to be neat and organized, guess that helps when you have a lot of papers and things to deal with.

"Knowledge is good, it's the only thing that once you have it no one can take it away from you, at least not fully. Freedom is fleeting, and things break. So yeah, I like to read and learn what I need to know and sometimes the things I don't need to know but I'm simply curious about." She finished repacking her pack and stood. "We can make it to the East Passage by dusk if we speed up a bit."

"East what?" Pendry asked, stuffing his empty packets into his pack and standing up to pull it on.

"It's a small unguarded door in the wall. Well, it is guarded, but not by the King. We can't exactly go through the main gate with you being wanted."

"Yeah, still not used to being an outlaw I guess."

They headed down the road at a slightly faster walk.

Pendry blinked up at the thinning canopy of trees, thinking about being an outlaw.

I'm either an outlaw alone or an outlaw with an army at my back. I think I prefer facing this with an army rather than alone.

8

Jewel

I t was just after dusk as they hid in the brush looking at the walls of the city. They were huge fortifications, with parapets and ramparts. They were ancient, built of rough cut stones from the base of the mountains. The town of Hamndle was built next to the old quarry, but it had gone unused for a century. In the light of day, you could see the blue and green veins that ran through the stones, giving them an elegant, almost painted look. But in the evening gloom they stood dark and menacing.

Even though they were beautiful in design, Jewel hadn't wanted to see the walls again, but here she was and there they were. She took a deep breath and looked from side to side. *All clear.* They ran to the wall crouching low. When they got to the wall she started examining the stones.

"I thought you said there was a door." Pendry whispered urgently, as he looked around, one hand on a katshme.

"There is," Jewel whispered back. *There* she thought and she felt the small slit inbetween two of the stones. She pulled out a small knife, her katshme were too big, and slid it into the hole. There was a small click and an arch of the stones sunk into the wall. Jewel smiled, she loved these doors, even if she didn't like the walls or the city, these doors always amazed her.

"Oh," Pendry whispered behind her, apparently he liked doors like this too.

Jewel pushed the door in just enough so Pendry could squeeze in. She put her knife away knowing what was ahead, she didn't want to be killed before she was even able to see anyone.

She slipped in followed by Pendry. They hadn't walked more than two steps before the stones were pushed back into place and two people materialized out of the shadows.

"Who's there?" The voice was gruff but quiet, a man's voice.

"The Lion," Jewel whispered back. She hated that nickname but it was what people knew her by and at this point why fight it.

"Jewel?" the man whispered as he stepped forward pulling a small pocket light out and shining it at her for a moment. "All that is holy! I thought you'd taken up gardening and dancing with pixies," the man said, chuckling softly. "Come on, no need to keep our Lion out here waiting," he laughed quietly to himself.

"Samuel Mav. They have you out here pulling guard duty?" She smiled as they were led into a small door in the wall.

The city walls were thick, thick enough that in ancient times they had been fitted with catapults and there was still room for guards to walk around them. The door they had first entered led into a small room built into the city wall. The second door led them into a short narrow passage leading down the length of the wall. It was dimly lit with orange flickering lanterns.

Samuel turned and gave Jewel a hug, "Good to see you kid." He was an older man, short and grandfatherly. He had deep smile lines like he spent most of the time smiling, and he had. Jewel remembered him treating her like a granddaughter even after she became Commander.

"Good to see you, Mav. We need to get to the main. I need to talk to Ferga. This man has some information and he's looking to join."

"Ferga, right, follow me. We've had to change some of the passages due to the King's Guard and what." He led them down the narrow passage. Jewel had forgotten how cold the passages were. Thankfully, they were dry since they had made sure to weather seal them.

"Who's Ferga?" Pendry whispered.

Jewel turned to see that he was ducking and inching along sideways. She hadn't thought about the passage being too small for him. She bit back a laugh, he looked comical squeezing through the passage with his head tilted and hunched over.

"Oh, my cousin, the new Commander of the Gradiare," She whispered back. "Are you ok? I didn't realize these passages were so small, sorry."

"Yeah, I'm fine," he grunted as he squeezed around a corner, "I wouldn't expect someone as child sized as you to realize how small this passage is."

"I'm not child sized, that would have to be a big child."

"Fine, not child sized," he grunted as he continued to squeeze through the passage.

"Everything alright back there?" Samuel called over his shoulder.

"Yes," Jewel called out trying not to laugh at how ridiculous Pendry looked. "Just forgot how small this passage was."

"Oh, right, your friend there is a big guy, give me a second." There was a clicking and grinding noise and the passage became a little wider and a little taller.

"Ugh," Pendry groaned as he straightened and stood only slightly sideways. He seemed to relax a little. "That's better. How'd he do that?"

Jewel turned back to Samuel, "Thank you Mav, I forgot this passage could do that."

"You wouldn't have needed it ma'am," Samuel said over his shoulder, "I don't use it that often, it makes one more thing to do when leaving the tunnels."

"The walls were built to transport forces secretly from one point of the walls to another. There's levers and pulleys that push and pull the walls and ceiling, they get wider but it takes a while," Jewel whispered to Pendry as they walked down the tunnel. "We took over the tunnels about ninety years ago. The current king doesn't know about them as far as we know, but we keep guards on every entrance and exit that's noticeable."

"Are these tunnels in every wall of the city?"

"Yes, and under the city. It's how we've been able to move so easily and without notice." Jewel looked back to see Pendry nod slightly.

"Ok, that solves about half of the mysteries of the Gradiare."

They kept moving, turning into a doorway and down some steps into another passage. The passage continued down and grew colder as they went underground. It was one of those passages that, unless you knew where you were going, you could get lost very easily; perfect for new recruits.

"Sorry about the roundabout way, had some trouble with some grawn wrathes getting into the tunnels a month ago. Had to close down a section because of the mess they made." Samuel chuckled, "I haven't seen Wen that angry since, well probably when those goblins tried to take over the tunnels."

"How's he doing? Last I heard he and his family moved to one of the houses on the West side."

"Oh he's doing good, liking the house, they needed it with the baby." He turned back. "Did you hear, I now have twelve grand babies?"

"I hadn't, congratulations."

They continued on down the passage, Samuel talking about all his grandkids and how proud he was of them. He hardly seemed like he was looking where he was going, but it also seemed he didn't need to.

The passage split into three and they took the right, then it went up again and split into two and they took the left. The passages were tall enough for Pendry to walk normally now.

"This can't be real. How did I grow up in this city and never know about this?" he asked as they came to a door.

"Agh, no one knows unless we want them to, boy," Samuel said, pushing the door open.

They entered a stone hallway. It was in the section of wall that was buried underground. It was nicer stone than the passage, wider and brightly lit.

"You know the way from here, ma'am. I'll be getting back to my post. It was nice seeing you again." Samuel nodded respectfully.

"Thank you, Mav. Good seeing you too, and hearing about your family," Jewel said, shaking his hand. "Say hi to your wife for me."

Samuel turned back down the passage they had come from, closing the door behind him.

They walked down the hallway. It was the same rough hewn stones of the outer walls, lined with rugs and carpets. Memories flooded Jewel as they went, some good and some she wished she could forget.

"This is huge," Pendry said softly as he looked around. "How have you been able to hide from the King for so long?"

Jewel smiled. "Most of the headquarters is either under the city or in the walls. They were old store rooms and shelters in case of attack from when the city was first built. We even have some of the old abandoned buildings on the west side. To be completely honest I have no idea how the King hasn't figured out where we are. The most I've heard, he knows some of the west side houses but when they did that raid two years ago they only went for the decoy."

"You have decoy houses?" He asked in surprise.

"We did, I'm not up to speed on if we have any new decoy houses." They stopped in front of a set of double doors.

Jewel took a deep breath. "Don't say anything, at least not at first, and don't, just don't," she made a face as she looked at Pendry, *just don't act like a peace officer*, she thought.

"Don't look so lawful?" He asked, smiling his crooked smile.

"Yes, and you have some cobwebs in your hair."

He brushed the cobwebs out of his hair and straightened his sweater trying to look a little presentable. *The scruff might help him not look so officer*, she thought. but he had a way of standing that made him look trained.

She sighed, "Good enough." *They'll accept you eventually, just takes a bit to build trust.*

She turned to the door, suddenly filled with excitement at seeing her family again. She took a deep breath, readying herself for the crushing hug that would greet her. She opened the doors and they went inside.

9

Pendry

P endry didn't know what he was expecting but it wasn't what he saw. The room was big, with a vaulted ceiling. At the far end was a large table covered in papers and weapons. To the right was another set of doors and to the left was a large fireplace with two large oversized chairs like the ones back at Jewel's cabin. There was a desk and some chairs between the fireplace and the large table. At the desk sat a man who was at least as big as Pendry and had red curling hair and a big red beard.

The man looked up as they entered. When he saw Jewel he jumped up from the desk and vaulted over it, yelling as he did. "Yeah! Whoo!" He bounded over to them and picked Jewel up by her waist, spinning her around, laughing and jumping.

That was unexpected, Pendry thought as he waited for her to yell or get angry. To his surprise, she did neither.

"Put me down you idiot," Jewel laughed.

"Aw but I didn't think I'd see that beautiful face again," the man said, setting her down.

"You could visit, you know," Jewel said, straightening her sweater and tucking some hair behind her ear. She was smiling, and not just a sad tired smile, it was a full beaming smile.

She has a nice smile.

The man looked at Pendry and his smile grew, "You found someone, finally! Ah, is that why you haven't visited? Welcome to the family." The man grabbed Pendry by the hand and shook it firmly before Pendry could even process what he was saying.

"Ferga!" Jewel yelled. "That's a recruit I brought." Her face was flushed.

"Oh, well that can always be fixed up later. Nice to meet you. As you've now heard, I'm Ferga," He smiled jovially.

Pendrys head was still spinning from everything, but he had enough presence to respond. "Oh, um, Pendry, nice to meet you sir."

It finally occurred to him what Ferga had been saying. *Did he just say welcome to the family without confirming if I was family?* Pendry thought. *How strange and forward of him.*

"I think the information he has might be helpful or at least good to know," Jewel was saying.

Pendry had missed something, but it didn't seem important.

"Mmf," Ferga grunted. "Well, we can talk about that later, I was just finishing up here before going to get ready for the New Year ball." He smirked at Jewel, his blue eyes glinting, "You made it just on time."

"Oh, no, we won't be going to that, I didn't bring anything to wear and I was hoping to come quietly and leave quietly and not get into the whole family mess of things."

Jewel was waving her hands back and forth as if to wave off the very idea of a ball.

"Nonsense!" Ferga boomed, "If I have to attend and have all the mothers and aunties trying to match me up with their daughters, then you have to go and have them fawn over you." He smoothed his beard and flashed a big smile, "Besides you might take the heat off me coming with this strapping young man."

"No," she said firmly, looking agitated.

"Yes," Ferga said, getting a mischievous look to him, "yes, I like this plan more and more, come. I'm sure your mother has some of your old dresses and I have some nice clothes for this man, Pendry right?" he said walking them to the other set of doors.

He clearly isn't going to take no for an answer.

The next half hour was a blur to Pendry, there were several people he met and was introduced to. Somewhere along the line he was separated from Jewel and led by Ferga to a set of smaller rooms. They seemed to be dressing rooms of some kind.

"These things are usually formal, although formal for us means no holes or dirt, so." Ferga said, opening a closet and pulling out some clean dress pants and a clean linen shirt. He eyed Pendry, sizing him up. "No, you've been sleeping in the woods, showers over there, your shoes look passable, the scruffs fine." He handed Pendry the clean clothes and showed him to the shower.

He showered and dressed, trying to wrap his head around the whirlwind of everything. He'd just been hiking through an enchanted forest and before that he was a prisoner of the King's Guard. Now he was going to a ball with the leaders of the Gradiare.

Not something I ever thought would happen. Didn't think a gang would have parties, at least not balls.

He examined his arm. He wasn't sure how to take out the stitches, but the wound was now completely healed. He rubbed the scar and was surprised to see the stitches crumble off. He brushed them into the sink and washed his arm.

Whatever magic was in that worked nicely. Never had something heal that fast, he thought as he examined the pink scar.

He buttoned up the shirt and tucked it into his pants. He'd never liked the officer's balls that he'd been to, but part of that was getting dressed up in the dress uniform.

He came out to see Ferga combing his newly trimmed beard. As he was leaning forward, Pendry saw a smaller version of the Gradiare tattoo on Fergas neck. He straightened and smiled his broad smile at Pendry. "Right, let's go. This will be perfect."

"Why do I get the feeling I'm being dressed up to be fed to the wolves?" Pendry asked, following Ferga. He could hear music playing from somewhere, but he wasn't sure where exactly it was.

"Ah," Ferga said, winking at him. "That's because you are. I don't know how she did it all those years, being swarmed by suitors, but two years of it and I'm already over it. Leading I can handle, battle plans, infiltration yes, I can do those," he grimaced. "But the blatant flirting and throwing daughters at me," He shuddered, "that I can't handle. So yes, for tonight I'm passing that off to you and Jewel."

Pendry felt uneasy at the idea of being fed to the wolves but he understood. "Alright, but you owe me."

"Me, the Commander of the Gradiare, I owe you?" Ferga said in a mock indignant tone. "Works for me, I'm done with this garbage." They continued down the hall.

The music grew louder and they could hear voices of people laughing and talking.

"I am curious," Pendry asked hesitantly, "why are you having a new year ball in spring?"

Ferga laughed at that, "Because this is the real new year. Don't worry, you'll learn." He clapped Pendry on the back making him stumble forward a bit. He wasn't used to someone being the same size as him or so strong.

"Here we are," Ferga said, opening a set of double doors.

The room they stepped into was grand, not as large as some of the palace rooms but larger than he thought could fit in the underground headquarters. It had high vaulted ceilings and a large fireplace with a roaring fire in it. There were no windows for obvious reasons, but the room was well lit with a soft, amber glow. The music was loud but not overpowering. Jovial, dancing music and the smell of food and flowers filled the air.

The women were all in long dresses and the men were dressed similar to Pendry, in nice linen pants and clean shirts. Some had vests on, but most seemed to prefer a more relaxed look.

He found himself scanning the room for Jewel, trying to look for a familiar face. He almost missed her. She had her hair down in soft ringlets that fell past her hips. She was wearing a long, forest green dress and looked like she belonged in a fairytale, or one of those legends of princesses.

Ferga led him over to her smiling victoriously. "Here we are, all cleaned up."

Jewel turned and smiled at them.

She's beautiful. He'd noticed she was pretty when he first saw her. But seeing her dressed up and smiling made her look radiant.

He tried not to stare. She had changed her many small hoop earrings for gold ones except for the lowest one which was a larger gold hoop. She had on a thin gold necklace with a small flower pendant. The dress she wore went down to her ankles and had short, capped sleeves, he could see her tattoo completely. It was also a little lower in the front than what she'd been wearing the other day and he saw a thin, white line, the scar from the arrow. Overall it was hard not to stare.

She had been talking to an older woman who looked familiar. Her hair was dark with some gray in it, her face was soft with some small signs of age, she had deep blue eyes that seemed both sad and happy at the same time.

"Auntie Kessa, this is Pendry, he's here with Jewel," Ferga said, indicating him. The way he said it was very pointed.

"He's the recruit I brought, Pendry this is my mother," Jewel said glaring at Ferga.

That was why the woman looked familiar, Jewel looked like a much younger version of her mother, her hair and eyes were different colors than Jewels but aside from that they looked the same, even the same size and build.

"Nice to meet you," he said, shaking her hand gently.

She smiled sweetly at him, "It's good to meet you. Well you are handsome," she said turning to Jewel, "Don't you think he's handsome?"

Pendry could feel his ears grow hot and hoped that no one could see them under his hair. *This is what Ferga was talking about.*

"Mother," Jewel hissed, looking a little flushed herself.

"What, I'm not allowed to say that? Oh you know your sisters will say it." She turned to Pendry and smiled sweetly. "We do love a nice new face here."

"Nothing wrong with that," Pendry said. He tried to relax a little, *just like sweet talking the higher ups.* "Although I do think Jewel's face is a lot better looking than mine. Probably because of all that fresh air."

"Ah, nah," Ferga interrupted, "she's always had that face, made all the men stumble and the girls glare, until they realized she'd rather cut them than wed them," he said chuckling, then grunted as Jewel stepped on his foot with the heel of her boot.

"Well, I'm sure she followed in your beautiful foot-steps." Pendry continued ignoring Ferga who was wincing and leaning on him for support.

"Oh my," Jewel's mother said blushing, "Jewel sweet, are you sure he isn't going to be family? We could use more handsome men."

"No mother," Jewel said, exasperated. She grabbed Pendry by the arm and steered him away from her mother. "Come, Pendry, there's some people I want you to meet."

Pendry smiled and nodded to her mother before letting Jewel lead him away.

"What was that for?" She hissed at him.

"I'm a new recruit right? I figure it's always better to talk nicely and even butter up the higher ups." *That's what I had to do as a peace officer.*

"Yes, but not my mother. gah!" She looked flustered, "Look, my mom is not in that area of the Gradiare, in fact she hasn't been since I took over. Now she spends her time working with the families of the fallen or trying to play matchmaker. Just don't act too flirtatious with her or stand too close to me. They're already talking about us because I brought you." She looked around nervously.

He was about to comment on that when someone walked up behind Jewel.

"Well hello, Jewel. I thought you'd left the city." The voice was smooth and oily.

Jewel stiffened and turned. There, standing in front of them, was a man with blond slicked back hair. He looked as oily as his voice sounded.

"Hello, Gaidin. I see you haven't changed." There was an edge in her voice and Pendry noticed she had stepped back to be closer to him. Her hand strayed to where her katshme would be, but she didn't have them.

"Mmmm and you haven't changed either," Gaidin said, eyeing Jewel up and down while biting his lower lip. "Have you reconsidered my offer of marriage? Did living alone in the woods make you realize how you can't live without me?"

Eww. Pendry thought, *who is this gross, oily weasel? Not someone she trusts.*

"Did you reconsider my offer of being drawn and quartered?" Jewel said, straightening her shoulders and making herself look more commanding.

Gaidin sneered at her. "You'll change your mind, I always get what's mine." He reached a hand out as if he was going to stroke her cheek. She flinched and raised her hand like she was readying to fight.

Pendry's reflexes kicked in and he grabbed Gaidin's hand before he could stop himself. "Ok, no. You're making *my* skin crawl, and I've seen some things." He pushed Gaidin's hand down and moved to put himself between Jewel and Gaidin. "She said no, but if you need to hear it from another man, I'll be the one to knock it through your skull." He'd dealt with enough slimy, oily men who couldn't take no for an answer. He'd found the best way to deal with them was to simply take command.

Gaidin eyed Pendry as if he was a foul street urchin. "And what gives you the authority to make decisions for her?"

"Nothing, and I'm not making her decisions. I'm voicing them so you will listen. She said no, so back off."

Pendry was at least 6 inches taller than Gaidin and he was more muscular than him too, but that didn't seem to make a difference. Gaidin sneered again at Pendry and made a move to go past him, when out of the corner of Pendry's eye he saw Ferga's red hair.

"Gaidin," he said in a commanding voice. "This is our new recruit, Pendry."

Gaidin glared at Ferga then at Pendry. "Pleased to meet you," he said through gritted teeth. "Jewel, you know where to find me." He turned and sauntered off.

"Sorry about that, forgot 'that' would be here," Ferga said, turning to Jewel.

"It's fine, just as long as HE isn't here." She said nervously, smoothing her dress. She looked up at Ferga, looking suddenly scared. "You said you'd get rid of him. Did you?"

"Yes, first thing I did was to exile him. You won't be seeing *that* one." He gently guided her to the side of the room.

Pendry followed, curious about the oily man and the man that she no longer needed to worry about. She seemed different, not just in her appearance but also in the way she acted, more on edge.

She doesn't seem as comfortable here.

Ferga led her to a chair. Once she was seated he turned to Pendry, "I'll go get some refreshments. Good job with Gaidin. Um, keep an eye on her."

"Yeah," Pendry said, feeling a little unsure about what was going on.

He turned to Jewel, who seemed to be doing some breathing exercises. Her eyes were closed and her hands rested on her knees. He watched her for a while, wanting to ask, but not wanting to interrupt her trying to calm down.

She opened her eyes and looked up at him, "Sorry. Thank you for back there. I wasn't ready for that kind of interaction again." She shivered.

He sat down in the chair next to her. "I was wondering about it, seemed a little forward of him and creepy. I'm sorry but why, and eww." He turned to look at Jewel. She was smiling sadly.

"It came with the territory, everyone wants to be the head of the clan or head of the gang as you'd put it, or as close to the head as possible, so you get marriage proposals or offers of spouses from families. It gets to be too much." She sighed and leaned her head back against the wall. "Honestly, that was the best part of leaving. It was quiet. That's why Ferga got so excited to have us here at the party, takes some of the heat off of himself."

"Yeah, but that guy wasn't going to take no for an answer, is that common?"

The look on Jewel's face told him that it was and that she didn't want to say more.

Ferga walked up holding two drinks and talking with a new person, he was slightly slimmer and a little shorter than Ferga. "Look who I just found hiding in the drink corner," he said pointing to the man.

"Dannor!" Jewel jumped up and hugged him.

"Hey sis." He hugged her tightly, lifting her off the ground as he did. He had the same hair and eyes that Jewel had but his features didn't look like her other than that. He set her down and kissed her forehead.

"What have you been up to?" she said, eyeing him up and down. "Still have all your limbs?"

"Yes, all four limbs and both eyes," he said, smiling at her. "You ran into Gaidin, I hear." He made a face like the mere thought of the man made him sick.

"No, you're supposed to help lift her spirits, not bring them down with him," Ferga said, handing Jewel a glass of some pink liquid. She took it, smiling graciously at Ferga.

He sat down in the seat next to Pendry and handed him the other glass of the pink drink.

"Ah, sorry. Yes, lifting your spirits." Dannor looked up, then snapped his fingers and pointed at Ferga, "Did you tell her about Luna?"

"Luna?" Jewel asked.

"I didn't," Ferga said, smiling broadly, "but she's over there if you want to introduce them."

"Come on sis, this will cheer you up."

They walked off, leaving Ferga and Pendry sitting alone. Pendry sipped the pink drink, watching Jewel and Dannor walk away. The drink was floral and sweet, not bad but not what he was expecting. He turned to see Ferga eyeing him. He had the feeling Ferga could see through him, to read his thoughts and know what he was thinking or feeling.

Ugh, I probably gave away I'm a peace officer.

"So, um, Gaidin was it, what was that about?" he asked cautiously, trying to change whatever Ferga must be thinking about him.

"Mph, snake of a man, his father too. Slithering in where they shouldn't be. They have this family motto of,

I always get what I want." He snorted, "I think it's the first thing they say as babes. They're in charge of the supply lines, great at getting what's needed in and out in a timely manner. He's tried a little too hard to get Jewel to be interested in him. Even after the incident when everyone else backed off a little and gave her room, he wouldn't."

"Incident? You mean the arrow or the wall?"

"No," Ferga said looking a little uncomfortable, "It's not really my place to tell. You can ask her about it if you have the courage, but it was before all of that, well before. She says the arrow was the start towards her leaving but I think the incident really was it." His eyes seemed angry and far away like he was somewhere else and not happy about it.

His expression reminded Pendry of the look Jewel had just before fighting the King's Guard. *Whatever the incident was, it wasn't good.*

10

Jewel

Luna, as Jewel had expected, was the woman that Dannor was courting. She liked seeing her older brother blush and fumble his words. It was cute.

"Jewel, this is my Luna," he said, then blushed at the way he'd said it. "I mean...."

"No, I'm your Luna," she said to him smiling. She was a beautiful woman, tall and strong. Her skin reminded Jewel of chocolate and her hair like a storm cloud. She had a nice low, melodic voice and she walked like she was on air.

"It's nice to meet you, Luna. I'm sure Dannor would have talked you up, but I've been away for the last two years," Jewel said, shaking her hand.

Luna smiled and looked at Dannor lovingly, "That's ok, there's not much to tell. We met when we were both on the same assignment, him from the capital and me from Leanna. I'm sure you can read the report notes if you want, but there's not much I can say in this crowd."

Jewel smiled back. That made sense, Dannor had been in the spy and espionage side of everything since she became the Commander. "No need to read any notes. I'm not back to be back. I simply escorted a new recruit in and was planning to leave tomorrow."

Dannor narrowed his eyes at her, "No you don't, or you won't. You're not leaving tomorrow."

"Why wouldn't I leave tomorrow? I brought Pendry, I've made introductions. There's no reason for me to stay."

"There are things that have been at a stand still for months and we need you. The council was making plans to go out and talk to you or bring you in for a meeting."

They what?

Jewel was stunned. When she'd left there were rules. One was not bringing work to her or getting her for work. Another had been not to have her as a backup plan but to move on as if she actually was dead. She stared at Dannor for a minute, feeling the anger and disappointment rising, then turned to Luna.

"Would you excuse me? I have a cousin to chasten. It was lovely to meet you." Then she turned and practically marched over to Ferga. She could hear Dannor apologize to Luna and follow after her.

"Jewel. Jewel, I'm sorry. I wasn't trying to ruin your night. Part of the problem has been that we didn't want to get you," Dannor said, trying to keep up with Jewel. "But since you're here, it makes more sense for you to stay and help with..."

"Shut up," she hissed at him. She stopped in front of Ferga and Pendry who looked like they were having a good time. "What's this I hear about you getting ready to send for me?" she asked, trying to contain her anger. She crossed her arms and glared at Ferga.

Ferga looked offended, "I would not. Ferday and I have been fighting everyone to not bring you in." He paused and looked pointedly at Dannor, "Some people have been planting seeds that you should be back and that I'm not a fit Commander."

Jewel spun on Dannor, "You conniving imp! You knew my rules. You knew why I left. Did you actually believe me or did you side with HIM?"

"Jewel, it isn't like that. I always believed you. I've never sided with HIM." He looked pleadingly at her. "I never meant to take away your peace, but we need you to lead again."

"This is your leader," she said, pointing to Ferga. "This is your new Commander and you refuse to accept it. This is why I had those rules."

"Jewel, you haven't been here. You haven't seen what the King has been doing." Dannor continued to plead. "Leanna is the only city that doesn't have King's Guards. He's executing anyone and everyone who opposes him..."

She held up her hand, seething with rage. "No. I said to act as if I really was dead. If I had died, then you would have to deal with this on your own." She turned back to Ferga, flushed and feeling tired of people. "Is there anyone you'd like me to see before I call it a night and leave?"

She avoided Pendrys eyes, but she could tell he looked surprised and tense. *Stay focused*, she thought, *you can explain later.* This was not the good first impression of the Gradiare that she wanted to show him.

Ferga sighed. "No, but I had been hoping for a dance, I haven't danced since becoming Commander. If I dance with anyone not family, then the rumors fly. And your sisters were never the fun dance partners."

Is he pouting? Ugh, he is.

He had such a sad and pleading look in his eyes. She remembered all too well the pressures and hardship of being the Commander of such a large organization, and the rumors that they spread.

She sighed. She could resist Dannor's pleading looks, but Ferga was harder to ignore. "Fine, one dance. Then I'm going to bed." She turned to Dannor, glaring. "You can go. I'm still mad at you. Congratulations on Luna and all. I'll see you tomorrow when I'm more able to yell at you."

Dannor looked deflated and frustrated. "Fine, but only if you will listen before you leave."

She nodded. Satisfied, he turned and walked back to where Luna was. She didn't care that she was being commanding again. She was just mad that her own brother, who saw and knew what she went through, would be trying to get her back into this mess.

"Now," she turned to Ferga, "before I change my mind, name your song and dance, and know I'm a bit rusty on the partner dances."

Ferga jumped to his feet grinning broadly. "Not a problem, just let me lead and we'll be good as gold." He let out a shrill whistle and all music and talking ceased. "Clear the dance floor and strum out my song, the Lion and I are about to break the floorboards."

Jewel rolled her eyes and glanced at Pendry. He still looked confused by what had just transpired but was smiling, as if to say *what treat is this?* She smiled and took Ferga's hand.

Just try to enjoy the rest of the night, she told herself.

The floor was cleared and the lively music started. She pushed past all the frustration and turmoil she had already been through in such a short time. Ferga led her in, bounding onto the dance floor. She'd missed dancing with him. He'd always helped her feel like a kid when everyone else had made her grow up.

He spun her round and dipped her. The dance was almost a jig, but more formal and easier to do in a long dress than a jig. When he flipped her over his head she was happy she'd worn her under shorts like she used to.

She focused on Ferga, the dance, and the music, pushing the faces of the people watching them out of her mind. She'd missed Ferga, he'd been her second in command and had always been ready to help her focus on lighter things. He'd also been her biggest supporter of moving to the cabin. She should have known that he wouldn't have been a supporter of bringing her back.

"I hope you have the energy for two more dances," he whispered in her ear as he spun her out.

When he brought her back in she hastily whispered, "I said one."

He flipped her up over his head, then brought her down and dipped her low. She could feel her hair pooling on the floor. She'd forgotten to pin it up before dancing.

"One with me and one with your new friend," he whispered back. He led her round the room, radiating joy and looking like a giant of a little kid.

"Not happening," she muttered back. She caught a glimpse of Pendry standing and watching. He looked happy and intrigued by the dance.

The song was coming to an end. She remembered what Ferga liked to do before the end right before he did it. He spun her, not out or around, but in one spot. He liked to go as fast as he could until suddenly stopping and dipping her. The last time they'd danced, her hair hadn't been so long. She could feel it hitting him and spinning out behind her. She felt light hearted and happy. It had been too long. He dipped her as the music ended and there was applause.

He stood her up and let her catch her balance on him as he turned to everyone. "Join the dance," he said loudly, then he led Jewel off the floor. She gripped his hand, the room still spinning slightly.

"Why do you always do that to me?" She asked as he sat her in a chair. She could feel her face flushed and beaming.

"Agh, because you're the only one who can still walk after that."

"Yes, but not well."

"You're just out of practice," he said. Then he slapped Pendry on the back, "Your turn man. Show me what you've got."

Pendry looked a little surprised, "I'm not really used to this kind of dancing and I don't have anyone to dance with. I'll have to sit this one out." He rubbed the back of his neck nervously.

"Nonsense!" Ferga bellowed, he pointed at Jewel. "There's your partner and everyone knows the next song. I'll go tell the musicians what's the next song." He turned and was gone before Jewel and Pendry could argue with him.

Jewel sighed and looked at Pendry. "He's never liked being told "no" when he gets one of his schemes. It probably wasn't the best plan to give him so much authority."

Pendry sat next to her smiling, "Just because he said to, doesn't mean we have to. He left, there's not much he could do about it."

She smiled, "Ah, but you're the new recruit and have to do what he says. Maybe you could find someone else to dance with. If you dance with my mother, no one will gossip about you."

"That's not happening." For such a big man, Ferga was able to sneak up before either of them had noticed.

Why is everyone always trying to match me up with someone? Can't I just be happy alone? she thought, glaring at Ferga.

"Fine," Pendry said, giving Ferga a slight glare. He turned to Jewel, smiling at her. "You called me friend, we can dance as friends." He stood up as the song finished and held his hand out to Jewel. "My lady," he said with a slight bow.

She was reminded by the way he was standing with one hand behind his back and one hand held out to her that he had been a peace officer and had more formal training from the capital school.

She smiled at him and took his hand, then glared at Ferga, "I'll get you for this," she hissed.

Ferga was beaming as he shooed them to the dance floor and stood watching with a smug smile on his face.

"Sometimes I hate that man," Jewel whispered as they took their position among the other dancers and the music started. She could feel all the eyes in the room on them. She'd always tried to avoid being the topic of gossip, but a lot of the time it was hard.

I wonder how they'll spin this one.

"Ignore them," Pendry whispered as he led her into a waltz.

She looked up and saw him looking where he was leading, but smiling that crooked smile.

"Hard to when I know what they're thinking," she whispered back.

He spun her out then dipped her, it was slower than dancing with Ferga but just as fun.

"Let them think, let them talk," he whispered, smiling at her. "We know what's true."

He's right, it's just gossip. And truthfully, he'll be the one dealing with most of it once I leave.

He led her around the room, spinning and twirling her as they went. She couldn't help smiling. She'd always loved dancing and it was always better with a good partner, and Pendry was a very good partner.

She could feel her mood lighten and her heart skipped. This was what she'd missed when living by herself, the friends and family that made her feel happy.

The music stopped and Pendry ended with her right in front of Ferga. He bowed to her and led her to her seat.

"You said you couldn't dance," Ferga said, looking surprised.

Pendry shot him a confused look, "You sent me out there to dance and be made a fool?"

Ferga smirked. "Eh," he shrugged.

Jewel sat for a moment letting the good mood linger. Then she stood and turned to Ferga, "I've danced like you wanted, now I'm off to bed. It's been a long day of hiking into the city and I'd like to have some rest for that discussion with Dannor and the trip back to my cabin." She turned to Pendry and gave a small curtsy, "Thank you for the dance. If you'll excuse me, I'll be off to bed now."

She turned and made her way out of the room before Ferga could make her dance with anyone else. She could still feel eyes watching, but she made it out before anyone else stopped her.

11

Jewel

J ewel woke the next morning to someone knocking on her door. Before she could answer, the door opened and in walked her little sister, beaming at her. Her dark hair was half up and curling softly around her face. Her bright blue eyes danced and reminded Jewel of for-get-me-nots. She wore a long, full sage green dress with a cream and purple apron.

Lavender closed the door softly, then turned and bolt-ed to the bed and jumped on top of Jewel, hugging and kissing her.

"Oh, I missed you," she said, squeezing Jewel so tight she squeaked. "Oh sorry, it's just I didn't know you were going to be here until I woke up and heard you were here. I wanted to say hi before you snuck off."

Jewel sat up, hugging her sister and kissing her cheek. "It's ok, I missed you too. You weren't at the ball yester-day. Why? You normally never miss one." She brushed a wisp of hair behind Lavender's ear.

"Oh, I couldn't. I was on kitchen duty for breakfast. That's why I'm up so early." She bounced on the bed a little, moving herself to face Jewel. She had a smug look in her eye. "I hear you have a beau, and you danced the night away with him."

"Lav," Jewel said indignantly, "is that how they're telling it?" She groaned and stood up. "Pendry is a new friend that I brought as a recruit, nothing more." She scooped up her clothes and walked behind the dressing curtain. She caught a glimpse of her reflection in the mirror and stopped, *ugh* she thought, *why am I blushing?* She patted her cheeks, trying to stop the red from spreading. *That's not how it works.*

"Oh?" Lavender teased.

"Lavender," Jewel snapped playfully. She looked out from behind the curtain, "Stop. If it was like that I'd tell you personally and not let gossip spread to you first."

Lavender sighed and leaned back on her hands. "Fine, but you have to say it looks it, you sneaking in with a strange handsome man and then dancing with him. You never dance with someone without reason."

"Ferga made me," Jewel said as she dressed.

"Oh, that makes sense. I heard you danced with him first. Did he do that thing where he spins you so fast and you can't think clearly, then passed you off to the other guy, what's it?"

"Pendry, and yes he did." She stepped out from behind the curtain, finishing the last button on her blouse. "Is he taking lessons from Mom and Aunt Diana?"

Lavender laughed. "No, but he has been under the attack of the matchmakers. He probably wanted some breathing room, and you get to leave now, so why not throw you to them."

Jewel sighed. She knew the feeling. "Yeah, I get it, but still, Pendry's not leaving and he starts his time here with gossip. Probably not very wise on Ferga's part."

She moved to the sink and started to wash her face. It was nice to be back, the familiarity of it all, the people she cared for. The room that she'd grown up in. It was a sparse but neat room. She'd taken most of her belongings with her and only left a few things for if she ever visited. There was a small bed, a dresser with some clothes, a small desk that she'd hardly used, the changing curtain, and a small sink. The walls were cream and bare, no windows. Windows were dangerous in the hideout.

"I think it was very smart of Ferga," Lavender said, watching Jewel wash her face. "It got everyone talking about Pendry, and now everyone knows him and that you trust him. He made it so that everyone will trust him because you trusted him enough to bring him and dance with him."

Jewel dried her face and sighed. She had to admit that was smart and she hadn't thought of it that way. She untied her braid and started pinning it up into a bun.

"Well, enough about last night. How have you been? Find your own special someone?" She smirked at Lavender from the mirror.

Lavender rolled her eyes. "No," she said standing up from the bed. "I'm perfectly fine without that right now."

"Really?" Jewel asked, turning to face her. "But you were always talking about boys and who you thought was most handsome. I would have thought you'd have a, what did you call it, a beau." She smiled coyly at her sister.

"Ugh," Lavender groaned, swishing her skirt. "Just because I can admit when a guy catches my eye doesn't mean that I have to go chasing him, I'm not Shayla. No, I'm happy with my teaching and cooking jobs. I'd like to just focus on that for a while."

Jewel sat on the bed and started pulling on her boots. "Oh? I'm glad you like those jobs."

"Yes, I've been meaning to say thank you for setting me up with them, but it got a little busy. So, thanks."

"You're welcome," Jewel said. She'd finished her boots and stood looking around to see what she'd forgotten. Her katshme, she'd gotten so used to getting dressed without them that she almost forgot to put them on. She strapped on the belt with the katshme over her pants and eyed Lavender. Something was different.

"I'm really happy you like the jobs." Jewel straightened and realized what was different. "Did you get taller?" she asked, suddenly realizing her baby sister was at least two inches taller than her now. "Ugh, I'm now the shortest in the family. That's just rude."

Lavender laughed, and caught up Jewel's arm as they started out of the room and down the hall to the dining room.

"If you don't like that, wait until you see Ferday. He had a late growth spurt and is now almost as tall as Ferga, I think Dannor is upset because he's shorter than him now."

They could hear laughing before they even entered the dining room. Jewel knew Ferga's laugh, it was boisterous and filled a room. The other laugh was loud and jovial, but not one she recognized at first.

They walked into the large room. Like all the rooms, it had a vaulted ceiling and a large fireplace. There were rows of tables that were empty at this earlier hour, except for the one set with food. The walls were draped with tapestries, with one wall being covered with memorial name plates and the Gradiare crest.

Ferga and Pendry were laughing as they ate their breakfast. Pendry had a good laugh, once Jewel heard it she was reminded of their trip through the woods and the joke about the rock. It made her happy to hear him laughing. Ferga and Pendry seemed to be fast friends and to be getting along well.

That's good, she thought as they walked up to the table.

"There they are!" Ferga exclaimed, raising his coffee mug to them. "Hope you slept well in the stuffy rooms of this old hold after all the fresh air you've had."

Jewel smiled and pulled out a chair next to Ferga. "I slept well considering. It helped to be tired and dizzy after dancing with you." She smiled across the table at Pendry. "Good morning. Pendry, this is my little sister, Lavender. She was one of the morning's cooks."

Pendry smiled, "It's excellent food, thank you. And good morning to you both."

He looked well rested. He most likely hadn't stayed at the party long after she left. He was wearing some of Ferga's clothes and they fit well, only slightly too big.

Lavender handed her a cup of coffee and went to get some food. Jewel thanked her and turned to Ferga,

"What's your plan for the day? If you need me I can stay for the day, but if not, I'll be leaving after talking with Dannor."

Ferga sipped his coffee, then sighed in satisfaction. "Ah, I called an emergency council meeting. Since you're here and don't plan to stay, figured you could tell those old coots to stick it and flaunt your way back to that meadow you live in."

She glared at him, "I don't live in a meadow."

"You kinda do," Pendry said, smirking over the rim of his mug.

Is he enjoying this? She thought. She glared at him too. "And when have I ever told the council to stick it?" She asked, looking back at Ferga. She was trying to stay serious, but the glint in Pendry's and Ferga's eyes was making it hard to keep on track.

"Didn't you tell them to suck lemons when you were in the sick bay and they wouldn't leave you alone to recover?" Lavender asked as she set a plate of food in front of Jewel.

Pendry snorted and started coughing and choking on his coffee.

Ferga burst out laughing and slapped the table. "I'd forgotten that diamond of a memory. Oh, I wish I could relive that," he chortled, "You laying in bed covered in bandages and those ten grown men telling you they couldn't lead without you and you needed to get out of bed." He laughed and turned to Pendry, who was still trying to breathe normally. "She had only woken from her coma the day before and these idiots of a council are telling her to get up and lead, and before any of us can tell them to shut up and leave, she practically screams at them to suck a lemon and run into a wall and maybe then they would have an eighth of the pain she was in." He laughed even harder.

Jewel was trying not to blush at the memory, but she knew it was too late. "That medicine tastes like sour lemons," she said indignantly, "and I'd quite literally had a wall fall on me. I was simply trying to express that I was in no condition to lead and they needed to leave me alone. It didn't help that the meds made everyone look like giant purple grape people."

It was Ferga's turn to snort and splutter on coffee. "What in the, why?"

"I don't know," she said looking at Pendry who was still doubled over in his chair trying to breathe while laughing at the conversation.

He was wheezing and coughing, but managed to say, "I've had that stuff, it's not right." He sat up wiping tears and smiling broadly, "Not that I've had a wall fall on me, but I think it's used for coma patients. Ugh" he dried his eyes and chuckled, "I've never heard anyone describe it like that, but that's pretty accurate."

Ferga was wiping his eyes with a napkin and chuckling. "Anyway, that's why I figured you could tell the council to leave you alone. I think you're the only one they'll listen to on that."

Before Jewel could respond she heard someone singing as they opened the door, she turned to see a tall slender young man entering the room. His hair was redder and shorter than she remembered, and he was definitely taller and more muscular. He had on a billowy black shirt and black pants tucked into his boots. Draped around his shoulder was a gray cloak fastened with a red pin. There were several knives strapped to him. She counted at least two daggers across his chest, a set of katshme, a sword belted at his waist, and a small knife sticking out the top of one of his boots.

"Remember, my name!" He shouted the last line of the song then bowed to his imaginary audience. "Thank you, dear Lav," he said, reaching out to take the plate that Lavender was carrying to the table.

"Get your own food," she snapped deftly dodging his reach and sitting next to Jewel.

Jewel stood up and walked toward the man. "Hi, Ferday." She meant to walk calmly over to him but he had other ideas.

"Whoo!" he whooped. Running up and catching her up, he spun her around. "Finally, someone who isn't afraid of anything." He tossed her in the air and caught her neatly, still spinning.

"Put me down you idiot," Jewel said, thumping his chest. She couldn't help but laugh.

Why do they both always have to do that?

He hugged her close and kissed her cheek. "Ah, but I've missed my sparring partner and my Lion."

"Put her down and get some food," Ferga said. He'd recovered his senses. "We have a council meeting and who knows how long it will be."

"Ooo. An opportunity to see you tell those idiots to jump in a lake. I like it," Ferday said, setting her down.

"I never told them to do that." Jewel said, taking her seat again.

"Yes, you did," Lavender, Ferga and Ferday all said.

Pendry chuckled and stayed focused on his food. *He is getting a kick out of this*, she thought.

"Fine, when was that?" she asked as she started to eat.

"When you were fifteen and they told you to do as you're told and heed their advice." Ferga said, smirking at Pendry.

"After the incident when they said you'd made it up and were just trying to get rid of him, because he opposed you," Lavender said, sipping her coffee.

"When they tried to say you couldn't fight because you're a girl. When they said you had to be a good role model and marry. When they said..." Ferday said over his shoulder as he heaped his plate with food.

"Ok, I get it. I didn't remember being so opposed to the council." She rubbed her forehead. *Why am I here?* She had a slight headache just from the thought of all those council meetings.

Ferday sat down smiling boyishly at Jewel. "You were the most stubborn Commander the Gradiare has ever seen and the only one who ever retired instead of serving until they died." He sat back, then seemed to notice Pendry for the first time. "Hello, who's this?" he gasped, "Has our intrepid leader finally given in and found a match? Oh, has someone tamed this Lion? What's your name, good sir?"

Jewel was so flushed she was sure she looked like a beet. She couldn't talk. It was too much.

Why does everyone think we're together like that?

Pendry turned to Ferday and shook his hand, "Pendry, and I'm just a friend and a new recruit," he said smiling. He seemed to understand that Jewel was having a hard time with everything.

Ferday raised one eyebrow, "Hmm, friends can lead to more than friends, I'll accept that for now." He turned and started eating like he hadn't eaten in days. He'd never learned table manners, insisting they had no use and would only slow him down. "I'm suddenly excited for this council meeting. Haven't had one with a good knock down brawl since," he paused, "two months ago?" he asked, looking at Ferga. "But that wasn't a planned one. Not that any of them ever are planned. But this one is expected."

Pendry turned to Jewel, "Just what kind of council meetings are these?" He asked, looking a little concerned.

"Oh, you'll see. You'll love this," Ferday said wolfing down more food.

Jewel rubbed her head, that headache was growing worse.

12

Pendry

Pendry followed Jewel and Lavender down one of the long halls. The entire hideout seemed to be a maze of halls and rooms. All of the halls were lined with rugs and tapestries to add warmth. It was easy to forget that they were underground and that there was an entire city living above them. For an underground army hideout, it felt more like a village or a small town. There were signs of war with everyone wearing weapons, but also smiling and laughing. It was easy to forget about the fighting.

Pendry liked Jewel's family. He'd felt both accepted and slightly awkward at breakfast. They seemed like a family should be, at least what he'd always pictured it would be like to have a big family.

They seem close, he mused as they walked.

He watched Lavender whisper and laugh with Jewel. Behind him he heard Ferga and Ferday laughing and joking about what Jewel would do to the council. Even with the teasing and joking, he could tell that they all loved and respected Jewel. She'd obviously been a good leader and had some good support from her family.

Lavender looked back at him, then whispered to Jewel. Whatever it was, it made her blush and look indignant. She said something back in a hushed tone.

Pendry was feeling better after a full night of sleep with no wrathes screaming or eyes watching him. It helped to have good hearty food cooked and ready when he woke up. This wasn't what he'd pictured when he'd thought about the Gradiare. He had pictured hardened criminals and grim circumstances. Instead he got laughter, dances, and people ready to have him join the family before they even knew his name.

How have these people been the biggest enemy of the king? he thought. *It seems backwards. Everything just seems backwards now.*

He was broken from his thoughts by Ferday slapping his shoulder and whispering loudly to him. "Just looking does nothing for a relationship."

"What?" Pendry asked as he realized what he was referring to. He had been staring at Jewel as she walked ahead of him. "I wasn't." He started to say.

"Don't force him to her," whispered Ferga, pulling Ferday's arm off of Pendry.

Pendry turned to face the two men. They were smiling conspiratorially. If he hadn't known they were cousins, he probably would have thought they were brothers.

"He'll move when he wants." Ferga continued raising an eyebrow, "Right, Pendry?"

Pendry put his hands up slightly, "I'm not, I wasn't."

"Ah, the flustered mutterings of young love," Ferday sighed theatrically, putting a hand on his chest and gazing at the ceiling.

"What is it with you people and romance?" Pendry asked in a hoarse whisper. He was getting a little annoyed with the constant comments. No wonder Ferga had been so ready to pawn him off for everyone to gossip about, but now Ferga was one of the gossipers.

"Oh, that's easy. There's nothing to lift the mood of those constantly at war like good news. Young love or new babies, those are the best news. And young love leads to new babies," Ferday said, smiling dreamily. "It doesn't help when the majority of people are family in one way or another. That makes it so any and all newcomers are the point of all matches."

Pendry nodded, it made sense when he said it like that. "Ok, but why are you shoving me at Jewel?"

"Simply harmless fun. Partly because it's fun to watch her squirm and blush and partly because it says a lot about someone to see how they react to it." Ferday winked at him. "And you handled that very well. Confrontation is good in our circle."

"You were testing me?" He felt a little angry, but also intrigued. "Do you do this to everyone?"

"No." Ferga shook his head. "Jewel hasn't ever brought in a new recruit, so we had to take the opportunity where it presented itself."

"What are you talking about?"

All three men jumped and Pendry turned to see Jewel eyeing them with a stern glare, her green eyes seemed to flash in the dimly lit hall.

"Oh, just debating about what way you're going to tear down the council's pride." Ferga said, rubbing the back of his neck.

"And about who's going to pee his pants first. I think Renly." Ferday said, looking sheepish.

"Right," she said hesitantly. She didn't look convinced but she dropped the subject. "Ferga, is there anything I should be aware of before we go into the council meeting?"

"No," he said, confused. "Oh, well, actually you should probably know we have a leak."

Jewel stared open mouthed at Ferga. "What?" Her eyes darkened and her fists clenched, "What!" She growled again, louder and through clenched teeth. "You didn't–you were going to let me walk in there, not knowing that crucial piece of information?"

Pendry thought she was about to fight Ferga. She kept clenching her fists and her eyes blazed like they did when she fought the King's Guard.

A *leak*. He thought about the captain of the 11th who was killed. *Did he have something to do with the leak? But that wouldn't make sense about why he'd been killed.*

Jewel eyed Pendry and he had the feeling she was thinking the same thing. She rubbed her forehead. "Anything else before I go in there?"

Ferga thought for a moment, "No." He hesitated.

"What?" Jewel growled again, stepping closer to him.

"One of our informers was killed, and another one told us he knew who the leak was, but then he went dark," Ferga sighed, "To be honest, it's been a mess. The King's been making stricter laws and harsher punishments. Recruitment's been down, rehoming has gone up, but as fast as we help people out of the city more people come in." He suddenly looked worn and on the verge of breaking. "We've been planning the coup, but we lack the manpower, and no one is up for doing the reconnaissance and getting the information we need." His shoulders slumped and it was as if he aged twenty years in the minute of conversation. "If you haven't noticed, the hold is a bit sparse on people. Everyone we have that is up for the task of retrieving the information is otherwise occupied. But now is the best time to execute the coup. I'll explain more in the meeting."

Jewel sighed. Her eyes softened and her hands relaxed. "Ok, thank you." She smiled sadly at him. "You're doing great, Ferga, you really are. I won't let them put me in charge, but I have nothing against being some of that manpower you need."

He seemed to get his strength back and stood up a little straighter "Right, let's face the old coots, tell them what's what," he said, getting back his energy and vigor as he talked.

Jewel turned and gestured for Ferga to take the lead. He squared his shoulders and stepped forward, Ferday and Lavender falling in behind him.

"Careful what you say. Don't talk until I say," Jewel whispered to Pendry. "Just because we trust you doesn't mean they will. We've worked hard to get the council to where they are now, but they're a bunch of slow-to-move fast-to-judge old grumps."

Pendry and Jewel follow the others. "Noted. Let you rip them down before I say anything." He smiled down at Jewel. She was making a face that seemed to say, "Really? You too?"

They entered the council room, a large stone room with vaulted ceiling and a stone fireplace. A long table was off to one side. Half of it was covered with neat stacks of papers and the other half had trays of pastries and finger foods. Around the fireplace were about fifteen wood folding chairs arranged in a circle. Most of the chairs were filled with older gray-haired men. Some were older than others, but they all looked grim and hardened by war.

This was more the picture that Pendry had in his mind when he'd thought of the Gradiare, minus the pastries and maybe add in some strong drinks. He noticed among the older men were a few younger men. Dannor was one of them. He was talking in a low whisper to the older man next to him. He stopped and sat up expectantly when they entered the circle of chairs.

"Thank you for coming on such short notice," Ferga boomed. "Now, as you may have heard, Jewel came last night and brought a new recruit." He stepped aside and indicated Pendry and Jewel.

Pendry felt every eye of the council turn to them. He glanced at Jewel and saw her straighten and her face grow stony. It was more the way she'd looked when he first saw her. She had drawn up all of her defenses. He hadn't realized she'd lowered any.

He watched her stride forward, a hand resting on one of her katshme. She didn't even say a word before it seemed that every man in the room was on their feet talking. It was like they were children asking their mom for food or help. Not only were they talking over one another but some were even pointing at each other, pointing blame.

How do they get anything done?

Ferga pursed his lips and let out a shrill whistle. "Are you all babes that crowd your mother the moment you see her? Have some respect, men."

Slowly the men sat down, but Pendry could hear them grumbling to each other in low voices.

"Thank you," Jewel said, patting Ferga on the arm. She turned and addressed the council, "I'm not here to take over, I'm here to be extra brains and strength. Ferga is still in charge and I will gladly take a seat." She smiled at Ferga and took a seat near the fire. She indicated for Pendry to take a seat next to her.

Again he felt all eyes on him. He wasn't used to causing such a stir by simply walking into a room. *I guess that's what happens when the former Commander brings you in.* He thought as he walked over and sat in the seat that she'd indicated. He made sure to stand straight and tall. As a kid he'd had the habit of hunching down to make himself smaller when he was in front of everyone. He'd had to work extra hard to stand straight as a peace officer, but the habit sometimes came out when he wasn't thinking.

"To start off with," Ferga was saying, "It has been confirmed there is a leak." There was a collective groan and murmur that went up from the council. "And," Ferga continued, holding up one hand. "It has also been confirmed that our leak is not a part of the council, so we'll have no division and fighting." He took a moment and looked around the room.

"Do we know who the leak is?" one of the younger men asked.

"Not at the moment. We have sources who are looking into it as we speak. When I know, you will know." Ferga glanced at Dannor who inclined his head slightly. "Now, before we move on to the matter at hand, are there any other questions?"

No one answered, although they all seemed to have something they wanted to say, just no questions.

"We have been working towards infiltration of the castle and gaining information to finally come out of the shadows fully and lead a coup." He looked at Jewel, "This is where we've been divided. The risk of going into the castle simply to get a better understanding of the layout has been the reason we've never fully started the coup." He sighed. "That and the last coup we started ended in the loss of too many lives." Jewel nodded.

This must have been something she's dealt with before.

"Thanks to the most recent mission of Dannor and Luna we now know that the King fully intends to overthrow the peace officers and only use the King's Guard." He glanced in Pendrys direction.

He knows I was a peace officer, Pendry thought, *but I didn't tell him.*

Ferga turned towards Ferday and continued talking. "According to accounts we've heard, they're recruiting all loyal peace officers into the King's Guard and killing any who show slight opposition to the idea. Not only that, but anyone who openly opposes the King is being imprisoned, some even executed."

Pendrys stomach twisted. How many of his old friends were ok? Would any of them have joined the King's Guard? His closest friends were those who served with him and were now the people at the highest risk. He felt something touch his hand and looked down to see Jewel tapping his hand gently. He'd been clenching his fists so hard his knuckles were white. He relaxed his hands. He had to relax. These were the people to help his old friends.

"The King has moved from killing those who want him gone to killing those who don't like his rules. It's no longer those who stand against him because of what he believes, but those who simply question him." Ferga rubbed his eyes and looked worn again. "We received news that the Getrin brothers who run the newspaper were arrested yesterday for printing the story of the King's new ruling of papers needed for the inner ring. We don't know what he plans to do with them." He stopped and looked like he was trying to regain control of his emotions.

"The simple truth," Ferday said stepping in, "is that this can't go on. The kings have all been bad but this King has turned out to be worse than Seynaus, the very first king. He at least wanted people to rule over. At the rate that the King is moving, the city will be under strict lockdown and there will be so few people it will be all but a ghost town."

The air was heavy with those words. Pendry knew it was bad. He'd heard rumors of more peace officers joining the King's Guard and the rapid disappearance of other officers as well, but he never knew what was actually happening.

"We can't lead a coup, not when those being trained in Leanna have yet to finish and arrive." One of the older men said, standing, "We have to protect our own people before we protect those in the city."

"If we focus on our own people there won't be a city," another man said standing to oppose the first.

"Have you forgotten how many families with children are here under our protection?" The first man yelled back.

"And what about those families with children who live in the city and couldn't move to be better under our protection? Are they not worth our protection?" One of the younger men barked back.

"Men!" Ferga shouted, having regained composure. "We are not here to debate about if now is the time for a coup. We decided that two months ago. Now is when we need to act. We need confirmation to show the people of this city that the King will no longer protect them as a king should. There are fewer King's Guards since the King sent out a fleet of ships to make alliances with other kings. Now is when we need to act before he regains forces from Trenten."

"With what people?" There was a new man standing. He was one of the older men. By the way he stood, it looked to Pendry as if the man was used to getting away with challenging authority.

Jewel stood. She didn't walk to where Ferga was. She simply stood and all eyes turned to her. They seemed to plead with her to help, or more to challenge her to fix what these men couldn't. The man who had recently stood sat back down and retreated into himself.

"This isn't new. We started this in motion five years ago, picking up where my dad left off," she said in a calm but commanding voice. "We have never had enough to fully challenge the King and all his allies, and yet we still stand. I have a solution to the problem of attaining the information, a solution I've mentioned before but was told I wasn't allowed to do because of my position."

"No." She hadn't even finished talking before the first of the older men stood again. "There is no way we will let that plan pass."

Jewel didn't seem shaken, in fact she simply sighed. "Sit down, Renly," she said sternly. "Unless you're volunteering for the opportunity to get out into the field again." The man sat down sheepishly. "I didn't think so."

Pendry saw Ferday smirk at that, he had guessed she'd make him wet himself, almost but not quite, he was probably thinking.

"As I was saying, I recommended a small group of two or three people to infiltrate the castle and obtain information. The last time we had this opportunity it was decided that it would be a suicide mission, and no one was ready to volunteer. We missed our opportunity five years ago because of arguments like this, I will not allow that to happen again." There was a hum of agreement. "Since I'm no longer Commander, I'll be going as part of the group," she said it like it was a done deal and that it was normal to sign yourself up for a suicide mission.

There was an uproar. Men were standing and yelling and pointing. Again they reminded Pendry of children.

"A child couldn't handle such a mission!"

"Leave this for the men!"

"It's signing your death. Haven't we had enough of you trying to one up every able bodied man here!"

That last comment made Pendry want to laugh. What able bodied men? Certainly not the man who said it, who was hunched over a cane and seemed to be at least 90.

"Not even your own father could make it out alive."

Pendry didn't see who said that, but he felt the anger from his companions. He waited for Ferga to whistle but he didn't. Instead, he was treated to Jewel yelling at them.

"Shut up!" They did, but they remained standing. She took a deep breath and glared at them. Gritting her teeth, she seemed to be only just containing her rage. She continued in a slightly calmer tone. "Ugh, I'd forgotten just how insufferable all of you are. Sitting here in your safe hole in the ground, thinking that someone else will do the dirty work, but if anyone says they'll do it that isn't a man, it's a challenge to you. I'm not castrating you! If you're going to act like children. then go put a diaper on." She was fuming, her green eyes burning and venomous. She looked as if she were ready to start fighting them all right there. "How many of you went with my father? None! You're a bunch of cowards, and you always have been."

The men were slowly sitting down, Pendry saw Ferga slip something to Ferday and he had to suppress a smile. They knew she wouldn't stay calm.

"The point of the council is to vote for the good of the people, to be the voice of the people, and to bring wisdom from other points of view. The last time that happened was well before I was Commander. Instead, you're a bunch of stumbling blocks, tripping up any progress we can make against the King." She took a deep breath, "So if none of you can even handle the idea of this operation, you can leave before we plan it. Feel free to go back to your dominos and novels like the good old coots that you are." She was talking normally but there was still a fierce icy anger in her voice. It made Pendry happy he'd stayed quiet and was on her good side.

Ferga snorted and covered his mouth. Ferday had ducked behind Ferga, but Pendry could see him shaking from laughter. They were enjoying the show but also seemed to be in horror of it.

Jewel was doing a very good job of ignoring the two of them. "Before you're dismissed, was there anything else that needed to be discussed?" she asked calmly, her eyes softening slightly.

"Who's that man there?" one of the men asked, pointing to Pendry.

Jewel glanced over at him, like she'd forgotten he was there. "This is a new recruit and someone who has information to share for this operation. That's all you need to know at this time."

Got it, Pendry thought, *don't talk and definitely don't tell these men you were a peace officer.*

"Dismissed," Ferga bellowed in a hoarse voice. "You heard her men, no old coots." He snorted again. But they listened. All the older men left, leaving only the five of them and Dannor.

13

Pendry

The moment the last of the older men left, Ferga and Ferday burst out laughing. They were laughing so hard they were doubled over, tears streaming down their faces.

"You called them old coots," Ferday wheezed.

"To their face," Ferga chortled.

Jewel sat down in her chair and covered her face with her hands. They were shaking slightly and she was flushed.

Pendry wasn't sure where to look or who to address. "Is that normal?"

"Yes, unfortunately." Dannor was smiling but not laughing like the other two. He rolled his eyes at them and walked over to Jewel. He knelt in front of her, "You good? I'm sorry, I forgot how they treat you. I will make sure you get your peace in the cabin after this." He rubbed her back with one hand while the other hand rested on her knee.

Pendry realized he'd judged Dannor too fast. Yes he'd wanted his sister to come back and take on the responsibilities again, but he didn't want her hurt. He was still a caring older brother, even if he forgot the pain his sister went through.

They all care, he thought, *they all know the stress. All of these leaders are the same age as me or younger and they've been doing this for a decade.*

He looked around the room and suddenly these new friends didn't look like leaders or goofing off kids. They looked like steadfast companions who'd seen hell and lived.

They've seen war, he thought, *all those fights with the Gradiare that I've heard of, they were fought by these people. When they were children no less.*

He looked back at Jewel and saw her doing that same breathing exercise that she'd done the night before when she'd run into Gaidin. He felt bad. Here she was putting herself through the trauma she'd experienced of being a child Commander and for what? For him. He hoped that wasn't the answer but he had a feeling it was at least partially true.

"Ok," Ferga said, wiping his eyes and sighing, "that was good, I needed that. Oh, that will be a good memory to look back on at the next meeting."

"Jewel," Ferday said standing slowly and wiping the tears from his eyes. "I know that always leaves you shaking, but oh heavens, no one can talk to the council like you." He snorted at the memory, "You said you weren't castrating them." He squeaked and fell back to the floor hooting and laughing.

"Now, who's going with you on this operation?" Ferga said, chuckling as he walked past Ferday.

"She's not going," Dannor said, standing and turning to face Ferga. "You were against her even coming here to talk to them, now you're all for sending her on this suicide mission?"

Ferga's eyes darkened, "I was against forcing her back in. I was against taking away her peace. She's already here and she volunteered. I will never tell her what to do." Ferga's voice was low and threatening, "She's in charge of what she does. She was and always will be the Lion of the Gradiare and I have always been there to support and help where she needs. Where have you been?"

The mood had suddenly shifted. The air again felt heavy. Ferday jumped to his feet the moment Dannor turned to face Ferga. One hand on a dagger, all humor gone, he looked ready to fight his older brother to protect his Commander.

Whoa, wait, I know families fight, but like this? Pendry thought, watching the three of them and wondering what he should do.

"Enough," Jewel groaned. She was sipping on a drink that Lavender had just given her and she looked more in control. "I said I'm going and I mean to go," she took a deep breath, "I'm small enough to go unnoticed and most of the King's Guard still think I'm dead. I can handle myself."

"Most?" Dannor asked, turning to her. "What do you mean most, shouldn't all of them think you're dead?"

"We ran into some on the way in," Pendry said quietly, thankful they didn't start fighting. "My fault really, I guess I should tell you all about why I'm here and how we met."

He looked at Jewel to make sure it was ok. She nodded so he continued. "I'm, or I was, a peace officer. I was on the road to being captain of the 10th, but-" he hesitated, then remembered his friends. They needed him and this was how he could help at the moment. He took a deep breath and continued.

He told them of the murder he'd witnessed, about the arrest and about being escorted to the Keep. "I'm not sure what you've heard of the Keep. It was built a few years ago. It's somewhere between here and Trenton. I heard rumors that it was built into an old Dragons cave. I used to think that couldn't be true, but now I think there must be one somewhere around there. I'd heard the King's Guard brag about all the Gradiare they would be locking away there, never heard if they ever did." He leaned back, remembering the dismissal journey through the woods. "I was escorted by two King's Guards. I managed to pick the lock on the prisoner wagon and fight them. I was injured in the process. I think I was stumbling around that woods for a day and a half or so. That's when I stumbled on the cabin and Jewel. I passed out at that point." He glanced at Jewel. "It was when Jewel realized that the King's Guards were still looking for me and Greta was in danger that we decided to come here."

"Are Greta and the boys in danger?" Ferga interrupted.

"No," Jewel smiled at Ferga. "We made sure they were safe, then cleared the road."

"When you say cleared the road, you mean...?" Ferday smirked at his sister.

She nodded. "Yes, unfortunately Monty got away."

"He didn't just get away." Pendry cut in, taking up the narrative again. "He bolted the moment he saw you were ready to fight. I've never seen him run so fast. He left those two King's Guards to fight you alone. I'm not sure if you know Monty, but he won't keep quiet about Jewel being alive." He stared at the floor, deciding not to recount the encounter with the faie. "We didn't run into any other King's Guard on the way in. It was pretty uneventful."

He looked up at the faces of the others. They were all staring at him with a mixture of horror and disgust. He suddenly was acutely aware of how dangerous his position was. If they didn't like that he was a peace officer, there was no way he could think of that he could take on one of them let alone all of them. Even if they did accept him, he felt sure they didn't like him anymore.

"That pig!" Ferga blurted out. "Sorry, if you're finished," he asked Pendry. He nodded. "That selfish pig is always making sure he's safe and always looking for new ways to feed the King's insanity," Ferga growled.

"It's too bad he knows who you are," Dannor sighed, "Although I think at this point only the newer King's Guard wouldn't know you on sight."

"Urgh, if I see that Monty, I think I'd like to, well I think I'd take great pleasure in killing him," Ferday said making air choking gestures like he was choking an imaginary Monty.

Pendry looked around the room surprised, "You don't hate me?"

They all stopped and looked at him surprised, even Jewel looked confused about why he'd asked that.

"Why would we hate you?" Ferga asked.

"Because I was a peace officer."

Ferga waved his hand like he was shooing a fly. "Ah, that's nothing, most of our recruits were at one time either peace officers or working for the King in one way or another. Some of our best men were once extremely close to the King. That's never been a big deal. Plus, I figured you were when I saw the way you acted at that ball last night."

"Oh," Pendry blinked, it made sense but he'd thought they wouldn't like him once they found out who he was. He wasn't really prepared for them to not care about his past. Or that Ferga had already figured him out and simply didn't care.

"Besides," Ferday chimed in, "if she trusts you, then we trust you."

Pendry glanced at Jewel. *Does she trust me?*

"Come," Ferga said, taking a deep breath, "There are better places to talk and I'd like to have some good food to eat while we make plans for this operation."

Pendry stood and went to follow them, glancing back to see how Jewel was doing. She was whispering with Lavender and seemed to be doing better, not shaking, and calmer. He turned and followed Ferga and the others out.

14

Jewel

J ewel followed the men at a slight distance. She hated council meetings. She hated how many of the men who'd been on the council from the time of her father's leadership were still there. It was a dumb system. In order for new council members to come on, they had to be voted on, and that was only if there was a vacant spot. If they wanted someone off they had to vote on that as well. The system was designed for active war. The members weren't supposed to be too old to fight. They were supposed to be active. She'd worked to force an age limit for how old council members could be, but that had been a fight that she hadn't won until after she took the arrow, and it looked like they still weren't actually following that rule. Then there was the problem of gender, they hated having her there, even when she was the Commander they'd hated it. They'd only put up with her because of the order of succession, another dumb thing she'd changed the rules on. Now it had to be passed on to the second in command. Ferga had been her second and Ferday was now his second. It still had to follow the family line. but it would hopefully never fall to a child again.

No one will ever have to go through what I did. No one will have their childhood ripped away from them. No one else will have to demand respect at the age of fourteen. No one will have to fight challengers, lead battles, and plan attacks before they are an adult. At least not in the Gradiare.

She loved her people, she cared for all of them. But the council seemed to always act like she was some war hungry, hormonal teenager. She'd never even fully grieved the loss of her dad. If the council had seen her cry, they would have forced Dannor or Ferday into the role of commander. No, she hated that time of her life, but she didn't regret what she did for her family.

"You good?" She was startled by Pendry walking next to her.

"What?" She'd been so focused on her thoughts that she hadn't heard what he said.

"You good?" he asked again softly.

"Yes," she smiled, "Just frustrated with the council. Always a fight. Always the worst battle."

Pendry grimaced, "I think I see why you wanted to be done. It's not just fighting the enemy. You were fighting your comrades too."

She sighed, "Yeah. They don't make it easy." She looked at the three men walking ahead of them, "They helped though, took some of the brunt, some of the burden. They helped a lot."

He smiled, "I can see that. Your sister seems to help a lot too, although she doesn't seem to be here."

"I asked her to make me some crestym and bring me some of those candies from my pack."

"Ah, that sounds like a good plan." He nodded and smiled at the memory of the treats. "Ok, I have to ask. Lavender? Jewel? I'm almost nervous about what names your other sisters have."

"Oh, rude," Jewel said laughing slightly, "Actually I was named after my mom's great grandma and Lavender was named after my dad's great grandma. And I quite like the names." She chuckled, "My other sisters are Gwen, Shayla and Marina. Besides, you're not one to talk. Who names their kid Pendry? Or is that also a family name?"

Pendry grimaced, "No, my dad said he picked it, said it sounded like a hero's name but not those ordinary heroes." He shrugged, "I don't know, he didn't really like to talk about it. I kinda always got the feeling my mom liked the name and he didn't know why but he just went with it."

"It does kinda sound like those hero names from a fairytale. Maybe that's why your mom liked it," she said, turning back to look at where they were going.

They were at Ferga's study now. The other three had gotten themselves situated around the table in some of the big comfy chairs. Jewel liked those chairs, they were the same chairs she had in the cabin. One of the ways they'd found to finance the Gradiare was in the making and selling of these giant comfy chairs. She'd heard a rumor that even the King had one of them without knowing they made them. She liked that rumor too.

"Now," Ferga was saying, "Jewel can't just go alone and we don't exactly know our way through the castle..."

"I do," Pendry interrupted as he sat in the chair next to Jewel.

Everyone turned to Pendry who looked proud that he could help.

"How do you know your way through the castle?" Dannor asked, confused.

Pendry leaned back in the big chair, "My badge number, it started in a 5, the 5 means someone close to you died in the line of duty. It also means that you start by getting a privileged position because of that loss. I spent my rookie years as a palace peace officer."

What? Jewel thought, trying to remember if she'd ever heard of a palace peace officer.

"A what?" Ferday asked.

They were all completely confused. Peace officers weren't in the palace, that was only the King's Guard.

Pendry smiled. He seemed pleased to finally be the one with the knowledge. "The King likes to keep a close eye on the peace officers. He said it was good leadership, but after hearing what he's doing, I think it was more to have his hand on the peace officers better," he sighed. "Anyway, the palace officers are mostly for show. It's not for anything other than to put on a resume to get higher and better jobs as an officer."

"And you had it as a rookie?" Ferga asked, grinning.

"Yeah," Pendry continued, grinning back at him. "We had to walk the halls and because the King was going through a please-the-people phase while I was there, we directed people touring the castle where they were allowed to go. I basically have that whole place memorized."

There was a stunned silence for a minute. They'd had people join who knew the castle but never ones who had it completely memorized.

"Wow, Jewel," Ferday said, "couldn't just bring any peace officer. Had to bring the poster boy of the peace officers who had the palace layout memorized." He smirked at Jewel then turned to Pendry, "You have my blessing."

Jewel was trying to think of something to say, when the door opened and Lavender came in carrying a steaming mug and a small purple pouch. She set them down in front of Jewel and kissed her forehead.

"Thank you Lav," Jewel said, squeezing her hand before Lavender headed back out.

"No fair, you get crestym and the storm candy?" Ferday said, leaning over the table and peering at the mug.

Jewel blew on it and sipped it, relishing in the warm comfort that washed over her. She sighed in satisfaction. "Ah, but I stood up to the council. I get the treats." She took another sip and smirked at her younger brother.

He plopped back in his chair with a look of indignation.

"I'll leave you some when I head home." She said, laughing. The crestym was already boosting her energy and giving her that lovely lighter, able to handle anything feeling. She pulled a candy out of the pouch and popped it in her mouth to help alleviate her sour mood.

Ferday perked up at that, "I'll take that offer."

"If you're done being childish," Dannor said, leaning forward in his chair, "Pendry, could you guide Jewel to the

King's official rooms? We need proof that he's planning a lockdown of the city. We need the people of the capital and those in outlying towns to know the King has no intentions of caring for his people. Luna and I found and took down a group from the King that was to take control of Leanna. The Lord there is one of our strongest allies. In the process, one of the men tried bargaining information for his life. That information was that the King plans to place the capital under siege and starve out anyone who opposes him. That's the proof we need to get to show the people."

Pendry nodded, "I know where his offices are."

"Good," Dannor said, leaning back and looking like a weight had been lifted. He let out a sigh. "I feel like now is the best time to tell you all that I had it confirmed this morning who the leak is. I was going to say something sooner, but felt it would be better if you didn't hear it in front of the council the first time you heard. In any case, it shouldn't be a problem to carry out an order of execution," he said looking at Ferga. He had an iciness to his voice that Jewel knew all too well.

Ferga looked confused, "We aren't the King. We don't just execute people from one offense. Who is it, that you'd jump straight to that?"

The name came to Jewel seconds before Dannor said it. "Leon."

The name hung in the air like a lit piece of dynamite waiting to go off. Jewel could feel the glances at her. She focused on the crestym. Inhaling the sweet caramel smell of it, sipping it slowly. Her stomach twisted and a knot formed in her chest, it would be him. She could hear someone asking if she was ok, but it was hard to focus. She felt dizzy and her vision blurred. The weight, that horrid weight, she felt like she couldn't breathe. She could feel herself getting drawn into the awful memory. That horrid day, the incident. The smell of him, the look in his eyes, she could hear her own scream ring through her memory.

"Who's Leon?" Pendrys voice brought her back to the present.

She looked up to see her brothers and Ferga eyeing her, the concern on their faces said it all. 'Sorry,' they said, 'sorry we couldn't protect you more.' She turned to Pendry who looked just as concerned, but more in a, 'What happened, how can I help?'

"Um," Jewel cleared her throat. "Leon is the man who tried to attack me." She swallowed, it was still hard to talk about, "Or more the man who did attack me. He was one of the council members and asked for a private meeting. Ferga was on the other side of the door. Otherwise..." She couldn't. He was getting that confused pitying look everyone always got.

"He tried to kill you?" Pendry asked, "But I've seen you fight, I don't think anyone who's seen that would think they even stood a chance."

"No." she said shakily, "and it was years ago. I was twenty, I think. I'm not sure. I've worked to block most of it out." She looked away from Pendry. She still struggled to talk about it. This was why they called it the incident. This was why they called him, Him. The memory of it still clung to her mind. She felt like she could smell him, like he was right there breathing down her neck.

She turned back to Pendry and tried to put on a brave face. "He was kicked off the council and Dannor took his spot. We came up with rules and safeguards to make sure it wouldn't happen again." She could see in his eyes he understood. He seemed sad and angry, but like he understood that she still couldn't talk about it and that she was ready to change the subject.

Now he's going to think I'm weak. Why does everyone get the same look when they hear about it?

"I think execution should have been handled right away," he said, turning to Ferga.

"Mmm. The council didn't believe it. The most they conceded to was to have him off the council," Ferga said gruffly. "It wasn't until I took over that I exiled him to Hamndle. But it appears that isn't enough," he sighed. "Is your source reliable?"

"Yes, although they asked for anonymity, but it's a very reliable source."

"Then yes, Dannor, you may carry out the execution order. Make it look like an accident. But go alone, I trust Luna, but I'd rather no one else even have the knowledge of this order."

Dannor nodded. "If you don't mind, I will leave for that at once." He stood up and kissed the top of Jewel's head. "I'm sorry again for everything."

She smiled at him, and handed him a candy from the bag. "It's not your fault." He took the candy and left.

It wasn't anyone's fault. There should have been rules in place from the start. Being the first woman Commander showed every fault in the leadership. Jewel thought as she watched her brother leave. *Leon wasn't the first to try anything. He was the only one who was supposed to be a mentor, an ally, who did. One I wouldn't have thought to do anything like that.*

"Now," Ferga said, smiling grimly at Jewel. "You two need to come up with a plan to get into the castle, and decide if you need anyone else. Also, plan a backup, and your escape in case of capture. I'm not having you survive that wall only to be captured and killed." He stood and headed for the door calling over his shoulder, "I have meetings to attend to and coots to calm. Thank you for the rousing morning."

15

Pendry

P endry staggered back to his room. It was late and he was tired. He felt as if he could fall asleep standing up. He'd done that before, and it wasn't fun. He made it into his new room and managed to kick his boots off before falling into the bed. He thought about the happenings of the day.

They had talked and planned for hours. They now had a pretty decent plan as long as nothing horrible went wrong, and they had a plan in case something horrible did go wrong. And on top of that they had a plan for if they got captured. Although that confused him, that plan was basically just Ferday does his thing, whatever that was.

Best of all he'd caught a glimpse of what Jewel was like as Commander. She faced a horde of men twice her age. She'd fought them just as ferociously as she had the King's Guard, and she never drew her katshme. He smiled, trying to picture what she'd been like as a Commander when she was still a kid. It made sense, all the stories of how terrifying she was. How much more would it have been to see her fight like that as a kid? He remembered the story of the capture of Kevka; they said she'd taken the entire stronghold on her own. He wasn't sure how much of that was true, but he didn't doubt it anymore.

He didn't know what he'd liked more, actually seeing her put the council in their place, or the reactions of Ferga and Ferday. He chuckled as he remembered them laughing. They all had such boisterous laughter. Even Jewel, when they'd been laughing in the enchanted woods, had a loud and boisterous laugh.

They seem to take every opportunity to laugh and enjoy themselves. He thought as he rolled over and tried to sleep. *It's nice to feel accepted without having to prove anything.*

He remembered one of his first days in training. All the new recruits had been made to stand in the rain in full peace officer armor, holding a large wood staff on their shoulders. Every hour a new staff was added. They'd stood there for hours. If they gave up, they were publicly humiliated in whatever messed up way the trainer could come up with. He'd met his best friend during that training. They'd kept each other going and helped each other through the rest of training. He hoped Brent was ok. He'd been facing a promotion to be the captain of the 6th. If they were targeting the higher up officers, then he would be one of them.

He pushed away the fear for his friend. Now was the time to rest, later was the time for action. He was happy he could help, even if it was a suicide mission. Maybe he could at least make sure Jewel made it out.

She deserves to go back to her peace. How does some-one attack someone so strong and terrifying? No, you've learned already how dangerous it can be to judge.

He fell asleep before he even realized his eyes were closed.

He woke up the next morning, not even sure if it was morning, since there were no windows in his room. He decided to assume it was morning.

He washed his face, brushed his teeth, and examined the stubble that was now turning into a short beard. He'd have to talk to Ferga or Ferday about borrowing some trimmers. He wet his hands and fixed his messy hair.

Not great but ok, he thought, then he turned and picked up his boots from where he'd kicked them off the night before. *Needs a polish,* he thought, then realized he didn't have to polish his boots here unless he wanted to. He smiled at that. Polished boots are nice, but always having polished boots had felt too much. Why polish them practically every day when they got muddy the minute you started your shift?

He looked back in the mirror, realizing he didn't have to shave if he didn't want to. He took a better look, trying to decide if he liked the beard. He wasn't used to a beard and decided to ask for a trimmer and, if anything, he'd be able to clean it up a bit. He pulled on his boots and headed out to get food. He heard Ferga before he'd even made it to the door. The sound made Pendry smile.

Halls filled with laughter and yet we couldn't find them. He chuckled at the thought.

He walked in to see Jewel and Ferga talking and laughing. She was telling him about something that one of Greta's boys had said and he was finding it hilarious.

Pendry got himself a plate of food and sat down across from Jewel. "Good morning," he said, then remembered he didn't know if it was morning. "Actually, how do you know what time it is or even if it's morning?"

"Morning," said Ferga, still laughing "Ah, we get that a lot." He turned and pointed to the mantle over the fire. "For one we have special clocks that tell us the day, time and if it's morning or night."

Pendry looked at the mantle. There was an ornate clock with a circling sun above it and a box with a small calendar under it. He couldn't read the date or time from where he sat.

"Second," Ferga continued. "We have specialized crystal lights that simulate the sun coming up."

It occurred to Pendry that his room had been bright with what had felt like sunlight but there were no windows. He was tired of feeling so slow to notice things.

Maybe I'm just taking in too much, so the little things are slipping through.

"It's ok," Jewel said. He must have looked a little disappointed that he hadn't noticed. "Most people are used to windows, so they don't notice the lights, and the clocks blend into the background."

He smiled. She seemed in a better mood after getting some sleep. That incident with the council had really left her shaken. "Ah, you're just being nice to me," he said, waving off the comment.

"Oh, she's not being nice. Everyone does it. Also, she's not nice." Ferga chuckled, then winced as Jewel kicked him under the table. "See, not nice." He groaned as he rubbed his leg.

Pendry smirked and blew on his coffee. He noticed that Jewel only had a cup of coffee in front of her. *That's odd*, he thought, *Did she get up so early she already ate?*

Lavender walked over with a plate of food and set it in front of Jewel. "Hardest job is making sure you eat. Do you just starve when you're on your own?" She plopped down in the chair next to Jewel. "Eat, or I'll be the one you're scared of."

"I'd pay to see that," Ferga muttered as he ate his food.

"Shut it," Lavender snapped, pointing at Ferga, then turned back to Jewel. "You eat. I'm not leaving until I see you eat. The only time you ate yesterday was breakfast. I kept getting plates back from your meals and yours hadn't been touched."

Jewel looked incredulous. "I eat. I just don't eat when I'm not hungry, and I'm not hungry when I'm working." She sighed and started eating.

He hadn't noticed her not eating during the meetings yesterday. He'd been so focused on the planning and strategizing. He'd only managed to eat his food because he'd learned years ago if food's in front of you, eat because you didn't know when you'd get food again.

"She eats at the cabin," he said before he'd stopped to think about how that sounded.

They turned to eye him curiously.

He felt his ears get hot, "I mean she at least had food ready when I woke up and made food at dinner." For some reason he felt awkward and embarrassed saying that, probably from the teasing the day before. Before he could embarrass himself more, the door burst open and in danced Ferday.

He always seems to make an entrance.

"Morning, my adoring fans. So glad you could make this meeting of the fan club." He stopped and kissed Lavender and Jewel on the head, then eyed Ferga, "Do you need a kiss too?" He said in a babyish voice.

"Get your food and stop messing around, Day. And if you kiss me again I'm going to let you taste the table," Ferga said gruffly.

Again. Pendry wondered. *They kiss each other a lot. Is that just a family thing? Or is that something every family does?*

Ferday got his plate, stacked it high with food, and joined them. "So my lovely people, we have our plan, but we don't have our day. I realized as I was falling asleep that that one very important detail hadn't been planned. What day would work best?" He said that last part to Pendry. Of course, he'd just taken a bite. He held up one finger while he quickly finished and swallowed.

"What day is today?" He asked, reaching for his cup of coffee.

Ferday looked at the clock, "Sunday."

"No, what's the date?" Pendry said, eyeing the clock. *How can he see the small numbers and day from so far away?*

Ferday raised an eyebrow, "The 16th, why?"

"Because the King's birthday is the 17th and he likes to have a large ball. There will be extra guards, but not at the side we're planning to enter in by."

Ferday eyed him in an odd way. "Do you need glasses Pendry? Why didn't you just look?"

"I did look," Pendry said, confused. "How can you see it from here? It's just a bunch of squiggles."

Ferday turned to Jewel in mock horror, "This is the guy we're trusting to lead us through the castle? He can't even see."

"I can see," Pendry said indignantly, "I just can't see something that small this far away. We'll be ok. There's nothing in the castle we need to see that's like that."

"Didn't you say you thought you were heading to Leanna but ended up at the cabin?" Ferday asked. He had a growing look of concern for the mission they had planned.

Pendry groaned at the memory of that. "I'd never actually left the city. I do have the city layout memorized and the castle memorized. There's nothing to be concerned about with that." He turned to Ferga, who looked a little concerned as well.

Great, now they don't trust me for the mission.

"Well, in any case," Ferday continued. "We can plan for tomorrow evening being the operation." He poked Pendry, "I need to see your skill in hand to hand fighting, so after breakfast we'll go to, nope, Sunday." He thought for a moment, "Ok church then sparring practice."

"Church?" Pendry asked, again everyone turned to him confused.

"Mmm." Ferga cleared his throat. "You went to the King's chapel, right, with all the deities and such?"

"Yes?" He hesitated, a little confused himself.

"We don't follow his self-made religion. You can join us if you want, or you can do what you would normally do for a worship thing. Actually, I'm not sure what they do there. But if you don't want to join us you don't have to. We can meet up again after lunch to go sparring," Ferga continued.

Pendry looked around and realized they all looked like they were dressed a little nicer than they had been the day before and none of them had weapons.

"I've never really been the religious type. Just went because I had to," he said, trying to ease his anxiety. "I'd be happy to go with you all."

16

Pendry

Church was not what Pendry thought it would be. He wasn't used to everyone singing together. He had trouble focusing on anything because there were so many people. They'd met in the council room, but instead of the small ring of chairs, there were rows of wooden folding chairs. Everyone had song books and some religious book that he didn't recognise. That was different too.

He sat in between Ferga and Ferday, and wasn't too surprised to realize they could sing really well and very loud, although it didn't seem like they were trying to be loud. They had those voices that were always loud.

It wasn't even that long, not compared to the King's chapel service. That could last half the day if the King wished, and that had always been dry and boring with a lot of random incense burning and muttering. It occurred to Pendry that he hadn't actually paid much attention to the services. He already liked this church more, simply for the lack of incense and muttering. He'd never liked that, probably because he never took the time to learn what they were for or if they had any significance. He usually spent those services wishing he could be anywhere else, doing anything else.

He remembered one time when Brent and he had spent the whole service kicking a pebble back and forth. That was the most memorable service. They'd joked about bringing a pebble every time, but a fellow officer who was a little more religious took to sitting between them.

The service ended after an hour, and everyone started talking and shaking hands. Several people went up to Jewel and said how happy they were to see her. There were a lot of people coming up to Pendry and shaking his hand and introducing themselves to him. He couldn't remember any names after, but it was nice to feel welcome.

"Jewel." Her mother walked up and took her by the hand, "Your grandmother is here, and she's asking for you to talk to her. She's so happy you came."

Kessa led them off to the other side of the room where a lady who looked ancient as time sat and knitted.

She looked up and smiled, placing her knitting down and reaching out to Jewel. "Oh, come here, you little imp. I've missed you." Her voice was soft and warm. She had the same green eyes as Jewel, although the same features as some of her other siblings. Jewel hugged her grandmother and knelt in front of her, "I hear you chastened the council again. Good for you. No one else here is brave enough to stand up to those idiots."

"I hear you used to do the same when you were younger," Jewel said, laughing.

"Me? No, never." Her grandma smiled smugly. "Maybe once or twice."

Pendry had never seen someone so old. Her skin was thin and withered, but her eyes had an odd gleam and youthfulness to them like she was secretly planning some mischief. He wondered at her. At the same time that she looked ancient, she looked fierce and conniving. Her hair was completely white and tied up in a loose bun. She sat in a wheelchair with an old quilt over her lap.

"How old is she?" Pendry whispered, leaning close to Ferday's ear.

Ferday chuckled, "That's the question. I can't remember, old."

"I may be old, but my ears are still good."

Pendry and Ferday froze like two naughty children. They turned to see the old woman glaring at them and Jewel looking pleased they were caught.

The old lady smiled, or was it a smirk? No, it was definitely a smirk. "Young man, I may be old but I can still fight as well as anyone half my age, and I don't hesitate to defend my honor."

Pendry felt a chill go down his spine. He'd never met a lady this old and he'd never had an old lady threaten to hurt him.

Does everyone here have two moods? Fight or love, this is going to take some getting used to.

"I'm 102. There, does that satisfy you? Impudent rogues," she said, looking pointedly at Ferday.

Pendry stared open mouthed, "You're as old as the kingdom."

"Pendry!" Jewel gasped looking embarrassed. He felt embarrassed. He hadn't meant to say it out loud.

Now she's mad at me again. Am I ever going to feel comfortable around these people?

"Sorry," he muttered, ashamed that he hadn't held his tongue.

"Ha." Her grandmother gave a mock laugh. "Nearly as old. This regime is 120 years old. My parents helped overthrow the old regime and establish the new one, only for the new king to betray them."

"It helps to be a gold vein, long life," Ferday whispered to him.

"You will be lucky if you live to your next birthday, my impertinent grandson,"she growled, glaring at Ferday.

"Ah, but I'd be lucky to look half as beautiful as you when I get to be half your age." Ferday said bowing low.

"You notorious flirt," she chuckled and waved him off.

Pendry smiled. She might be feisty, but she was still a grandma, and grandmas had always seemed to like him. Maybe he could make up for any offense he caused by his previous comment. He sat in one of the nearby chairs.

"You must have some of the best stories. Adventures, love and heartbreak, a life full of family and friends." He glanced at Jewel out of the corner of his eye, hoping he was making up for what he'd said. "I'd hope to live half as long and love half as much." He couldn't quite see Jewel's face unless he turned to face her but he thought he saw her stiffen a little.

I said something wrong again.

Her grandmother smiled and laughed. "Oh Jewel, tell me you're keeping this one for yourself. Don't let one of your man-hungry sisters get ahold of him. You have my blessing."

Oh, that was it, I presented an opportunity to match-make.

"No!" Jewel said patiently, rubbing her forehead.

Man-hungry? He was trying to picture Lavender being man hungry, then he remembered she had other sisters.

"We aren't here for a blessing, nor do we need one. We're just here to say hello before we go." She stood and kissed her grandmother on the forehead. "I love you," she whispered before turning and walking away. Pendry thought he saw her brushing away a tear.

What was that about?

"Right," Ferday said giving Pendry a playful slap on the shoulder, "we need to go see how well this one can fight." He walked over and kissed his grandma just as Jewel had done. "Love you, you're my favorite great-great grandma."

He turned to go and she called after him,

"I'm your only great great."

She chuckled, then leaned towards Pendry and whispered conspiratorially, "Don't worry, she's a romantic at heart and longs to be swept off her feet." She winked at him, "Has she told you she loves gardenias and lilacs?"

"Gardenias and lilacs." Pendry whispered back, deciding it would be easier to just go along with it than start a fight about how it wasn't like that. "Got it, thank you. I'd better go with Ferday," he said hastily. He stood and followed, looking back to see Ferga take his seat and start talking to the woman.

They really do have everyone playing matchmaker. That's going to take some getting used to. There's a lot to get used to in this new life. He followed Ferday out of the council room, not entirely sure what to expect for the testing he was about to face.

17

Jewel

The sparring room was just how Jewel had arranged it and left it. It was a large stone room, similar to the other rooms in the hideout with the exception of no fireplace. In one corner, the floor was covered with mats; in another corner, there was a large selection of fighting dummies. Weapons lined one wall, ranging from wood practice ones, to dulled practice ones and finally some sharpened practice weapons. There were thick targets for short distance knife throwing practice. The archery range was in a different room down in the tunnels. Near the practice dummies there was a stack of extra mats that could be used if needed. In the corner near the wall of weapons, there was a cabinet that had assorted ropes and hooks that were used for grappling and wall climbing practice. The beams of the vaulted ceiling were gouged and battered from years of being used for such practice.

She took a deep breath. This was what she needed. She needed to focus on the mission and training for it. Seeing her grandmother had made the reality of her decision fully sink in. She wasn't planning to come back from this. She was too tired, too tired of fighting to live, too tired of seeing her loved ones fight, die and suffer. Sure it was nice at the cabin, but she'd felt guilty and like she didn't give enough. She'd made up her mind sometime during the planning last night that she wasn't coming back. She'd had this feeling before where she didn't want to live. She'd actually had it several times since the incident, but after the arrow to the chest it had grown worse. She'd been her most reckless and rash that whole year, but after the wall it had gone away. Now it was back with a vengeance, and she aimed to succeed this time. Pendry could deliver the information. She would make sure he made it out safely.

She stretched and caught a glimpse of herself in a mirror. She didn't remember there being any mirrors in the sparring room. She had a sad, almost dead look in her eyes.

Fix your face, she thought. *Don't let them see you like this. They don't need more worries.* She blinked a few times and practiced a smile. *Better, think of something better, that always helps.*

She turned at the sound of Ferday and Pendry entering. Ferday was asking Pendry about his fighting training and Pendry seemed a little confused. She wished they hadn't planned to go with her, but someone had to come back alive and someone had to lead her in.

Ferday's the backup. She told herself, *Pendry will be the one you have to protect. He's the one to bring back the information needed for the coup.*

"I'm not sure what the words you're saying mean exactly, but I did have training in hand to hand, with the sword and in Jempa," Pendry was saying to Ferday.

Ferday raised an eyebrow, "Jempa? Right, ok, well, let's start with your hand to hand."

"I'll be testing him on that," Ferga said, strolling in, rolling his sleeves up. "You can spar with Jewel and make sure she isn't rusty." He smiled mischievously.

Ferday looked hesitant, "Couldn't you spar with her? Last time I did that breath-work of hers unnerved me a little too much. She also almost made me see my insides."

"Nope. Perks of being in charge, I get to pick who I fight, and you're no less unnerving than she is." Ferga walked up to Pendry and led him over to the mats on the floor.

Pendry looked stiff and nervous. *Hope he can handle the level of fighting we do*, Jewel thought as she watched them walk to the mats.

Ferday groaned. He walked over to a cabinet and pulled out some thick leather body armor and tossed one to Jewel. He removed his cloak and strapped on his armor. He drew his katshme, rolling his shoulders to loosen his muscles. "Please don't hurt me." he said in a timid voice, but his eyes were already glinting and he looked excited.

"You wanted to fight me," Jewel quipped, smirking at him. She'd already strapped on her armor and drew her katshme. "You just wanted Ferga to feel like he won the argument."

"Eh," he shrugged and started spinning his katshme.

Jewel started spinning her katshme, she could feel the smile spreading across her face. "Double tap?" She asked, feeling her roar starting in her gut.

"Sure, if that's what you need," Ferday said as he lunged forward.

The roar ripped from her throat, as their blades clashed and she glared at Ferday. He'd always managed to start with silent breath work, but it only took a second time of their blades striking for his maniacal laughter to start.

Focus, she told herself. She liked sparring with him, but she'd forgotten how distracting his laughing while fighting could be.

She let herself be lifted over his head and spun down behind him, swiping at his feet. He jumped out of the way and turned back to face her. His face was flushed and he had that insane look in his eyes. His ceaseless laughter made him look like a madman. His katshme spun towards her and she blocked and ducked, spinning her body around and kicking at his head. He managed to block with an elbow.

She decided to try something different. His blades came down on hers and she blocked them, sliding under and wrapping her leg around his leg and coming up. He was thrown off balance and started to fall forward. She kicked her free leg out and pushed them back just as he was regaining his balance. He hit the floor and she straddled him, pointing her katshme at his throat and pinning his arms with her legs.

He was breathing hard. "When'd you learn that trick?" He tapped the floor twice and she climbed off him.

She shrugged, "Lots of wrestling and tumbling with Greta's boys. It helps give ideas on how to fight." She sheathed her katshme and helped him up.

"Ugh," he groaned, flexing his arms, "I forgot how strong you are for being so small. Good job though, definitely not rusty."

"I keep up on my training."

"Did I at least break the record? What was that, three minutes?" he asked looking excited.

"That was about two minutes, and no, the record with Shayla was two minutes and your previous record was a minute and a half." She smiled coyly at him.

He sighed. "Well, at least I broke my past record."

There was a thud and they turned to see Pendry hit the mat. He was up almost as fast as he hit it. Fists up and ready to keep going.

"Enough," Ferga groaned. "You're good, can even take a hit and keep going."

He was panting and out of breath. Pendry looked a little winded too, but was still smiling like he'd only just started. They turned to Ferday and Jewel.

"Right," Ferga said. "Swap, you said you can do sword fighting, Ferday can test you on that."

Pendry eyed Ferga warily, "You just called it quits because you wanted your strength to fight Jewel."

Ferga chuckled, "You can fight her if you've the energy for it."

"Yes!" Ferday practically screeched. He cleared his throat, "Ehm, sorry, I'm always ready to see if someone can best her."

Pendry hesitated, "I'm not able to use the katshme, and I wouldn't feel right to fist fight." He shrugged, and smiled looking a little relieved that he wouldn't have to fight her.

"She knows Jempa," Ferga said, still a little breathless.

Jewel glared at Ferga. He just had to say that. She glanced at Pendry, his smile faded and he seemed hesitant again.

"No, that's not important right now. We're testing Pendry's fighting abilities, not putting on a show," she said, still glaring at Ferga.

"Ah, but we need to test his Jempa and neither of us know it," Ferga said, smirking at her. "Now you two hop to it. We'll rest and judge how you do."

Jewel sighed. He was right, but she knew that he was doing it just to pick on her. She rubbed her forehead. "Fine, just give me a minute," she said, unstrapping her katshme and taking off her guard plate. When she turned back, she saw Ferday and Ferga huddled close and whispering to Pendry.

Great, she thought, *now what? Are they giving him pointers? Do they really want to see me bested that badly?*

She walked over slowly and quietly, not wanting to intrude, but curious about what they were saying.

"Just don't pin her down." She heard Ferga whispering before he turned, saw her and backed away nervously. "Right, ehm, good luck Pendry," he said, patting him on the back.

Jewel rolled her eyes. They didn't need to give him that kinda talk. She'd learned Jempa because of the incident. It wasn't the kind of grappling fighting she'd seen others do.

That's why she liked it. It was developed specifically for all sizes and facing any opponent. It was the best fighting to keep your opponent at arm's length. There wasn't even a proper stance, whatever you were comfortable with and depending on who you were facing.

She sighed and glared at Ferga and Ferday as they scuttled out of the way, grinning like school boys.

"I'm sorry," Pendry muttered rubbing his neck. "We could just attack them." He smiled smugly.

She chuckled at that, "Nah, it's part of the job, testing the rookie's skills to see where he's at before a mission. It's also part of those two's personal goals to tease and make jabs at me." She glared pointedly at the two men leaning against the wall. Ferga made a shooing gesture, smirking while he did.

Jewel rolled her eyes and stretched her arms a bit. She turned back to Pendry and charged.

He wasn't surprised. His Jempa was good. He deflected her swings and kicks. She was trying to read him, where was his strength, where was he weakest. It only took a few kicks and hits before she got it. He had a strong stance, good bracing and good movement. But he liked to stay standing on the ground.

She caught his kick and flipped him. His balance wasn't great when he kicked. He was able to land on his feet, but he seemed unsteady.

Got it, she thought, *he's not good with the acrobatics of Jempa.*

She waited for him to charge this time. He led with a kick.

Obviously he doesn't realize his weakness in this stance. We can work on that later, she thought as she ducked below his leg and got in close.

She used a similar move to the one she pulled on Ferday, wrapping one leg around his waist and grabbing his neck. She vaulted herself over and behind him, kicking off his back and rolling when she hit the ground. She came up and watched Pendry stumble forward, catching himself as he hit the ground. He got up and turned to face her but she had already run up, caught one of his arms and swung her body around and over his head, pushing her knee into his shoulder. He hit the ground again.

He was panting and staring at her like he wasn't sure what to think. She stayed for a moment catching her breath, her knee still on his shoulder and her hands pinning his arms.

Her hair had come undone and was now hanging in a loose braid. She heard Ferga and Ferday whooping and clapping. She looked up at them as they walked over, she looked back down at Pendry.

"You good?" She asked, "Not too hurt?"

He smiled his crooked smile, "I'm good, but um," he looked at her knee, "you're still pinning me."

"Oh, sorry," she said, getting up quickly, and started fixing her hair.

"Nice one," Ferday was saying to Pendry, "I think most wouldn't have lasted that long. That was at least two minutes."

"Yeah?" Pendry asked, standing and flexing his shoulder. "I don't think I've ever seen anyone use Jempa like that. Who taught you?" He smiled at Jewel.

"Oh, a man named Everett. He used to be a peace officer back in the day and trained them. I think his dad was the one who developed Jempa."

Pendry was staring open mouthed at Jewel. "Everett trained you! That's awesome! I wish I could have been trained by him, but we all thought he was dead. He trained my dad when he was a new recruit."

Pendry looked like he had a newfound respect for Jewel, or maybe it was envy that she'd trained with Everett.

"He's very much alive. He lives in Hamndle. He's actually the one who started our training base there," Jewel said, finishing rebraiding her hair.

"Right," Ferday said slapping Pendry on the back, "Now let's test your sword skill. If it's anything like your other fighting, this will be quick."

Pendry looked offended at that. "I'll have you know that sword fighting is my strongest fighting." He followed Ferday over to the wall of weapons, to pick out a practice sword. Then strapped on some body armor.

Jewel turned to face Ferga, "Do you still need to test me?"

"No, I'm good, I see you're still very capable." He hurriedly said his hands up.

Jewel chuckled, and went to sit on the sparring mats. She was still trying to catch her breath. She'd kept up on her practice and training but it'd been a long time since she'd trained with other people.

She and Ferga sat together watching Ferday and Pendry fight. He was good. Ferday had a fascination with blades and had taken to learning how to use as many as he could, but even with his expertise, Pendry was keeping up.

She noted his footwork. In Jempa it was his weakness, but with a sword, it was his strength. She could tell he was tired, his black hair was wet and there was sweat dripping from it. Even still, he seemed to be enjoying himself.

He fits in with these insane people. That's good to know. He'll probably make friends fast. She thought as she watched them fight. *I feel better knowing that they'll all get along without me.*

There was a flick and Pendry disarmed Ferday. Ferday simply raised his eyebrow and nodded.

Pendry all but collapsed on the floor and groaned, "Ugh, is there any chance of a rest before anything else?"

"We're done," Ferga said standing up. He walked over and helped Pendry to his feet. He took the sword and handed it to Ferday. "We now know you can handle yourself well enough and you're right, your strength is with a sword. We'll find you one that works for you and you can take it with you tomorrow." He took a deep breath, "Now, you all reek, I think it's time you all hit the shower before we meet for dinner."

"You're no rose bud yourself," Ferday said as they started out of the sparring room.

Pendry smiled wearily at Jewel, "That wasn't so bad."

She couldn't tell if he was asking or telling. "Hmm, you need to work on your Jempa, it wasn't hard to find your weakness." She turned and headed for the door.

"Wait, what weakness?" Pendry asked, following after her.

18

Pendry

P endry felt better after a hot shower, he pulled on the clean clothes Ferga had given him and dried his hair with the towel. He'd forgotten to ask for trimmers but he didn't mind the short beard. He rubbed the towel on his face to make sure it was dry and hung the towel up.

He stepped out into the hallway. He was always surprised to see the halls practically empty when he knew there were so many people living in the Gradiare hideout.

Something else to ask about, he thought.

He entered the dining room and realized he was the first, aside from Lavender who was setting out food and drinks. He walked over to her.

"Do you need any help?"

She smiled up at him. She wasn't as short as Jewel but she still needed to look up at Pendry. "No, thank you, I'm all done, just doing some finishing touches." She looked back at what she was doing, "The others will be here soon." She had an almost singsong way of talking, like she was used to talking to kids more than adults.

He nodded and started walking around the room. There were things he hadn't noticed before, paintings and tapestries. Some looked like they were of legendary heroes and the monsters they defeated. Some were of battles, he didn't recognise some of the creatures in the battles. There were paintings of men in armor and women in dresses, but none he recognized. On one wall there were plackets with names. The wall was practically full from ceiling to floor and to either side. There was still a little room on the right, but not much.

He stepped back to get a better look and felt a hand lightly press on his back to stop him. "Oops," he started to say, then he turned and saw Jewel come around from behind him.

She had left her hair down to dry after her shower and was wearing a long skirt and an oversized pullover sweater. She looked more like the forest girl he thought she was when he first met her.

"You're good," she said, smiling sadly. She was looking at the wall of names. "These are those who've fallen in the fight." She walked up and let her fingers gently caress the names as she walked down the wall to the right. Pendry followed her, watching her gentle and reverent movements.

It must be hard, losing so many loved ones. Dad's name plate is up on the memorial wall in the castle. He had a sudden sick feeling as he fully realized his dad had died protecting this wicked king. *If he knew, he wouldn't have. He did what he thought was right.*

She stopped and looked at one name that was not far from the end, she looked so sad he had the sudden urge to hug her. He pushed it aside, not wanting to appear rude or ruin the friendship they had started to build.

"This is my dad, he..." she stopped and seemed to choke on the words. "He died fighting," she managed to say. She continued on down the wall to where there were no names.

Pendry stopped and bent close to read the name, Dani-hue Lovenwrite. He hadn't known what Jewel's last name was. He looked up to see her staring at an empty spot on the wall.

I wonder if she's scared we won't make it? Pendry thought, as he stood and looked at the other names that lined the wall, a vast majority of the names said Loven-write. Mounted above the names was a large crest, the same as the tattoo. A dagger with a ribbon tying on the two dandelions, one at seed and one in bloom.

"I've never had the chance to ask, what is the meaning behind the Gradiare crest?"

Jewel looked up at the crest. "A dandelion is nearly impossible to kill, as are we. And even if we are killed, the seed of what we stand for is spread far. Simple but poignant."

"And the ribbon, why the three loops?"

"The three points of leadership. The Commander, the council, and the generals. You'll meet the generals sooner or later."

A comfortable silence fell over the room as they both stood looking at the crest, each lost in their own thoughts. The revery was broken by the entrance of Ferga and Ferday. They were laughing about something. Jewel smiled and seemed to have slipped out of her sadness just as easily as he'd seen her slip into her guarded look before facing the council.

"Are you two ever quiet?" she asked, walking over to the table, her long skirt swishing as it brushed the floor.

Pendry turned from the name he'd been reading and followed her. He watched her climb into one of the large chairs and realized that she was, in fact, barefoot. He smiled at that. Even with all the fighting and war, she was still rebellious in her own way. She was still that forest girl he'd met back in the cabin.

He got himself food and sat down across from Jewel. She was sipping tea and looked like she was comfortable and content.

Lavender set a plate of food in front of her. "Eat," was all she said before she turned and walked away.

Jewel furrowed her brow and narrowed her eyes at her sister's back and continued to sip her tea.

Ferga and Ferday were talking about something, but Pendry was only half listening. He'd noticed how easily Jewel could slip from one emotion to another when she wanted. It seemed like a useful skill, but a dangerous skill for others to be unaware of. He looked at his food and thought, for probably the hundredth time, what it must have been like being forced to be Commander of such a large organization at such a young age. How lonely that must have been, having to give orders and make decisions for adults to follow.

It was a good meal, lots of joking and laughter, and, as always, the food was good. They finished up and moved their chairs to be in front of the fire, drinking tea and watching the fire flicker and crackle. Its orange and red flames cast dancing shadows on everyone as they were put under its spell. They sat in silence for a while, until Pendry decided to ask something that was nagging at him.

"I'm curious," he paused, trying to think of how to ask. "Why is it that you're all the leaders of this organization and yet all under thirty? I understand that some of you have been doing this since you were teens, but I've seen the people you lead. Is there some reason that no one older took over?" He felt it was a stupid question, but it was something that had bothered him for a while and he felt he had to know.

"It's a family position," Ferga said, leaning back in his chair. "Our great great great, I think it was, grandfather founded the Gradiare to oppose the king. He never thought it would take this long to overthrow him, but that was the plan. It was set up to be similar to the king's succession but after two generations they realized that wouldn't work. The leaders were dying off faster than heirs were born," he sighed. "So they decided to change it. It's still only those who can trace back to the founder who can claim the role of Commander, but they have the option to pass. Then there were some years of hiding and growing forces, small opposition, not too much. But even after that, there was still too much death. We are quite literally the oldest of the line who chose to take up the roles."

Pendry felt like that was a nice way of saying we were forced into this and had to make do with what we had.

He glanced at the others. They seemed to be off in their own worlds. He'd seen veterans look similarly when they were reliving the past, but it was eerie to see that same look on the faces of people his own age.

Ferday sighed, "Ah, not much more we can do about it. The council is slow to change and has never liked that we aren't cowering children." He turned to Ferga, "Were we ever cowering children?"

Ferga chuckled, "It's hard to be cowering when that one is in your family," he said pointing at Jewel.

"Why are you blaming me?" She asked, looking confused.

"I'm sorry, but were you raised with you?" Ferday asked, turning to her. "You, who even before you took on the role of Commander, decided to sneak into a council meeting, and were so angry at how they talked to Dad, you gave yourself away and tried to attack the man who so offended you. You were grounded for a week."

Pendry chuckled. He could see her being that kid.

"Don't forget about the time she read that book," Lavender said, sitting up in her chair. "The one that scared her with the stories of the faie, so she decided she needed to go face one, and dad had to track her down and bring her home." She giggled, "You were so scared, you wouldn't talk to us about it. I think I still don't know the full story."

"Wait, what?" Pendry said, turning to Jewel, "That's how you met one the first time?"

"First time!" Ferga bellowed. "Ha! You would go back and face it again. Wait, how did you know about that?"

He turned to Pendry, brows furrowed, then he turned to Jewel. He looked back and forth a few times, "You, she," he paused. "Did you see a faie on your journey in?"

Pendry was staring at Jewel again. She looked like she was trying to send him a message to stop, but he didn't care.

"Ugh, yes," she snapped, "We ran into a faie ring, or more, he walked into one and I had to get him out."

"Seriously?" Ferday asked incredulously. He turned to Pendry, "Seriously. You met a faie and lived? I thought Dad was the only one to ever do that." He turned back to Jewel. He looked confused, concerned, and possibly intrigued. "How did you do it?"

Jewel smiled, looking mischievous and like she had secrets. "I talked to it," she crooned.

"What!" The other three exclaimed.

Jewel kept smiling knowingly and looked at Pendry. She held his gaze while she sipped her tea, still smiling that mischievous smile, her eyes gleaming and laughing.

Gardenias and lilacs, he remembered, *those are her favorite flowers.*

Why was he thinking of that? He felt a rush, almost like adrenaline, but different. He couldn't place it. His heart started pounding and he felt his palms go clammy. Jewel broke her gaze from him and looked at Ferga who was asking her something but Pendry couldn't focus. He blinked and saw Lavender staring at him with a look of surprise that slowly turned into a smirk. He sat back and forced himself to focus.

"Yes, Dad did it, that's how I knew it could be done. He gave me his books so I made sure I knew what to say and I always have the tools to fight one when I'm going through the enchanted woods," Jewel was saying, still smiling mischievously like she was enjoying their confusion and intrigue.

Pendry picked up his cup of tea and noticed Lavender was still eyeing him with a slight smirk. It felt like she was trying to read him. It was a little unnerving.

What's she looking at me like that for?

The conversation continued about other adventures and mischief Jewel had gotten them into. Apparently, Pendry found out, before taking on the role of Commander, she'd been very mischievous, and she'd always had that attitude of *watch me*. He also realized that the other three had always followed her lead.

"There was that time," Ferday reminisced, "when there was that full moon, or was it a harvest moon? We were at the cabin on the lake, and dad had told you to look out the window late at night and see the pixies dancing. And you," he said pointedly, "you waited for everyone to be asleep and snuck out the window to go dance with the pixies. I woke up and you weren't there and Lav was sitting at the window crying because she thought you were going to get hurt or in trouble," he laughed.

"I was five," Lavender said defensively.

"Yes," Ferday continued "and I thought we were all going to get in trouble, so I was getting ready to go out there to get her, when I hear Dad laughing from the next room." Ferday laughed again, "Turned out dad knew you'd go out and dance with them and he'd waited up to see you do it."

"I didn't know that part," Jewel said with a sad smile. "I'm glad he saw. It was fun and memorable."

"Right," Ferga said, slapping his knees, "this is fun, but you all need to be well rested before tomorrow, and sleep in. The mission is at night." He stood up at the same time as Lavender, and offered her his arm. "My lady, shall I escort you back to your room?"

She took his arm and smiled at him sweetly.

"Yes you may," Ferday said gleefully and he bounded up and took the other arm. "Although, I don't usually go by my lady."

They went off laughing and Pendry realized he was alone with Jewel. His heart started beating faster. He felt that same rush as before.

Why? What is making me feel like this?

She sighed, drank the last of her tea and stood. Her bare feet made hardly any noise as she walked to the table and set her mug down.

Pendry stood feeling unsure of what to say or even if he should say anything.

She turned to him and smiled, "Good night, I hope you sleep well." Then she turned and walked out.

Pendry stood there. He realized only after she left that he hadn't said goodnight. He made his way to his room, still feeling off.

I hope I'm not coming down with anything, he thought as he went into his room.

He sat on his bed and took off his boots. He laid back and stared up into the dim room. When he closed his eyes he could still see her looking him in the eyes, with that mischievous smile.

Maybe she just unnerved me. He thought, *No, I've felt that before, and this isn't that.*

He rolled over and picked up the green rock he'd pocketed on the journey in. He rubbed its smooth surface, remembering the way she'd laughed at him. He wished she'd laugh like that more often. He liked that laugh. He liked that mischievous smile, and the way she cared for everyone, taking time to share in their life. He liked the way she was always ready to fight for what was right.

He set the rock back on the bedside table, still trying to figure out that feeling. It wasn't fear. It wasn't adrenaline, although it felt very similar. He fell asleep before he'd fully figured out what it was, but it was there on the edge of his mind, almost tickling his thoughts.

19

Jewel

J ewel sat on her bed. She stretched, feeling refreshed and well rested. Today was the day, the last day. She sighed and got dressed. She felt almost relieved, and at the same time, sad. All the stories last night had made her realize how much she'd missed her dad. Every story where she'd felt the most like herself and the most free had her dad in it somewhere. She'd stopped living the day he'd died. The day she took over, that little girl who danced with pixies and went out to fight faie, died.

And today the rest will die. She was at peace with it. She'd mourned and had a good evening with her loved ones. Now she was ready to be fully at peace.

As she dressed, she remembered the last time she saw her dad. He had kissed her goodnight and told her he'd take her riding to the caves. It had been a long time plan for them to go and explore what creatures lived in them. He'd promised that by that autumn he would set aside time for it. She'd woken up to him being captured and imprisoned. Two days later, he was executed. All plans and attempts to rescue him had failed. It was the main reason the council had always been opposed to any new attempt at starting a coup.

The day he was executed was the day her childhood ended and she became Commander. All thoughts of going to the caves had ended. She'd gone there eventually, but it wasn't the same. Instead, it had been a mission to find some magical crystals that turned into forming alliances with the ogres that lived in the caves, who then taught them how to make lights with the magical crystals.

She took a deep breath. Now was not the time to be lost in thought. She quickly twisted her hair into a bun and started pinning it up, walking out as she made sure it was in a tight, secure bun. She couldn't have her hair falling out and getting in her way. She'd even put a few extra pins in one of her pockets.

She walked into the dining room pushing all thoughts of the past out of her mind, feeling good and ready for the mission. She got herself food and sat down, smiling at Ferga.

"Good morning," she said happily before turning to eat.

She could feel Lavender and him exchange a look, and she knew they were concerned. The last time she'd had this up and down in emotions was the day the wall fell on her. She'd thought that was going to be her last day too. She'd planned it to be. Although she hadn't meant for a wall to fall on her. That had just happened.

"You seem in a good mood," Ferga said cautiously.

"I am," Jewel said, picking her words carefully. "I'm excited to be done with this mission after so many years of talking about it. I'm happy to help, and go back to the cabin."

Lavender raised an eyebrow, she crossed her arms. "Is that it? Nothing happened last night?"

Now Jewel was confused, "No, should something have happened last night?"

Ferga and Lavender exchanged looks.

"What?" Jewel asked, feeling her good mood slip.

"So just to be clear, you're just happy you get to go back to your rest in the cabin and nothing happened after we left last night?" Lavender asked, leaning on the table.

What is she going on about?

"No, I finished my tea and went to bed. I think Pendry was still finishing his tea but I'm not sure." She was really confused now.

"Ok," Lavender said, standing up and walking away. Apparently satisfied with that answer.

That was weird.

The door opened and Pendry and Ferday walked in. Pendry had shaved and looked more soldier-like than he did with the beard. He was holding a sword and Ferday was telling him about their armory and forges. Pendry was examining the sword and seemed to be only half listening. Jewel understood the feeling, Ferday could ramble when it came to swords and forging. He had talked her ear off on more than one occasion.

She turned back to her food and coffee. She was determined to enjoy this last day with everyone. She didn't want to see them hurt, and they'd done so well without her.

Yes, this is how it should be. She thought. *I did my part, and no Commander should retire. It will be how it should be. They can finally move on without me.*

Breakfast was as it always was, good food, good conversation, and good company.

I missed this.

She sipped her coffee and glanced at the sword Pendry had set on the table. It was a beautiful broadsword, good for two-handed or single-handed combat if strong enough. The pommel was carved to be a flower bud, and the grip was wrapped with beautiful blue and green leather. It had what looked like leaves carved into the cross guard. It was strikingly beautiful, especially compared to the more plain swords most members of the Gradiare favored.

Hello again.

"What do you think?" Pendry asked, as she eyed the sword.

"It's beautiful, are you going to name it?" She said feeling the soft leather of the hilt. She'd seen this sword once before, and would have claimed it, but she preferred fighting with katshme.

"Ferday says it already has a name." He turned to Ferday. "What did you call it?"

"Firebloom," Ferday said leaning back in his chair and pushing his empty plate away. "It was the sword some family member used until they couldn't fight anymore. No ones ever claimed it because they want manly swords." He said the last part in a mock deep voice.

"Why do they want manly swords? Isn't it manly just to use a sword?" Jewel asked, putting her coffee down and picking up the sword.

"Yeah, most of our new recruits are young or feel like they need to act tough. But not this guy; he walked straight up to that one and said, this will do," Ferday said playful slapping Pendry's arm.

"Well it will," Pendry replied, "It's a good sword and I don't care if it's not, as you put it, manly." His brows were furrowed but he wasn't flustered.

"It's made out of Firebloom. It's a magical metal from the Giants in the south," she said, caressing the carved leaves. "You met the previous owner of it."

"Who was that?"

"My grandma." Jewel smiled. "She was the first woman in the Gradiare to be a general."

"Oh, I'd forgotten she was a general," Ferday said smiling. "I think she's the only grandma I've ever met that I could picture still being up for a fight."

"Why is the metal called Firebloom?" Pendry asked, "I was thinking the flower carved on the pommel was a Firebloom."

"No, it's said that once Firebloom has been forged it will look like it's on fire. Not sure why only sometimes, Grandma said it actually looked on fire whenever she would fight with it."

"Guess we'll be putting that to the test," Ferday said as he got up to get more food.

"It's a good choice," Jewel said, putting the sword back on the table. "Nice job."

She sipped her coffee and let herself drift into her thoughts.

One last fight, one last mission.

She breathed in the smell of her coffee, then felt someone looking at her and opened her eyes to see Pendry watching her. He'd looked at her like that last night; maybe he was reconsidering the mission.

I won't let you die, she thought. *No one else will die.*

She set her coffee down, "We should gather everything together and go over the plan again before we get into position." She stood and smiled, then turned and walked out of the dining room.

There, now I can take a few minutes to focus and prepare myself, she thought as she walked out of the dining room, turning and walking to her room.

20

Pendry

P endry wasn't sure how far they'd run, but the tunnels were almost harder to run through than the woods. How long had it been since they'd left Ferga? Would they still have time? He focused on Ferday who was in the lead. He ran through the tunnels so nimbly it was like trying to follow a deer, his gray cloak billowing and fluttering behind him. Even though he had knives strapped all over him, he never made a sound more than a soft step.

Pendry held his new sword steady at his side. For its size, it wasn't as heavy as he thought it would be, probably something to do with the Firebloom metal. He didn't dare glance back for fear of tripping over something in the narrow tunnel, but he could hear Jewel's soft step behind him.

They must practice all this running as quietly as possible. Either that or it's some magical power of a gold vein.

He still hadn't placed that feeling. At the moment, he was feeling the adrenaline pumping through him, but before, it was softer than adrenaline. It had a similar effect of making him feel like running or jumping or just doing something.

"Right," Ferday said as he stopped suddenly. He turned back to them, grinning. "We've made it to the inner edge of the castle wall. You can tell from the stone work," he said pointing at the different, older looking stones. "We need to go up and get into position outside the castle. I'll be in the spy hole. You two know what to do. And remember, if anything goes wrong and you need backup, smash the bead."

He turned and started climbing a ladder that Pendry hadn't noticed until then. He was breathing heavily. Jewel and Ferday seemed to be only slightly winded. He looked down at the piece of leather wrapped around his wrist. On it was what appeared to be a clay bead, but he'd been told it had a magical powder in it. The trick was that if you broke it the powder would float to the wearer of the opposite powder. So if they needed Ferday, break the bead and he'd see the powder and come help. It sounded ridiculous to Pendry but he was getting used to the ridiculous being real.

It was his turn to climb the ladder. Ferday helped him out of the hole in the ground. But before he could turn to see if Jewel needed help, Ferday pulled him close and whispered, "You protect her, you hear?" His usual happy jesting voice was now dripping with menace. "She fights so well because she has no will to live, so you protect her." He pulled away and gave Pendry a serious and meaningful look.

Pendry felt like he'd been struck by lightning. No will to live? That didn't make sense. But Ferday had said it so seriously that Pendry believed him. He hadn't seen Ferday ever be serious about anything, not even when they were planning this mission.

Why doesn't she have a will to live? He thought, *She has family and friends who love her and would follow her anywhere, people who would die for her, and she doesn't want to live?*

He watched Ferday help Jewel out. She was smiling and looked like nothing was wrong.

"Right, off you two go, have fun. Stay alive." Ferday whispered cheerfully, as if he hadn't just put the fear of God into Pendry. He turned and melted into the shadows.

Jewel turned and closed the hole they'd climbed through, then turned to Pendry. "Lead on," she whispered.

He turned and led her around the buildings, keeping close to the wall. There, he pointed to the door in the side of the castle but didn't say anything. They crouched in the shadows watching for the change of the guard.

He glanced at Jewel, she seemed so calm and relaxed. He remembered how she'd seemed happier that morning and even lighter. He'd heard of people who came out of a depressive episode happy and lighter just to kill themselves. He hoped that wasn't her. He wasn't sure what that feeling from earlier was, but she was his friend and he wasn't going to see her hurt.

Gardenias and lilacs. I might just have to find her some flowers after this, maybe that's why I keep thinking of them.

He looked back at the door and saw the guard turn and march off down the path. They had one minute before the next guard came around the corner. They ran, crouching and keeping quiet as they went. They slipped in through the door, Pendry silently thanked whatever god was real that it opened silently and inwards.

They crept up the stairs and stopped just before the hall. Pendry peeked out and checked for any guards. All good. He led Jewel down the hall and deeper into the castle.

He was starting to wonder if something was wrong. They hadn't seen any guards, when Jewel caught his hand and pulled him into a dark hallway. He heard them then. It wasn't the King's Guard. They wore metal armor, that had been what he was listening for. It was peace officers in their leather protective gear. They walked past their hiding spot. Apparently they hadn't noticed them either.

Pendry waited until the footsteps had completely died away. He slowly leaned out of the passage and looked both ways. All good. Before he stepped out he realized Jewel was still holding his hand. He looked down at their hands, feeling that small rush, then at Jewel. She wasn't looking at him, she was looking down the hall behind them. He glanced back but only saw darkness. He squeezed her hand and she turned to him, he pointed to the now empty hallway. She let go of his hand and he started out. They were almost there. It was only two more turns and they were at the door.

He stood guard while Jewel picked the lock. Once they were in, she closed the door and locked it. The room was big. There was a still smoldering fire in the fireplace that gave a dim orange glow to the room. It was hard to see much detail in the light, but Pendry knew this room: its large desk and ornate chairs, its gilded lamps and gaudy rugs. This was where he'd been given his dad's captain's hat in honor of his sacrifice. He could still picture that day. He'd kept the hat in his chest back in his barracks. He shook his head trying to clear away the memories. Now wasn't the time for that.

Jewel turned and pointed to the large desk and they both walked over. She started gently sifting through papers, trying to leave things how they were. She shook her head. Nothing. Pendry walked around the desk and knelt as he started opening drawers and sifting through their contents. Jewel followed him and looked over his shoulder.

He suddenly realized he wasn't looking at the papers. He was instead acutely aware of how close she was behind him. That feeling was back, making him catch his breath. Maybe he really was coming down with something.

She reached over him and pointed at a piece of paper. He looked closer, that was it. The order to lock down the city. He picked it up, under it was another order. This was for the peace officers to comply or face punishment. He picked that one up too and handed both to Jewel. Then something caught his eye, a small gold ball, or a hilt. It wasn't important. They had what they needed.

He closed the drawer and stood. Jewel was examining the papers. She set them on the desk and reached into her pocket, pulling out some thin film. Pendry couldn't remember what it was called, but when it was placed over a paper, it would take on that paper. She placed one on the first order and one on the second. It took only seconds for the film to take on the traits of the papers. She picked them up, folded them, and handed them to Pendry. He bent down and slid them into his socks, just like they'd planned, one for each sock.

He stood and saw Jewel pulling off two more films, folding them up and slipping them into an odd compartment in the heels of her boots, again one for each boot. Then she folded up the papers and stuffed one into her pocket and gave the other one to Pendry.

The idea had been, if caught they had something to find. If one was caught, the other could still get away with the information. They'd brought a few sheets of the film just in case they came across extra information, which was easy, since the film was so thin.

Now they just had to get out. They crept to the door as quietly as they could. It was quiet on the other side. Jewel unlocked the door and slowly opened it. All clear. Pendry stood guard as Jewel locked the door behind them.

They headed back the way they came. So far it was going a little too well. He felt uneasy about how it was going, but stayed focused and kept his eyes and ears sharp.

There was a noise ahead of them. He grabbed Jewel's hand and pulled her into another dark corridor. He didn't realize until the noise died down, but he was hugging her to his side. She looked a little confused, but not upset.

Ferday really shook me, Pendry thought, his heart pounding.

He looked around the corner, all good. He led her out and down another hall. He was still holding her hand, not quite ready to let go. He had a feeling something was really wrong.

It shouldn't be this empty, even with the King's birthday party.

He led her down another passage and heard guards coming. He stopped and waited for them to fade. They didn't. It was like there was one big line of King's Guards marching through the hall.

Need to find a different way out.

He turned and realized it wasn't just at the end they were heading towards, it was also behind them. He cursed inwardly. He had to make sure Jewel got out safely. If he didn't, he was sure Ferday would kill him, and he would probably help him with that. For now, they were stuck in a passageway and on either end guards marched through the halls. It felt as if it went on forever, Pendry felt his heart pounding in rhythm to the marching.

I have to get her out.

He felt her squeeze his hand and realized it was shaking. He took a deep breath to steady his nerves. They were safe for now. They just had to stay put until it was clear. He tried to focus on something other than the noise of the King's Guard. He found himself focusing on Jewel's hand in his. It felt so small and soft compared to his. He suddenly had that feeling again.

No, that's not what I should be focusing on, not now.

The noise ahead finally faded and he inched forward, the hall was empty. Jewel squeezed his hand again. He looked back at her. She wasn't looking at him. Across from them was the passage they'd ducked into to hide from the peace officers. There was something there that Pendry couldn't see but Jewel could. She looked concerned but not too scared.

He led her out into the passage and started to pass the one they'd hidden in, when Jewel pulled him back suddenly. An arrow flew out of the passage and stuck into the wall.

Out of the dark passage came a slender evil looking King's Guard with a crossbow. He smiled wickedly at them. Pendry let go of Jewel's hand and drew his sword. The blade gleamed and glittered like it was on fire. The man lunged at him swinging his crossbow. Pendry blocked it and punched the man. He crumpled to the ground. He sheathed his sword and saw Jewel sheath her katshme. They stuffed the man back into the passage that he'd been hiding in.

"Why didn't you say something earlier?" Pendry whispered.

"Because he was sleeping on duty," Jewel whispered back. "And we were trying to be quiet."

Pendry nodded, satisfied with that answer.

They stepped out of the passage and turned down the hall, walking straight into three peace officers.

"Pendry?" one of them asked.

He shoved them aside, grabbed Jewel's hand and started running towards their exit. He heard the whistle being blown and heard the King's Guard coming for them from every direction.

They were surrounded.

21

Jewel

J ewel drew her katshme, she heard Pendry draw his
sword. They stood back to back and faced the King's
Guard that were coming at them from both sides. The
hall was too narrow to see how many they were facing.
They were coming too fast to stop and think.

*Couldn't just have a quick quiet mission? Not that I've
ever had one.*

Jewel lunged into the fight, katshme spinning, roar
ripping from her throat. She saw the guards stumble back
then surge forward. She took down the two in the lead
before they'd even had a chance to swing at her.

She leapt off the back of one and sliced through another's helmet as she came down. They swarmed her and she
was forced to change to a more grounded fighting style.
She still managed to hold her own, ducking under swings
and cutting through the guards. Then one slammed her
with a shield and she hit the wall. Her katshme fell to the
ground. She was dazed but looked up just in time to see
the man swinging his sword at her.

She dove under and came up behind him facing a different guard. She kicked his sword out of his hand, caught
it deftly, then slashed his throat.

No, she thought. No, *don't kill people with their own weapons.*

She turned and stabbed the man who'd struck her.

Where's Pendry? I need to get him out.

"Pendry!" she called out. There were to many guards and she knew she couldn't hold them back forever. Pendry needed to escape.

Two men fell and Pendry stepped over them. His sword looked like it was on fire with a strange silver flame. He looked formidable and heroic, like the paintings of the heroes in legends. She'd never seen him in a real fight before. All those smiles and the glinting smugness were gone. In its place was a soldier, ferocious in the face of battle.

"I'm good. You ok?" He had a wound on his left forearm and his lip was bleeding.

"Fine," Jewel said, blocking a sword. "You need to go. Run, get to Ferday!"

He looked confused, "What? I'm not leaving you to die." He caught the arm of a guard as he swung and twisted making the guard drop his sword. He threw him back into the crowd of guards, causing them to stumble.

"Someone has to get the information back to Ferga." She stabbed and then quickly blocked a sword before it hit Pendry.

"I said I'm not leaving," he growled as he stabbed the man she was fighting.

She glared at him, "When I say go, you go."

"I don't follow your orders, you're not my commander." Pendry smiled his crooked smile. "Besides, Ferday ordered me to protect you."

"What?" Jewel asked, then spun to block another attack. She hated fighting with a sword. They were awkward in such a small space and harder to use your whole body. She kicked the man in the face then slit his throat.

"Forget what he said," she yelled, "and go." She spun around and brought her sword down on a shield. She grabbed the edge of the shield and flipped herself over it, bringing the man strapped to it down in a full arc, slamming him into another King's Guard. She turned and saw Pendry still fighting.

Why won't he listen? Someone has to get the information to Ferga.

Something hit her on the side of the head and she hit the wall. She pushed herself up feeling even more dazed. She could hear Pendry calling for her but she wasn't focused on that. Her vision blurred, and turned a hazy red. She could feel herself fighting, though she didn't see much of it.

How can I protect the people I care about if they won't listen? She thought. *Those idiots need to let me go, and that idiot needs to listen and leave.*

Her vision cleared and she was using a different sword to fight two men at once. She could see the back of Pendrys' head. He turned and looked like he was trying to say something. He was being overwhelmed.

I have to get to him, I can't let him die.

Then she felt a sharp splitting pain on the side of her head and everything went dark.

Pain was all she felt, dull in some spots, intense and throbbing in others. She heard herself groan.

"Don't move. Don't fight it. You might black out again." Pendry's voice sounded muffled but close. There was a muffled ringing that grew louder.

She tried to move. Pain shot through her head, she sat up straighter. The pain intensified. Her vision was blotchy and ragged.

"Ugh." Was all she managed to say. She tried to touch her head where it hurt but she couldn't move her arms. She groaned as her eyes began to focus and the room stopped spinning. "What happened? Where are we?" She finally managed to groan out, her mouth was dry and felt dusty. "The last thing I remember was fighting the King's Guard."

I'm not dead, I should be dead.

She tried looking around the room but moving made the pressure in her head increase.

"Yeah, we fought them all right," Pendry said. He was sitting opposite her and to the right a bit. He was tied to a chair and looked as though he had been beaten.

"What happened to you?" She asked, concerned by the sheer number of cuts and bruises on his face and arms.

"Me?" He sounded a little taken aback that she was asking about him. He shook his head slightly like a thought he had was absurd. "Well, Monty apparently is not a coward when his foe is tied up. He also doesn't like being called a coward." He attempted to smile but only managed a grimace. "You were knocked out by someone that came up behind you, while you were fighting two other men. He ran in from behind and hit you in the head with the hilt of his sword. Knocked you out, made me think he killed you." He looked like he was trying to be light hearted about the whole thing, but Jewel could see him shaking slightly. "Not sure why they didn't kill us. Monty said something about telling the King about his birthday present."

As she looked closer she thought she saw tear stains.

That can't be right, she thought, *He doesn't care that much. my vision must be acting up.*

"So I now know what your skull looks like," Pendry said, clearing his throat. "I really could have gone my whole life not knowing and I would have been fine. Also, that was a lot of blood." He was shaking, and there were some tears welling up in his eyes.

"Are you ok?" She asked genuinely confused, "I've been through worse and I heal fast, I'll be fine. Were you hurt?"

Pendry turned to her, he looked angry. "No, I'm not ok, I thought you were dead, I thought you were dead and that it was my fault. I should have protected you more and I'm sorry." He coughed and grimaced. "I'm not hurt, not like you are. I've seen people killed, I've lost friends before, but..." he paused, "just don't die."

He was looking at her with such a caring, pleading look. It wasn't a look Jewel was used to. Concern, yes, but from family, not from a friend.

He's not supposed to care that much. No one is supposed to care. Why would he care? He barely knows me.

Before Jewel could say anything else, the door opened and Monty strode in. He had a wicked smile on his face.

"Good news. The King himself wants to come and personally see to the torture and execution of the two of you. Ah, our little injured Lion is awake." Monty smirked, knelt down in front of Jewel, and pointed at Pendry, "This fool has been crying for you, did you know that? 'Don't hurt her, don't touch her.'" He said with a mocking laugh.

He stood up, laughing harder. She could hear the guards in the hall laughing with him. Suddenly, he grabbed her by the neck, lifting her and the chair she was tied to into the air.

"I'll hurt who I want and do what I want," he growled at her.

Jewel choked, and gasped, trying to fight him, but she was tied up and weak from blood loss. Her already ragged vision of the room was growing dark. The pressure was building in her head, and the ringing in her ears grew louder. She could hear Pendry yelling at Monty as if he was muffled with cotton.

Here it comes, she thought, *this is my death.*

She didn't want to die like this, tied to a chair, unable to fight, but she didn't think she could hold out much longer. Her lungs burned and the pressure in her head grew until she thought her head would explode.

Not like this! I don't want it to end like this!

Suddenly Monty dropped her. She felt weightless for a moment, then felt the chair break as it hit the ground. Everything went black.

22

Pendry

J ewel was a crumpled heap on the floor, not moving, not breathing from what Pendry could see.

Monty looked at her in disgust, then turned to Pendry. "If she wakes up," he smiled wickedly, "and if she doesn't, she is how we'll torture you." He said leaning close to Pendry. He stood laughing wickedly, then turned and left.

Pendry heard him slam and lock the door behind him. He hadn't stopped staring at her body on the floor.

She can't be dead. They tried before and she can't die.

"Get up," he whispered. "Get up," he said louder this time. The tears were flowing freely now. He strained against the ropes, pulling until his hands were numb.

He stopped to catch his breath and let the blood flow back to his hands. He looked around the room, trying to see what he could use.

It wasn't a large room, no bigger than a spacious parlor. There was one small window high up on the wall and a large vent halfway up the other. On a table near the door were her katshme and his sword Firebloom, but that wouldn't help at the moment. He knew they were somewhere in the King's Guard bunkhouse but he wasn't as familiar with it as he was with the castle or the peace officer's stations. He slumped against his bonds, discouraged that he couldn't think of a way out.

Why wasn't it me? he thought. *She'd be better at getting us out. I've never been in a situation like this.*

His face hurt from the beating he'd received. His arms ached from the cut during the fighting and being tied up. He looked at her still form. Why couldn't he have prevented this? Why had he not been there to protect her? Again the thought came to him, *gardenias and lilacs.*

He felt like he almost could place why he was thinking that. But he decided to push the thought away and focus on getting out. He'd make sure there was time to figure that out later. Then he looked at the chair Jewel had been tied to. It was splintered and broken on the floor around her. It gave him an idea.

This will be loud and I won't have much time, he thought. *Let's hope they think it doesn't matter.*

He leaned forward, trying to pull the chair up enough to get the back legs off the floor. Then he threw his head back and his body with it. The chair rocked but didn't break.

Not hard enough.

He tried again, still nothing. The third time he leaned as far forward as he dared and threw his whole body back. The chair broke, hurting his arms more, and he thought he'd hit his head.

Fix that later.

He slid his bound hands under himself and tucked his legs through them. With his hands in front he was able to untie the knot at his feet and then pull at the knot at his wrists with his teeth. He then slipped the now loose ropes around his chest over his head.

Once untied, he scrambled over to Jewel. She hadn't moved. She was pale and there was more blood. He scooped her up gently. She was breathing, but it was shallow and ragged. The wound on the side of her head had half healed but was bleeding again from the fall. There was a red hand print that wrapped around her neck. He gently wiped the blood off the side of her face with the sleeve of his shirt. The sight of her laying there limp made a rage start to build inside of him, it was unlike any anger he'd ever felt.

"You will not die here," he whispered, his voice cracking. "I broke the bead; I'm not sure how long that takes to work, but Ferday should be here soon."

He hugged her close, she was so small and limp. It wasn't fair, none of it was. The fact that she'd been used her whole life, the fact that all she wanted was peace and instead she was given war and an army to command. He thought of the story of her dancing with pixies as a kid. He wanted to give her that freedom and peace to go dance with pixies again.

I'll get you out. I won't let you die here.

There was suddenly an odd rush and pop. He looked up to see Ferday standing with his back to him, smacking small smoldering flames on his shoulders.

"Glory be, this bunk house is huge," he said, turning around and smiling at Pendry. "Found you."

"Ferday," was all Pendry could say. He choked on the lump in his throat.

Ferday was by his side in a second, "Oh, they did a number on you didn't they?" he said, looking at Pendry's face. He then looked down, seeing Jewel laying half bound and unconscious with a gaping head wound. "Lord, they really have it out for her," Ferday hissed. He knelt and cut the remaining bonds. Then he took out some bandage tape and a jar of ointment from one of his pockets. "Best field dressing for a gold vein." He said, applying the ointment and taping the wound closed.

"How did you get in here?" Pendry asked.

"Mm, cloak of transport, it's one of those nice to have, not nice to use, magical items." He gestured at the cloak he was always wearing. "Practically sets me on fire every time I use it. Would have used it for the mission, but you can only go places you've already been."

"Then give it to me and I can go to the King's office and kill him now." Pendry growled through gritted teeth

Ferday looked at him sadly, "That's not the plan. If you do that, they'd have more to use against us, saying we're the bad guys. The King still has allies, and they could twist that into any story they want. No, as easy and nice as that would be, it would set us back too far. People need evidence, that's why we're here." Ferday looked at Pendrys boots, "Still got it?"

"Yeah," Pendry sighed. He knew Ferday was right. The King was too controlling and manipulative. He probably wasn't in his office anyway. "They only took our weapons."

Ferday looked around and saw the weapons on the far table. "Right, well I have an escape plan for you, but I don't think the weapons will fit. I'll take those."

"Wait, shouldn't the guards be swarming us? I was kinda loud breaking my chair," Pendry said, looking around.

Ferday smiled mischievously, it looked a lot like the smile Jewel had made the other night, but not quite. "I took out the two guards at the door. Others will be here soon, but we have a few minutes." He stood up and reached out, "Do you need help?"

Pendry shook his head and stood, slowly lifting Jewel. She was so limp she looked dead. He tried not to think about it.

Ferday ran to the table and scooped up their weapons, he flipped the table and pushed it in front of the door to block it. He then walked to the vent halfway up the wall.

"What are you doing?" Pendry asked, walking over slowly so he wouldn't jostle Jewel.

"Getting you both out. Last time I was captured, I managed to escape through this vent." He pried off the cover with the tip of his dagger. "It's big enough to squeeze through, and for some reason they don't think we can fit. Guess they think it's smaller than it is or something. Not sure what it's for but it makes a great escape route." He turned to Pendry smirking. But his smirk turned to a frown as he watched him walk over. "She'll be ok, you did good. She's tougher than she looks and she's been through worse." He grimaced as he looked at her, then took a deep breath. "She's hard to keep alive sometimes. I'm not sure when it happened, but somewhere along the line she started fighting without care of dying."

"But she'll be ok?" Pendry asked, feeling the lump coming back into his throat.

Ferday smiled sadly, "Yeah, it'll take more than a small head wound to kill her." He tapped the open vent, "Now, you two go in and I'll close this up, then I'll open the window over there a bit. Let's have them chasing their tails," he said with that mischievous grin. "Don't try and go too far, it narrows a bit after about 15 feet or so, you'll still be able to fit but I don't think you'll be able to carry her through. I'll meet you in the vent and we can come up with a plan then."

"You're just making this up as you go aren't you?" Pendry asked, furrowing his brow.

"Yes. Now go."

He tucked Jewel into the open vent, making sure not to bump her head. Ferday helped him crawl inside. It was only just big enough for them to both fit laying down; it was difficult for him to crawl through holding her. Somehow he managed to hold her up with one arm and pull himself forward with the other. He tried using his legs and feet a bit, but that made it difficult to hold Jewel still.

Once they were in far enough, the light dimmed and he heard Ferday put the vent cover on. There was the loud crack of metal on metal.

He must have dented the cover so it couldn't be opened.

He stuffed down the panic that tried to climb out of him at the thought of being trapped in the dingy, narrow vent. He took slow even breaths and slid slowly forward into the vent, continuing to hold Jewel with one arm and pulling them forward with the other. After a minute he stopped and listened. Nothing. He decided to rest for a while, his injured arm ached every time he moved. He flexed his arm and tried to look at the cut; it had looked worse when it first happened but it wasn't as bad as the one he had when he first met Jewel.

There was a noise and he decided to try going deeper into the vent. He only made it a little farther before his arms gave out and he decided to rest again. He tried to lean his body off to one side so he wouldn't crush Jewel with his weight, but the vent was narrower here, like Ferday said it would be. That meant wait. He decided to try relaxing a bit. He couldn't hear anyone coming, but that didn't mean they were safe.

He was just beginning to wonder where Ferday was when he felt a movement. He looked down to see Jewel move a little. She groaned, then her eyes snapped open, they were dilated and scared.

She started to scream. Pendry quickly covered her mouth, trying to shush her. She slapped him, flailing her arms around and beating him on the chest. It wasn't her normal calculated hard hit, it was a fear induced fight. She kneed him in the stomach and punched his chin. Even without her full strength, it hurt and rattled his jaw. He was forced to take his hand off her mouth and hold her hands down so she wouldn't make more noise with her flailing and give away their position.

"Shh, it's me, Pendry," he whispered as loud as he dared. "Everything's ok, we're escaping. You need to stop moving and making noise." Her arms relaxed, and he loosened his grip. "There," he said, stroking her hair that had started to come loose, "I don't know where you are, but you need to listen to my voice. You're safe for now. We're waiting for Ferday to come back and help us get out."

Hope no one heard that.

He realized she was shaking. At first, he thought she was seizing from the head wound, then he noticed she was crying. She covered her mouth with her hands to muffle her crying. The realization of what she was reliving hit him harder than any punch or blow he'd taken.

Leon.

The man had attacked her when she was younger. He didn't know the details but Ferga had said that he'd heard her scream and had pulled him off her and that she'd never quite seemed the same. Ferday had mentioned that the incident had been what prompted her to learn Jempa, a fighting style that didn't let your opponent get close unless you wanted, where you use your opponents weakness as your strength.

Pendry sighed. Too much, she'd been through too much. He pulled her into a hug and whispered softly, "It's ok, you're safe, no one will hurt you and no one will touch you." He wanted to hurt all of them, Monty, Leon, anyone who'd hurt her and caused her to be scared. "I'd move over but we're in a vent that Ferday had the bright idea to use to escape. I'm sorry."

He set her back gently, but she reached up and wrapped her arms around his neck burying her face into his chest. He gently wrapped one arm around her again, bracing against the wall of the vent with the other.

He let her cry. He'd never seen her cry before, but he'd never seen her this scared, not even when they'd faced the faie.

She'd probably never felt so helpless as she did when Leon attacked. He thought, *She won't have to be so scared again. I'll make sure she gets her peace.*

She was starting to calm down and taking deep breaths. Still shaking and clinging to him but no longer crying hard.

Gardenias and lilacs.

It came to him then, why he kept thinking of that, and why he felt so angry at the thought of her being hurt. He wasn't quite ready to dwell on that feeling and he wasn't sure he should. *Definitely not now,* he thought. *First we get out, then there'll be time to think about that.*

"Everything ok?" He looked up to see Ferday laying in the vent ahead of them. He was smoldering a little, but he didn't seem to notice.

Pendry nodded, but he didn't let go of Jewel. She didn't seem ready.

Ferday watched for a while. He seemed to understand and was in no hurry to break into the moment.

She took a few more deep breaths, then let go of Pendry. He laid her down slowly, and watched her wipe her tears.

He felt a stabbing pain, seeing her injured and crying.

"Sorry," she said softly, trying to smile. "Did I hurt you?" She reached out and touched the new bruise forming on his chin. He winced, but smiled.

"All good," he murmured. "Nothing that some ice can't help."

"Well, we can get some ice if you two are ready to go," Ferday said smirking at them.

Jewel twisted her head around and smiled. She'd just noticed Ferday. "We're fine. Sorry, had to fight the past. Thank you for the rescue." She twisted the rest of her body around so she could crawl on her own.

"Oh, I get that all the time when I'm on stakeouts with Dannor," Ferday said twisting around and heading down the vent. "Did I tell you about the time he threatened to feed me to a sea monster?"

Pendry let her go ahead and follow Ferday. He followed a little ways behind.

23

Jewel

Ferday led them for what felt like forever, but Jewel thought that might be just her feeling that way since she was injured.

"Not much farther. You hanging in there?" he asked over his shoulder.

"Yes. Nothing to worry about, it's just a small head wound." She tried to convey that everything was ok, but her vision kept getting these strange blotches and it hurt to breathe.

After a few more minutes he stopped, twisted his legs in front, and kicked a grate off. It clattered to the ground. Ferday had always been flexible, squeezing into the smallest places imaginable. She watched him push his way out without even checking first. He also had a tendency of being needlessly reckless. Suddenly his head popped up and he grinned at her.

"Right, come on my little big sis." He reached out and she gladly let him help her.

He set her down near the wall and let her slide down to sit. He checked her head and was muttering about something. She couldn't focus on it. Standing had made her dizzy and feel faint. Her vision grew worse. The blotches were now large, dark and ragged, filling most of her vision. Her head screamed with pain, nausea rose into her throat. She couldn't tell if it was from the pain or being dizzy.

"How is she?" Pendry asked, walking over. She wasn't sure how he'd gotten out but that didn't seem to matter.

"Seems a bit drained, but the wound is already closed and seems like it'll be fine."

They're talking about me like I'm not here. Maybe I'm not really, she thought as her vision slowly cleared and she realized she was clinging to Ferday's arms and staring blankly at Pendry.

"I don't think she can walk," Pendry said, kneeling down and looking at her closer. "Are we safe here until she's recovered enough?"

"No, there's an entrance to the Gradiare tunnels just ahead and I've stowed your weapons in there," Ferday said pointing with his head. "Can you carry her? I'll take lead and clear the path if we run into anyone."

"Yeah," Pendry said, reaching out to pick her up.

"No," she finally managed to say, pulling herself up against the wall and letting go of Ferday. "I'll manage, it's not that bad." She took a step forward and felt her legs give out. Pendry was ready and caught her, her vision started to blur again.

Whoa, maybe I can't.

"No you can't," Pendry said, scooping her up before she could complain.

"Follow me, quick. I think I hear someone." Ferday turned and ran down the passage.

"Hold on," Pendry whispered to her. She didn't complain, and just held on. He ran after Ferday and followed him into a doorway in the wall that must have been the tunnel.

Everything went dark and for a moment, Jewel thought she was passing out again. Then her eyes adjusted and she realized the door had just closed.

She looked up and saw concern and worry on Pendry's face. He was looking down the tunnel. He held her close, and gave her the feeling he didn't want to let go any time soon. She felt his arms flex and saw his jaw harden like he was clenching his teeth. There was something about the way he was handling this, like he was protecting his injured arm back when she'd first seen him stumbling to her cabin. He was protecting her like she was a part of him, but that didn't make sense. No one was supposed to protect her. No one cared that much.

I'm supposed to care, not them. I'm supposed to risk myself for them, not them for me. I'm supposed to die.

"Let's go," Ferday said standing and holding their weapons under one arm.

Pendry followed Ferday down the tunnel, holding her close.

She found herself watching his face, trying to read it. In the dim light, he looked formidable and heroic, like he had when fighting.

She felt a rush of emotion in her chest, almost like adrenaline but gentler. She thought about his crooked smile and the look he'd given her that morning across the table, the same look he'd given her the night before. She couldn't place it, but she felt it was important, this feeling in her chest.

Later, she thought, *that can be solved later.*

She let her head rest on his shoulder and closed her eyes.

When she opened them again she was facing a fire. She could hear hushed voices. She hadn't meant to fall asleep. How long had she been out?

She rolled over and realized she was laying on two of the big chairs in Ferga's office that had been pushed together. There was a large blanket draped over her and a pillow under her head.

Not injured enough for sick bay, she thought as she continued to roll over. She winced as she moved. Her head throbbed. *Not long enough for it to be fully healed.*

She pushed herself up a bit and looked over the arm of the chair. She could see three figures sitting around the table and leaning close together, talking in hushed voices. From the sound of it, they were Ferga, Ferday and Pendry. She couldn't quite make out what they were saying, but they sounded serious and urgent.

"That's not going to work," Ferday said a little louder. The others hushed him and they continued in their low voices.

Jewel sat up, ignoring her pain, she crawled out of the makeshift bed and stood with the blanket wrapped around her. Her hair was a mess, hanging limply in the bun she'd done before the mission. She gave herself a second for the room to stop spinning, then walked over to the table, moving slowly so she wouldn't hurt herself. She was still slightly dizzy and her vision was hazy.

"Look, there's not much more we can do. We've sent out the message to our outposts, but now is when we need to attack, before they get a chance to learn what we know, before the King's allies arrive," Ferga said in an urgent whisper. He was about to continue when he saw Jewel standing and watching them. The other two turned to see what he was looking at. Seeing her, they jumped up.

"Why are you standing? Get back to bed," Ferday said in a gruff but concerned tone.

"Don't strain yourself. Here, sit here," Pendry said gently, offering her his chair.

She didn't move, she stayed looking at Ferga. She knew what they were talking about, and from the look on his face he knew she wouldn't like it.

"You," he said looking regretful, "you know we have to, it's the only way."

The others looked back and forth between Jewel and Ferga. They knew each other so well having worked so closely all those years. He didn't need to say anything, she knew what he was thinking.

Jewel took a tentative step forward and felt herself sway slightly. Pendry grabbed her elbow and led her to his chair. She sat and curled into her blanket.

"I know," was all she could manage to say. She was still too weak from the blood loss, but was trying not to show it. "How long was I out?" She managed to ask after a moment of pause.

"Just a couple hours," Pendry said, sitting in the seat next to her. He still looked battered and worn but more relaxed than before.

"You went in on the night of the 17th and I found you around midday on the 18th. It's still the 18th, sometime around 11:00 I think," Ferday said glancing at the clock.

"Ok," she muttered. Her eyes wanted to close but she forced herself to stay awake.

"Should we wake Lav to help, maybe get you some crestym?" Ferday asked, turning to go. "She would want to know you're up."

"No," she said, smiling half-heartedly. "I'll be ok." She turned to Ferga, "I know what you're planning, and it's dumb. You don't have the forces here and you can't overthrow the King on your own." She took a ragged breath, "But, you can plan a small attack, at the same time spreading the news of what the King is doing as a rumor, getting his people against him is your best option."

Ferga nodded, "I wasn't planning a full frontal attack, but now is the best time for an attack." He scratched his beard and leaned back in his chair. "The rumor is something I hadn't thought of, but you're right. We need the people to turn against him. The King's biggest weakness is the people and we should turn it against him."

Jewel laid her head back in the chair, fighting to stay awake.

"Pendry," Ferga said quietly, "would you escort Jewel to her room? She needs rest, as do you. Ferday and I need to plan. Thank you for your work on the mission."

Pendry nodded and stood. He reached down and helped Jewel to her feet. She was still wobbly and felt as though all the blood had drained from her head and she was going to fall. He scooped her up, blanket and all, then he turned and walked out.

I can walk, she wanted to say, but she knew it would be a lie. She couldn't even stand without almost passing out. She rested her head on Pendry's chest and fought to keep her eyes open, only to give in after a moment.

She opened her eyes to him setting her in her bed. He adjusted the blanket so it covered her better, then unlaced her boots and gently tugged them off.

That was nice of him, he didn't need to do that.

She closed her eyes and nestled into the pillow. Then she realized he was taking the pins out of her hair and setting them on the table next to her bed.

"You don't have to," she murmured, her eyes still closed.

"Can't have you hurting your head more, and I don't mind," he said softly. He finished and she heard him walk to the door.

"Thank you," she murmured into her pillow.

"You're welcome," he said quietly. "Goodnight." Then she heard the door close.

24

Pendry

Pendry washed his face the next morning. It had been a long day and a long night, but he didn't feel like he could sleep any longer. He checked the cuts and bruises on his face in the mirror, then checked the cut on his arm. It really hadn't turned out to be as bad as it first appeared and didn't require any stitches, just some taping. He closed his eyes and leaned on the sink, the weight of the memories from yesterday's events felt too much.

He groaned. All he could picture when he closed his eyes was Jewel, limp and bleeding from her head. He took a shaky breath and decided to go to the dining room to see if she was up. Even though he had been the one to see her to her room, he felt as if she was still lying half dead and bleeding somewhere.

He entered the dining room to see Lavender fussing over Jewel. The tight feeling in his chest relaxed.

"I don't care how late it was, you should have woken me so I could see you were ok," Lavender said, as she combed Jewel's hair.

"Sorry," Jewel replied weakly. She was in that same long skirt and sweater as the other night. "I didn't actually stay up, I woke up and went to my bed. That's it."

Pendry felt his shoulders relax as he walked over. He didn't even bother with food, he just sat down across from Jewel and watched her get her hair done. She didn't have a bandage anymore and he could see a curved pink scar just at her hairline.

She smiled softly at him, pulling her knees up and holding them. It made her look small in the large chair.

"Oof, you both had it rough," Lavender said, eyeing Pendry. "We have some medicine for bruises; I'll get it for you after I'm done here."

Pendry smiled. He felt relieved seeing that Jewel was ok. And more than that, she was healed already. "I'm ok, no rush." He sat back and let himself relax more.

That was too much, he thought, *I don't know how they handle this. Maybe that was a once in a blue moon mission.*

"Did you sleep well?"

He sat up and saw Jewel watching him. "Yes. Well, as well as I could, considering."

He watched Lavender braid Jewel's hair and heard the booming voices of Ferga and Ferday as they came down the hall. She smiled knowingly, then closed her eyes and let herself relax into her sister. She looked so peaceful.

How can she be so calm after all of that?

"I told you they'd be here," Ferday said bounding into the room and up to Jewel. He knelt down and gently kissed her cheek. "How are you my little big sister? You look better."

"I'm doing better, thank you Day," she said smiling, her eyes still closed.

"Glad to hear it; I've made plans for you to have transport back to the cabin," Ferga said, sitting in his usual spot. He passed a mug of coffee to Pendry and smirked, "Lav do we have any of that stuff to heal bruises for the poor man?"

Lavender glared at Ferga, "I said I would get him some as soon as I'm done here. I just used it on Jewel's neck, just give me a minute. And there, I'm done." She draped the braid over Jewel's shoulder and kissed her cheek before walking away and calling over her shoulder. "I'll get you that stuff."

"I'm ok, I've been through worse. Honestly," Pendry said as he picked up his coffee. He didn't want them to worry about his bruises when there were more important things to do.

Ferday walked back to the table, set a mug of coffee in front of Jewel and sat next to her. "Eh, we've all had worse. Doesn't mean you can't be better."

Jewel sipped her coffee and turned to Ferga, "I'm not leaving yet. You've only just started and you need all the help you can get."

"You barely made it out of there alive. I'm not sending you back in there," Ferga said in a commanding voice.

"That's because there were two of us and a hundred of them. I'll be fine. Really, I'm feeling much better after some sleep." She smiled. She did look better, but she also looked tired and like she needed more rest.

Why is she pushing herself? Pendry thought. *Just go rest.*

"Only if you're with me," Ferday said. "I'm not having you push yourself and getting hurt again."

Jewel sighed, "Ok, I'm ok with that. I'll follow your lead."

Ferday got that mischievous smile. "Really? I'm in charge of you? Ooo, I like that idea."

Jewel smacked his arm playfully, "Don't get too excited. I said I'd follow your lead, not that you're in charge." She smiled.

"Here we are," Lavender said as she came up behind Pendry. "Here, look here and I'll help put it on." She was holding a jar of cream and a small round pad of gauze.

"Get ready for stinging," Ferga said, wincing at the memory.

"It's not that bad," Lavender said as she started to apply it to the bruises on Pendry's face.

It was pretty bad. It felt like he was being cut with a tiny knife or that she was rubbing lemon juice on a hundred paper cuts. He tried not to wince and just hold still so she could apply it.

"It is that bad. Actually, no, it's worse than a little stinging," Ferday said. Pendry glanced over and saw him wincing and grimacing while watching Lavender apply the cream.

"You're all babies," Lavender snapped.

"Have you ever used it, Lav?" Jewel asked. She was grimacing too.

"Not for a bruise as big as you all seem to get, but yes I have."

"Then you're the toughest of all of us," Ferga said, chuckling.

"There, all done," Lavender said as she examined Pendry's face. "That bruise on your chin is at an odd angle. How'd you get so many?" She closed the jar and put it and the round pad in her apron pocket.

"Um." Pendry hesitated and glanced at Jewel and Ferday. He wasn't going to say how Jewel had hit him and why. And he wasn't ready to talk about the beating he'd taken from Monty. "Just fighting."

Ferday nodded. He seemed to understand, but Jewel looked sad and like she wanted to say sorry, but didn't.

There was a pang of guilt. He felt bad about the whole vent situation. He didn't mean to scare her, and he hoped he'd never cause her to be so scared again.

"Ehm." Ferga cleared his throat. "Anyway, we need to strategize and plan; I have a meeting with the council and I will not put you through that again," he said, taking Jewel's hand. "You lot get some rest and recover. We'll meet in my office with the other generals around noon for the strategizing meeting. And you." He turned to Jewel, "Rest. I mean it. I'm glad you're doing better." He stood and kissed the top of her head. "Looking forward to fighting alongside you again, my Lion."

He strode out of the dining room. Ferday gulped down his coffee and jumped up to follow. They were alone. Sometime while Ferga had been talking, Lavender had left, and Pendry hadn't noticed.

Jewel slowly stood with her coffee and walked to the chairs in front of the fire. He watched her, wondering if she was well enough to walk. Her braid hung down almost to her knees and swished while she walked. He watched her slide into one of the oversized chairs and curl up with her coffee to watch the fire.

Pendry stood, took his coffee, and sat in the chair next to her. He sighed, realizing just how sore and tired he was.

"Sorry about the bruise," she said, still looking into the fire.

"Not a problem. I'm sorry you had to go through that, and then relive it." He watched the fire. It was mesmerizing and soothing to watch.

They sat like that for a time, just sipping their coffee and staring at the dancing flames.

"You don't have to stay, you know," Pendry said softly. "I'd hate to see you hurt again."

She chuckled, "Don't worry about me, I've had my fair share of pain and I don't mind a little more if it means the job gets done."

He turned to her; she had that sad smile playing about her mouth. He felt the urge to yell, to get angry. She couldn't be so blind that she didn't see how much everyone cared. He closed his eyes and took a deep breath.

"Everyone loves you. You know that, right? They want you safe. They want you to have the rest you deserve after all the pain you've been through." He opened his eyes and stayed looking at the ceiling. He heard her stir, and felt her eyes on him.

"You don't know me," she said quietly.

He turned to her again. She was studying her skirt, her lips pursed and her green eyes dark. "I know what I see."

He said sitting up, "I know what they've told me. Ferday said you fight like you want to die, like you have nothing to live for."

She looked at him confused, "He... he said that?"

"Yes." He set his mug down on a nearby table and leaned forward, "Look, I realize that you're used to sacrifice, but you've done enough. No one wants you to die."

"But maybe I don't want to live." She said it so sharply that Pendry felt like she'd stabbed him. He looked at her; she had that hardened look she had when they first met.

But I want you to live.

"Why don't you want to live?" he asked gently.

"What's there to live for? I've served my people, I've done my job. I should have died three times now." She took a ragged breath, her eyes were wet with tears building up. "After this, if I'm still alive, I just go back to my cabin alone to live. But live for what? Yes, it's peaceful and yes, it's nice, but I'd rather die fighting so others can enjoy that peace."

"And what if you weren't alone?" Pendry asked, staring at his hands. He wasn't ready for this. He didn't even know exactly what that feeling was. Yet here he was.

No, he thought, *I'm talking to a friend in need. A friend in need of a friend, now more than ever.*

"I don't know," she muttered, turning to the fire. "I wouldn't want someone to waste their life just to make me feel a little better."

"Why do you think it would be a waste?"

"Because there's better things they could be doing with their life."

Pendry took a deep breath, "And what if that was the best way they could think of to spend their life?" He turned to her and chuckled, "You can't argue that some dreams are small. Just because you dream big, with over-throwing the King, doesn't mean everyone dreams that big."

She smiled softly and snuggled down into her chair. "Not all of my dreams are so big," she sighed. "I might be coaxed into believing that someone could dream that, but I think it might take a lot." Her eyes looked heavy and she seemed to need rest. "Thank you for listening," she muttered as she closed her eyes.

Pendry sighed and stared at the fire for a moment, then he stood and walked over to a chest similar to the one he'd seen Lavender get a blanket from the night before. He pulled out two blankets and walked back to Jewel. She was still holding her coffee mug. He smiled, gently took it and placed it on the nearby table next to his. Then he draped a blanket over her. He then went back to his chair and sat in it, deciding he needed more sleep too.

I can talk to her after the attack, he thought as he drifted off to sleep. It was easier to sleep with her laying in the chair next to his where he could see that she was safe.

25

Jewel

J ewel was startled awake by the sound of dishes clattering. She remembered she was still holding her coffee but when she looked it was gone. She sat up and saw Pendry curled under a blanket in the chair near her. He was so tall that his legs hung over the side of the chair. That made her smile. His bruises had cleared and he looked so peaceful.

He really is very handsome. There's no point in denying it, she thought as she watched him sleeping peacefully. She watched the gentle rise and fall of his chest as he slept. He'd been so considerate of her after she was injured. *For someone so tall and strong, he is very gentle and kind. I don't think I've ever met someone like him.* She felt that same rush of emotion, almost like adrenaline, twisting her stomach and making her chest hurt.

Suddenly the dishes clattered again and he started awake.

"Wha-?" he started to say.

He had nearly jumped out of the chair from the noise. As soon as he was up he looked disheveled, his thick black hair sticking up at odd angles and his shirt twisting around him. She had to cover her mouth to suppress a laugh. He looked at her and relaxed. He smiled and laid back down. Lavender walked past with a stack of dishes.

"Is everything ok?" Jewel asked, trying not to chuckle.

Lavender stopped and groaned, "Oh, I'm sorry, I didn't mean to wake you. We're getting food ready for the strategizing meeting. The kitchen is a little short on people today, so I'm trying to do three jobs. Nevermind, not important." She glanced at the clock on the mantle, "Actually you two should get cleaned up and ready to go. I didn't realize the time." Lavender hurried off out of the dining room.

Jewel glanced at the clock, half an hour until the meeting. She stood up from her chair and stretched. She felt cramped after sleeping in a ball, but a little stronger after resting more. She glanced at Pendry and saw him stretching too.

"Right, I'll see you there." She turned and headed for the door, feeling slightly embarrassed at the memory of the conversation they had before she fell asleep. But at the same time, that dark heavy feeling was lifting, and she felt a little lighter.

Maybe I just needed to talk with someone.

She was just outside of the door when she heard him call to her.

"Hang on," Pendry said as he caught up to her.

"Is everything ok?" she asked, trying not to focus on how his hair was sticking up.

"Yeah," he said, rubbing the back of his neck. "I just wanted to make sure you were good, you know, after our talk." He said it hesitantly like she might get upset with him.

She smiled reassuringly to him, "I'm ok. Thank you for checking." She turned to walk away, he followed.

"I just want to make sure that you aren't going to do anything reckless," he said, catching her arm. "During the battle later. Just..." he hesitated, "just remember that people care for you and they want you to make it through."

He said it with that same look, the look that she didn't understand. That feeling grew, the soft rush of emotions and adrenaline.

"Ok," she said, giving his hand a squeeze. "I'll be as safe as anyone can be in a battle."

"Thanks," he said, letting go of her. He didn't move, she had the feeling there was more he wanted to say, but he didn't say anything.

"Was that it?" She asked, tilting her head slightly. *He looks a little lost.*

"Yeah." He muttered, but he still didn't move.

"I'm going to go clean up. I'll meet you there, ok?" She was a little concerned that there was something important she was missing.

"Yeah, I'll see you there," he said, still looking hesitant and lost.

This time she turned and walked down the hall instead of waiting for him to move first.

What was that about? she wondered.

She took a shower, letting the hot water soak into her stiff muscles and run through her hair. If she wasn't in a rush, she'd have stayed there longer to let the heat help her relax more. Instead, she cut herself off after a few minutes.

Quickly dressing in some easy fighting clothes, pants and a loose blouse. She braided and pinned up her hair and tied on her boots. Then she strapped on her katshme. Before heading out, she checked the new scar. It had just missed her temple and was a thin jagged pink crescent shape. That would fade, just as all her smaller scars had. She was more concerned about the slight pain she had when she moved suddenly. She moved on to examine her neck. There were no marks, but it still burned a little when she took a deep breath.

Not a big deal, there's still time. Healing takes time.

She half expected to see Pendry still standing in the hall, unsure of what to do, but he was gone. She continued to Ferga's office and was greeted with the smell of food and coffee.

She was also greeted with cheers from the generals. Several of them rushed forward and shook her hand. She liked the generals; they were a great group of people. There were five generals total, Ferday was one. There were two women among the men. All of the generals were young compared to the council, and she knew them all very well.

"I'm so glad to see you here," Lacia said, rushing forward to embrace Jewel. She was a tall slender woman with bright blue eyes and short blond hair. She led the archers. "I was hoping I'd get to see you before you left."

Jewel hugged her. "Good to see you too, Lacia."

"Right on time for the first major battle since that wall incident," Tristain said, shaking her hand. He was a large burly man, with short cropped brown hair. He led the brunt of the attacks.

They all played a role and they all were good at that role, following orders and working as a unit. They'd all trained together and fought together. She couldn't imagine a better group of people to fight with.

She saw Pendry talking to Ferday. He'd showered and taken care of the hair that had been sticking up everywhere. Now it was its usual messy black curls. She walked over and saw them examining something and laughing about it.

"What's this?" She asked, walking up behind them.

They turned and in Pendry's hand was a pair of glasses, not the kind you use all the time, but the kind you use to test your vision with. There were little levers on both sides and several layers of lenses.

"We were testing his vision, and it turns out he does need glasses. They won't be ready for tonight's battle, but we now know no archery for this one," Ferday said laughing. "Oh, try them on again. Show her how ridiculous they look."

Pendry put them on. "I don't think it's ridiculous at all." He looked at Ferday with a very serious expression.

Jewel had to bite her lip to keep from laughing. They were absolutely ridiculous. He turned to her and she snorted, that was even worse.

It's good he still has a sense of humor.

"Oh I think it's perfect," she said, trying to hold in her laugh.

"Go on. You can cackle at me again. I'm not above being the brunt of a joke every now and then," he said, smiling his crooked smile.

"I don't cackle," she said, chuckling.

"Does she cackle?" Ferday asked grinning, "Oh let's hear it."

"She does," Pendry said, taking the glasses off and handing them to Ferday. "Haven't you heard it?"

"No, she never actually lets go and laughs, not since we were kids, and even then she hid her laugh." Ferday glared at Jewel, then turned to Pendry, "Wait, how did you hear her real laugh?"

Pendry chuckled, "Just a joke after that run in with the faie."

"I told him to be careful what rocks he picked up after he put one in his pocket," she said, still fighting her laughter.

"Oh yeah, those purple ones explode," Ferday said seriously.

Pendry looked back and forth between them. He looked like he was just believing them when Ferday snorted.

"I'm sorry, your face," he said, doubled over laughing.

"Seriously? Do you both have the same brain or something?" Pendry asked, chuckling and rubbing his nose.

"It's a joke from when we were kids," Jewel said, laughing slightly. That feeling from before was back. "Gwen, our oldest sister said she'd found a pet rock, but then she lost it and asked us all to find it. Over the years we teased her about it but then it turned into a 'careful of the rocks' joke." She was trying to catch her breath and stop laughing. She didn't want to cackle.

"Ah, I miss that grouchy old know it all," Ferday said, wiping his eyes. "Hard to believe she has two kids and another on the way." He shuddered, "Ugh, her as a mom."

"She makes a good mom. She made a good sister too. That's why you don't like the idea of her as a mom."

"Can you imagine when Dannor becomes a dad?" Ferday shuddered again. "Oh I think that's worse. He's so boring."

Jewel rolled her eyes. "He's only boring to you because you hate sitting still and following his plans."

Ferday laughed. "One time he tied me up to the mast of that little sail boat we used to take out on the lake." He turned to Pendry. "He insisted I was scaring the fish off. All I did was sit."

Ferga entered the room then, grumbling and looking like a storm cloud. All laughter died.

"Confounded old so and so's." He plopped down in a chair and rubbed his face. They all gathered around the table and sat.

"Jewel, I don't know how you never killed anyone in those meetings," he sighed, then slowly sat up and took a more commanding position. "You lot make me feel like there's hope yet." He took a deep breath, "Now, before we begin, I say we eat. Planning is better with a full stomach."

26

Pendry

P endry had never been in a meeting like this, especially before a battle. Everyone had a chance to talk and be listened to. But at the same time, it felt as though everyone was talking at once. There was a lot of planning, lots of food and, surprisingly to Pendry, there was a lot of laughter.

They're getting ready for a battle, planning the attack and still laughing and cracking jokes. Maybe it's just a cultural thing, Pendry wondered as he looked around the room.

He'd caught some of the planning, but since he wasn't in charge of anything, he didn't worry about catching all the details. He learned that Ferday led the stealth charge, and they would go in before anyone else. They were to secure the main gate to the inner ring of the city. A woman named Jenaveve led the 75, though he wasn't sure why they called it the 75. She was to lead the charge to secure the market gate. And a man named Wen was in charge of the tunnels and the hidden traps under the city.

There's traps under the city? How many secrets were built into this city?

He learned that they weren't planning to take over the castle, just the outer ring of the city. They needed to control the gates until reinforcements arrived. Those would arrive in the next week or so. But they needed to take hold of the outer ring first. With reinforcements, they would be able to take the inner ring and press on to the castle.

There were maps spread out on the table, some of the city and some of what looked to be the Gradiare hideout and the tunnel system. He knew the city had been built slowly over time. They'd started with the castle and the wall around it, then as the city grew and they needed more space, they built a wall around it. When they outgrew that, they built a second, larger wall around it. He could see the sectioned wards, 11, 10, 9 and 8 were all in the inner ring of the city. 7-1 were located in the outer ring of the city.

"We need to get the information out to the people, too," Jewel said as she pushed her empty plate away. "The only way any of this is going to work is if the people are against the King."

"Yes," Ferga said, rubbing the bridge of his nose. "Ideas?"

"Have Marina and her medic team go through the city telling people. Use more of the record film to make more copies of the orders from the King and have them put them up in strategic places." Ferday suggested, "They'd probably be more open to listening to them. She's said how her team has helped those in the city and have been working on building a good reputation with them." Ferday sat forward, furrowing his brow. "I can send for her if you think that would be a good plan."

Ferga nodded, "Yes, I think that should work. Then the medics would be out and able to help where needed. Let her know that only those who want to should do it."

There was some more planning, placement of archers and when the frontal attack would happen and where.

"Right," Ferga said, "you all know what to do. Make sure everyone knows this isn't our usual fight. What we have here is all there is. We aren't likely to succeed and there's a high chance a good number of us won't make it, so make sure to say goodbye to your loved ones and that everyone with you is ok with that."

Somehow the meeting came to an end, and the most of what Pendry knew he was with Ferday and Jewel, and that they would be going in before the rest. He didn't understand why they had made it sound like they didn't have enough people. With five generals, there must be 500 people behind them. Sure that wasn't enough to face an army head on, but it had to be enough to win in a surprise attack.

He followed Jewel and Ferday to the armory to prepare. They were talking about the best options for armor when it came to stealth. They decided leather, not the best for protection, but the best for stealth. They were the only ones in the armory, but Ferday and Jewel didn't seem to mind.

"Shouldn't there be others getting ready?" Pendry asked, looking around.

"No, all the real soldiers have their own armor," Ferday said, clapping Pendry on the shoulder. "Jewel even had her own stuff, but it was damaged beyond repair when that wall fell." He turned to Jewel pouting. "And you never had more made; I guess the meadow is safer."

Jewel rolled her eyes, "It's not a meadow. Those are full of flowers."

Pendry smirked, "It's definitely a meadow. I remember a lot of flowers."

She glared at him, "I lived there for two years, I think I would know if it was a meadow." She picked up a leather breastplate and started strapping it on. "It's a field. If I scatter wildflower seeds, then yes, it would be a meadow."

"Ok, forest girl." He smirked.

She looked up at him sharply, a slight smile playing at the corners of her mouth and a glint in her green eyes.

Ferday handed Pendry a set of leather armor to strap on. "I'm assuming that since you were a peace officer you know how to put this on."

Pendry nodded, still smiling at Jewel. "Yeah," he turned to Ferday and saw a knowing gleam in his eyes. "Ehm," Pendry coughed, "yeah, I know how to put it on." He felt his ears getting hot as he turned and set the armor on a table and started strapping it on.

"By the way," Ferday said sadly, "we'll be fighting at the entrance to your old ward, also you may run into an old comrade or friend. Are you ok with that?"

Pendry grimaced, "Don't really have a choice. I became their enemy the moment I was at the top of the most wanted list."

"Right, well just wanted to check with you." Ferday turned to get his own armor. "Once you're finished we'll begin our trek out."

"How many will be with us?" He asked, strapping on an arm brace.

"We're kind of it," Jewel muttered as she strapped on one of her shin guards. "Ferday is lead on the stealth and he gets his choice of who he leads. Most of the men and women he takes are down for the count or out on other assignments."

"Oh," he said surprised, "guess it's just the same thing we did the other night, minus the separating and the other not good stuff."

"Yep," Ferday said cheerily. "We're starting a just like old times." He walked over to Jewel and high fived her. "See you at Heaven's gate."

She laughed. "Not if I have a say in it."

Ferday turned to Pendry and laughed at the confused look on his face. "I always forget how bad that sounds to outsiders; it's just a thing we say before a battle. Sort of an acknowledgement that we might die, but we'll go together."

"Or keep each other from going," Jewel said as she finished strapping on her katshme.

"Ok," Pendry chuckled.

"Yes, we're a morbid lot, with twisted humor and stunning good looks," Ferday said stroking his hair.

Jewel laughed at him.

At least we get to see each other happy before we go fight to the death. Maybe that's why they're always laughing.

27

Jewel

They ran through the tunnels; it wasn't as far to go as the other night, but it was still far. Jewel liked working with Ferday. He moved quickly and always had backup plans for his backup plans, and was quick to come up with a new plan when everything went sideways.

They were heading for the main gate of the inner ring. They needed to close and lock it so they wouldn't be overwhelmed by King's Guard reinforcements. They were heading for the north gate, known as The Main. A second team, run by Jenaveve with the 75, was headed for the south gate, the market gate. Her team was bigger and on horseback, and even though the main gate was called that, the market gate had more people and traffic around it, so it made more sense to send the bigger group to the south gate.

Lacia was heading for the outer wall with her archers. Their job was to pick off the guards on the outer wall, then work their way in, taking down guards on the inner wall and being backup for those on the ground. Ferga and Tristain would be leading the main attack, charging in from the city main gate and sweeping through the outer ring towards the inner ring. It was a good plan. They had good people in charge with years of experience. The biggest problem was numbers. They always kept enough fighters in the hideout, but it was risky. If too many King's Guards were in the outer ring, they could easily be overwhelmed. They had to trust that they would be enough.

They made it to the exit near the gate and Ferday looked through the spy hole to check that the coast was clear.

Jewel leaned with her back to the wall trying to catch her breath. Pendry did the same on the opposite wall. She closed her eyes. Her head still hurt, and even though her throat healed fast, it hurt to run and breathe. She had to focus, there was a job to do. She opened her eyes and saw Pendry watching her.

"You good?" He asked breathlessly. "Your head doing ok?"

"Yeah," she nodded. No sense in having him worrying over her again.

"Right my cunning gremlins," Ferday said turning to them. "We have a situation. We can get out and to a cart over to the right a bit, but we have about two guards at the main gate. Guess the King doubled up security since we broke in."

They crept out the door onto Holding Street and hid behind the cart that Ferday had mentioned. Jewel peeked out and saw the two guards. The big gate was closed and barred. Only the small door in the gate for people to walk through was open.

That makes things easier.

"I have an idea," Ferday said smiling mischievously. "You're going to hate me."

Jewel turned to him confused, then concerned. "What?" She groaned.

"Well," he paused and inched towards Pendry. "Jewel, you're a beautiful woman, go flirt with the guards," he said hastily as he cowered near Pendry.

"That's your plan." She hissed at him, "Flirt? I've never flirted with anyone in my life."

Ferday shrugged, "Do you have a better one? It doesn't matter if you can't flirt. You're so beautiful you just have to talk to them and they'll think you're flirting." He turned to Pendry like he was searching for reassurance.

Pendry blushed and looked a little nervous. "Why are you looking at me? I'm not going to protect you."

"Back me up," Ferday said in a hoarse whisper.

His face reddened. "I, um, I have to agree that your beauty is intimidating and makes it feel like you're flirting just by smiling," he said in a rushed stumble.

He'd called her beautiful before, but this time it felt different. This time it made her heart skip and that rush of emotions came flooding in on her.

"Yes, smile and bat those gorgeous eyelashes at them," Ferday said gleefully.

"I will kill you both," she growled.

"No you won't. I'm your baby brother that you love, and for some reason you kinda like him." he said pointing at Pendry.

"What? Does she?" Pendry asked, turning an even brighter shade of red and getting that look in his eye. "That's good to know," he muttered.

Jewel could feel her face growing hot. She knew she was blushing. She glared at Ferday, "I will not go flirt with those guards." She was ready to smack Ferday for even suggesting it. "You flirt with them since it's your plan."

"Mmmm," he said, eyeing the guards, "can't, I don't do men."

"How can you tell they're both men?" She was getting flustered.

"I just can, and in any case you're so pretty that even if they're women, they'd like to flirt with you."

She stared at him open mouthed. "I am the past Commander of the Gradiare and your best plan is to send me to go flirt with those guards?" She was fuming and growling.

"Yes." He still had that gleefully glint in his eye.

She looked at Pendry and saw his face was still very red and he was burying it in the crook of his elbow. *He's probably red from trying not to laugh at how ridiculous this whole situation is.*

Ferday waved her off. "Go on Jewel, the family is depending on your flirting with those guards over there," he smirked.

She groaned. Why couldn't she think of another plan, any other plan? "When this is over, I'll get you for this." She started to leave then turned back to him, "I won't be leaving you any crestym." Now it was her turn to smirk. It made her feel a little better, but it wasn't enough.

She turned and snuck down an alley, creeping between the buildings and coming out away from the guys on one of the streets going into the city's inner wall. If her memory was right, this was 39th. She took a deep breath and started walking up to the guards.

What on earth am I doing? She thought as she walked up towards the gate. *Don't march, just walk normally. Wait, what's my normal walk? Ugh, I forgot how to walk. Why am I doing this?*

As she walked up, she took note of where they were, making note of what streets led in and where guards might come from. She glanced at the nearby roofs. The archers were a big enough group and agile enough that some might attempt to get this close to the inner wall. In front of the main gate was a wide open space. The road had been left big enough for carts to pass each other with space and there was even an open cobbled circle in front of the gate big enough to turn two carts at once. Some years they had held markets on this side of the wall as well, but those weren't as popular.

All of this went through Jewel's head as she walked up to the guards. That, and the thought of how do you flirt? She stopped a few feet in front of the guards, suddenly very aware of the fact that she'd never been in a situation like this.

"Hi, I'm needing to get through," she said, smiling sweetly. *Yep, that's how to flirt, right?*

"Sorry, we're now requiring papers," one of the guards said, eyeing her suspiciously.

"Where would I get these papers?" She asked, trying to remain calm and sweet. Out of the corner of her eye she saw Ferday and Pendry sneaking out and scurrying towards the inner wall.

Oh, I'll kill him. He made me bait. She thought. *How do I get out of this?*

The guard was still eyeing her suspiciously. "You need to go to the Letter House and show them your city entrance papers, then he'll help you get the entrance papers to the inner ring."

"Right," Jewel said, trying to look shy. "See, I'm new, and I don't really know where the Letter House is. Could you maybe point it out or help me get there? I keep getting lost." She tried fiddling with a strand of hair that had come loose the same way she'd seen one of her sisters do when flirting with someone.

The other guard stepped forward, "Why do you have armor and weapons? You shouldn't have been able to get weapons past the outer gate." He drew his sword and the first guard did the same.

Well that was dumb, she thought, as she looked down at her very apparent armor and weapons. *Where did those idiots go, right when I could use them?*

The door in the gate suddenly slammed shut; Ferday appeared behind the guards slapping out his smoldering cloak and grinning like a maniac. "Can't have you sounding the alarm too soon, now can we?"

Pendry jumped out of the shadows of an alley and tackled one of the guards, knocking him out as he went.

Ferday threw one of his knives, it lodged in the other guard's neck; he collapsed with a small gurgling noise.

"Ugh, great, now if I pull it out I'll be sprayed with blood," Ferday said looking down at the guard.

Jewel walked up and punched him in the arm.

"Ouch."

"Really, go flirt with them, that was your bright idea? It would have been better if you'd said, hey, go distract them."

"Yeah, but it's more fun to tease you," Ferday said rubbing his arm.

Pendry stood up, dusting himself off. "Eh, you're also kinda cute when you're flustered and trying to be flirty."

They both turned to him in surprise. No one said anything for a while, just stared at each other blankly.

Did he just? No, he can't, he doesn't. Not possible.

Jewel turned back to Ferday, deciding to ignore what Pendry said. "Did you secure the door? Inside and out?"

"Yes," Ferday said still staring at Pendry. He raised an eyebrow.

She turned to see Pendry shrug. "Ok if you're done having a silent conversation, then we need to continue with our mission." She glared at Ferday. "Go get that cart and start a barricade."

"Hey, I thought I was lead," he said flustered.

"That was until you told me to go flirt with the guards," Jewel said, glaring at him.

Ferday walked off to the cart, grumbling.

She turned to Pendry and fixed him with a hard stare. He stared right back, casually standing with his hand resting on the hilt of his sword and a slight smile playing about his mouth.

She wanted to get angry and yell, but she also wanted to laugh. Why hadn't she seen that she was meant to be the bait? That feeling was back, it made everything so confusing. She sighed, "Go make yourself useful with Ferday."

He smiled that crooked smile and stepped forward to say something, when an arrow pierced the gate between them.

28

Pendry

P endry drew his sword Firebloom and saw Jewel draw her katshme out of the corner of his eye. There in front of them were about forty King's Guards. He was reminded of the fight in the castle, and slowly placed himself between Jewel and the King's Guards.

Not again, he thought, *she's not getting hurt again.*

Two things happened then, almost at once, and he almost missed them.

The first was a loud roar as Ferga came rushing in behind the King's Guard with his troops, about thirty men and women. It seemed like they came out of nowhere. They poured out of alleys and hidden doors in walls, charging and yelling. He'd never seen Ferga fight with a sword. It was similar to Ferday, with the exception that Ferga had more brute force and could sweep several King's Guards with every swing of his massive sword.

The second thing to happen was a rush and a pop above them, and a flaming cart came crashing down on the King's Guard. It took out about half of them. Ferday appeared in front of Pendry, slapping his shoulders and extinguishing small flames. He glanced back, smiled roguishly at them, then drew his katshme and charged into the fray laughing maniacally.

There was a second or two where Pendry stood in awe at the sight of the two leaders of the Gradiare fighting. Ferga with his brute strength yelling commands to his men. Ferday with his laughing and spinning acrobatics.

It's no wonder that they're the most feared enemy of the King.

"Pendry!"

He was snapped out of his awe by Jewel calling him back to the present. From the right side of Holding Street came another group of King's Guards. It looked to be about twenty more guards. They let the guards come to them.

At first during the fighting it felt like they wouldn't make it. It was two against twenty, but then some started falling with arrows protruding from them. He then remembered the archers and felt they would be ok. He could hear Jewel fighting behind him. He caught glimpses of her fighting and the others fighting as well.

Focus, attention divided is how you die.

He blocked and slashed, using his full strength and size to his advantage. Even though he was strongest fighting with a sword, he wasn't used to fighting so many at once. Slowly the tide felt like it was turning. Then another wave of King's Guard came from the left of Holding Street. He'd stopped trying to count them, but he felt like there were more King's Guards than he remembered.

He ducked under a clumsy thrust and stabbed the wielder.

It's almost like they just grabbed anyone for sheer numbers, he thought as he moved to block another swing.

As he swung his sword, he realized who he was fighting; he almost didn't recognize Brent dressed in full captain uniform. His dusty brown hair sticking out from under the green captain's hat. He looked confused and angry.

Pendry looked and saw a group of peace officers standing near the inner wall, but not fighting, just watching. They had to have come in with the latest group of King's Guards, but they didn't seem to know what to do.

"Pendry. What is going on?" Brent asked, glancing around.

"Brent, you're fighting for the wrong side," he growled as he pressed his sword down against Brent's. "The King is wicked. He's planning to kill all those who oppose him. Not just the Gradiare."

Their swords came away and Brent swung at Pendry. It felt more like when they had practiced rather than a fight to the death. He blocked and glared down at his old friend.

"So we've heard, but how can I trust you?" Brent said, glaring back at him. "You disappeared, then we hear you're wanted and you murdered a dozen people."

"Dozen?" Pendry asked, stepping forward and pressing his sword down against his friend's. "I witnessed the King's Guard murder someone and they pinned it on me. Brent, they're killing peace officers who don't join them."

Brent hesitated and stepped back, letting his sword relax. "All the murders they pinned on you were peace officers. The Gradiare, you trust them?"

"Yes. I trust them. All they want is peace and safety for the people." He watched his friend, hoping he wouldn't have to fight him.

He seemed to be processing for a moment. "We'd heard a rumor, but you know rumors."

Pendry waited, expecting him to swing at him again. Instead, Brent straightened, smiled at Pendry then let out a piercing whistle.

"King's Guards the enemy, we join the Gradiare." He turned to Pendry, "That was all I needed; if you trust them, then I trust them." He turned and led the other peace officers in to fight the King's Guard.

We might actually win this. Pendry thought. He turned to let Jewel know only to realize he'd moved farther than he thought he had. He was now half way down the old market circle. He saw Jewel fighting three of the King's Guards at once. She looked worn and slower than normal.

He swore to himself and started running over to help.

Of course she's moving slower, he thought, *she wasn't recovered enough to fight.*

He kept his eyes on her and willed himself to run faster. As he ran, she kicked one guard in the face and turned to the others. To his horror, the guard that fell got to his knees and brandished his sword.

No. Pendry thought.

"No!" He yelled.

But he wasn't fast enough. He watched as the guard pierced her back. The sword came out the other side. He heard her scream and watched her fall to one knee. He made it in time to cut the head off the guard on the ground before he could move the sword and do more damage. The guard fell in an awkward backwards fall, almost knocking Pendry over. He nimbly moved out of the way, then turned to see Jewel, still kneeling, stab the guard in front of her then slit his throat as he fell.

She stood and turned, blocking the third guard as he swung at her. She was gritting her teeth and glaring through the pain. Even wounded she moved fast. Before Pendry could get to her, another guard came up behind her and pulled the sword out, she cried out, wavering in her stance.

Pendry lunged forward killing the guard behind her, then turned and cut the head off the guard she was still fighting.

She collapsed to her knees, her katshme falling to the ground. She swayed, looking like she was moving to stand. Instead, she fell backwards. Pendry dropped his sword and caught her. He slowly collapsed to the ground and pulled her close. The wound was bad. He stared at it for a moment, trying to think of what to do to stop the bleeding. He hesitated, then put his hand on it, hoping it would help slow the bleeding.

She cried out at his touch.

"Sorry." He could feel the tears sliding down his cheek. "I'm sorry, I didn't realize I left you alone."

She smiled faintly, her eyes fluttering to stay open, then muttered, "You're cute when you're flustered."

Her eyes closed and she went limp.

29
Pendry

P endry cradled her. He felt numb. He wanted her to wake up. To say something, anything, even if it was her getting angry at him for not being there for her, especially for that.

"I'm sorry, I'm not ready for you to die. Please, wake up." He looked around for someone to help, but he didn't even know who to look for.

The fighting seemed to have dwindled and was all but over. There was a blood curdling scream followed by an anguished cry. Ferday ran up and slid to a stop in front of Pendry.

"NO! She can't. I can't." He was crying and looking her over then back at Pendry. "Is she. I... is she breathing?" he finally managed to ask.

Pendry leaned down to listen for breathing, as he did he pulled her up. Her head lolled back and he felt a small breath on his cheek. He froze, there was a second, then a third.

"She's breathing," he said quickly, his heart pounding harder.

There's still time, she won't die here.

"Marina!" Ferday screamed looking around. "Someone bring Marina!"

It only took a minute for a young woman a little older than Jewel to run up with a large bag. She had short hair the same color as Jewels and dark blue eyes. She looked similar to Jewel, but not quite the same. She was taller and not as thin, but still muscular.

She knelt and opened her bag. "Is it straight through?" She asked Pendry.

"Yes," he said, pulling his shaking hand away. It was covered in her gold flecked blood.

"Right, you two get her armor off." She said, pulling on some strange gloves.

Ferday helped him unbuckle her armor and gently removed it. Marina peeled up Jewel's shirt to reveal a nasty gash about 4 inches wide.

Pendry winced and felt sick at the sight of it. *That's really bad.*

She pulled out a bottle of something and squeezed it into the wound. Then packed on some gauze and taped it down. "Roll her over so I can get the other side."

Pendry pulled her up towards himself, exposing her back. "I don't-" He started to say.

"That's good, I just need to bandage it," Marina said, packing gauze on it and taping it down. "Lift her up so I can wrap it and make it secure."

Pendry did as he was told and watched as she wrapped Jewel's waist with a roll of bandages. Blood started soaking through before she had finished.

Marina threw her supplies into her bag then stood. "Bring that stretcher here," she called to two people standing nearby.

They came over and laid the stretcher down. Pendry laid her on it and watched them carry her off with Marina leading.

He felt as if a part of him was on the brink of death, he wanted to scream, to cry. But he just stared after them.

I wanted to tell her, he thought, *I wanted to tell her after the battle, but...* No, he told himself, *there's still time. She won't die.*

He looked down at his blood soaked pants and armor. He felt sick, seeing so much of her blood on him.

He heard a noise and turned. There, sitting on the ground, was Ferday. He was weeping into his hands. He looked like he was ready to crumble. Pendry walked over and sat next to him.

They didn't say anything, Pendry watched as the peace officers rounded up the remaining King's Guard and led them off to a holding place. He saw others being carried away on stretchers, some with sheets over them.

He'd never felt so numb and so lost.

"Is she gone?"

He looked up to see Ferga standing over him. He was battered and had a small wound on his cheek. He was looking at Ferday, who was still weeping.

"No," Pendry said softly. "But it didn't look good."

Ferga sat down next to him and sighed. "Good, if she's still with us she can still make it." He paused, "What was it?"

"She was stabbed through with a sword," Pendry said shakily, he could feel tears starting to run down his cheeks and a lump forming in his throat.

"Ferday was the one who saw the wall fall on her and was the one who dragged her out," Ferga said eyeing his cousin. "He was also there when she took that arrow to the chest. She actually took it for him."

Pendry looked at Ferday, who had stopped weeping. He was trembling and crying softly.

Ferga continued, "The arrow should have killed her, but her heart, as it turns out, isn't where it should be. It's slightly off to the right instead of the left." He took a deep breath, "And the reason the wall didn't kill her is she's so small that she was protected by a stone that covered her. She was still gravely injured by both, but it's almost like she can't help but survive."

"Did we win?" Pendry asked after a moment of silence.

"Yes, we won the battle for the outer ring. It will be harder to win the inner ring. They'll know we're coming and have time to prepare." Ferga cleared his throat and continued. "Our allies should be here before the month is out. The King has allies but not as many, not anymore."

Pendry nodded, still staring off into space.

"I noticed some of your peace officers helped us. I'm assuming that was your doing."

He smiled weakly. "Yeah, they have a similar code. Uphold peace and order, to protect those who can't protect themselves."

"I hope more of them join our cause."

The three of them sat in silence for a while. Pendry wasn't sure exactly how long they actually sat there, but none of them seemed to mind.

"She'll live."

He looked up to see Lavender standing in front of him. Her face was puffy and her eyes were red like she'd been crying.

Ferday choked and cried. "Thank you."

Pendry looked around them and realized it was growing late and the street lights were being lit.

"Can..." he hesitated.

"She's not awake yet," Lavender said, anticipating his question. "You should all come in and get tended to and cleaned up."

Ferga stood first. He sheathed his sword and picked up Firebloom from where Pendry had dropped it and handed it to him. "Come on, let's get you in some clean clothes and tend to your wounds."

Pendry took the sword and stood. His pants were stiff with the dried blood. His skin crawled at the feeling of it. He didn't know what wounds Ferga was talking about, but he was ready to get new clothes and clean the blood off.

Ferga helped Ferday to his feet. "Enough blubbering, she'll live."

Ferday dried his eyes on his sleeve. "I wasn't blubbering," he choked out. "I was mourning a loss before it happened. There's a difference." He sniffed and hugged Lavender. "Thank you for the news, Lav. Now help me to the sick bay. I think I've twisted or sprained my ankle."

Pendry followed the two, Ferday hobbling and Lavender fussing over his small scrapes.

Ferga wasn't with them. He'd gone to see that there were guards posted and that the outer ring was secured. They hobbled along to a door in the wall.

Gardenias and lilacs, Pendry thought. *I'll have to see if I can get her some. Not sure if they're in season, but I can at least try.* He smiled to himself. He finally fully understood why he kept thinking of that and what he wanted to say to her.

30

Pendry

Pendry sat in a chair in front of the fire in the dining room after breakfast. He'd showered and changed into some clean clothes the night before. He'd been tempted to burn the blood-caked clothes but decided since they were Ferga's, he'd let him decide, and set them aside for now. None of his injuries were so severe to take him to sick bay. He had a small cut starting from his ear across his cheek. The cut on his arm from the mission had reopened but wasn't too bad. Overall, he'd come out relatively unharmed.

He felt better after a night of sleep and being cleaned up, but at the same time he felt unsure. He'd felt sure when his adrenaline was still pumping, but now as he sat staring into the fire, he felt conflicted. Maybe he didn't know what that feeling really was, and if it was what he thought, what if she didn't feel the same way? He'd never dealt with a situation like this before.

How do you tell someone? Do you just say it?

Lavender walked over and sat down in the chair next to him. "She's awake now, if you want to go see her." She sounded worried.

His heart started pounding. Part of him wanted to jump up and run to sick bay, but the other part of him felt hesitant.

What if she doesn't want to see me? What if she's angry at me for not being there to protect her?

Lavender touched his arm breaking his trance with the fire. "Did you hear me? She's awake."

He nodded, but still didn't move.

"I've seen how you look at her. I think she feels the same." She said softly, "Is there anything I can help with?"

He furrowed his brow. Ferday had said something similar earlier. "No," he said softly, "just working up the nerve to go and see her. It's-" he took a deep breath, "that wasn't easy to see."

She nodded, "I can go with you if you'd like."

He smiled, "You really are tougher than the rest of us." He stood slowly. "Yeah, I think I would like that."

She stood with him and put her hands in her apron pockets. "Oh, it helps to have a higher power to turn to. Come on, I'll show you the way to sick bay."

He followed her down the hall feeling sheepish and nervous.

"Oh," he said blushing, "your grandma said her favorite flowers are gardenias and lilacs. Do you know if those are in season and where I could get some?"

She smirked at him. "They aren't in season but I do know her favorite early spring flowers, if you want to bring her some?"

"Maybe later. Let's just go there for now," he said, rubbing his neck.

I'll have to think of something else.

He followed her down the passages to a side of the headquarters he hadn't been to. They entered a large room that was sectioned off with dividers. He could hear Ferday joking and laughing with someone, then he heard Jewel laugh softly.

Lavender pushed aside one of the dividers and there they were. Ferday sitting with his ankle wrapped and a crutch leaning against his chair. And Jewel lying on her side in the bed looking very pale and worn. Her green eyes were shining and she was smiling.

Pendry's heart skipped in his chest, and he felt that rush of emotion, almost like adrenaline.

They turned to look at Pendry.

"Ah, there he is," Ferday said standing, "the man who turned the tide and helped us win the day."

"What?" he asked, confused.

Jewel smiled softly. "Day was just telling me how you got the peace officers to join us and that was what helped us win."

He'd forgotten about that. He was so worried and focused on Jewel that he'd simply pushed everything else aside.

"Oh, right." He smiled, "I... it..." he seemed to be struggling to talk suddenly. "They were ready to help, just didn't know the full truth."

Ferday squinted at him, "You don't give yourself enough credit. Take the win." He hobbled over on his crutch and leaned in to whisper in Pendry's ear. "Don't hesitate to make your move." He stood back and winked at him. "Lavender my dear, would you help me get to the dining room; I feel as if I haven't eaten in a week."

"Didn't you just eat?" she said laughing as she took his arm. "Are you ever full?"

"Never, my favorite baby sister."

They walked off arm in arm, Lavender turning to close the divider behind them.

Pendry turned back to Jewel who was still smiling softly. He walked over and sat in the chair next to her bed.

"I thought you, I was afraid you'd..." He couldn't bring himself to say it. He looked down at the floor, his hand resting on her bed.

How on earth can I tell her when I can't even talk?

He felt something soft and looked up to see her holding his hand; she squeezed it gently. He looked at her hand for a moment, so small and soft, compared to his large rough hand. He looked up at her. Her eyes seemed to dance even though they looked tired.

"I'm fine. I'll be here for a few days, but I'm fine," she said quietly.

He scooted his chair closer to the bed, folded his arms on it, and laid his head on them, still holding her hand, and gazed at her.

She's beautiful. How did I take so long to realize that I... how could I not?

He stayed like that for a while, just holding her hand and watching her breathe. It was comforting to see her breathing after seeing her almost die. He watched her eyes slowly close as she fell asleep. She was still holding his hand. He made himself comfortable and fell asleep with his head on her bed.

He felt her stirring as he woke up. She rolled slightly and he sat up to give her room to move. She groaned as her eyes flickered open. She smiled at him, then moved like she was trying to sit up.

He jumped up and helped her sit up, situating her pillows to help support her. He sat on the side of the bed still fluffing the pillows when he felt her hand touch his cheek.

"You're hurt, is it bad?" She asked as she looked at his cheek.

He sat back a little and felt his cheek where she'd touched. He felt the small taped up cut on his cheek. It was small enough that he'd forgotten it was there. He hadn't even noticed when he'd gotten it during the fighting.

"This is nothing. Just a scratch, nothing serious, not compared to what you had." He smiled, "Don't worry about me."

"And what if I want to worry about you?" She asked, leaning her head back. "Not much you can do about that."

"Only if I get to worry about you," he said smiling. She seemed to be doing better.

She laughed quietly, and winced at the pain. "Fine, but you need to stop looking at me like I might die at any moment. I really am better."

"The last I saw you, you were bleeding out in my arms." He flinched slightly at the memory of all that blood covering him. "Sorry if I'm still hung up on it."

"Well, as you can see, I'm very much alive and not bleeding to death." She fiddled with her blanket. "Thank you, for being there. That's twice you've rescued me."

"I wouldn't call either of those rescuing," he chuckled. "The first time, I was captured with you; the second, I just caught you before you were injured more. In any case, you've rescued me twice."

"Oh, well, if we're even, then I guess I don't need to stick around here once I'm healed." She smiled that mischievous smile.

He had a sudden urge; he almost pushed it down but decided that now was not the time for that. He leaned forward and kissed her.

He pulled back slightly and started to say sorry, when she gently cupped his face, pulled him in and kissed him back.

He thought his chest would explode. He wrapped one arm around her and pulled her close to himself. He didn't want it to end, he wanted to stay in that moment forever, where she was kissing him and he was holding her close.

She pulled away still holding his face. "Ow," she muttered half laughing.

"Sorry," he said, starting to let go.

"It's fine, just not so tight." She rested her forehead against his.

They sat like that for a moment, then Pendry heard voices and decided he should get up. He kissed her once more, then set her back gently before he stood.

She seemed to have more color and her eyes glittered. She let her hands rest on her stomach. With her hair down and spread across the bed she reminded him of a painting of a princess he'd seen.

He sat back in the chair as someone opened the divider. It was Ferga. He had the same tape on his face to close his gash.

"You're up. Perfect." He bellowed and clapped his hands. Then he walked over and kissed Jewel's forehead. "No more fighting for you. As soon as you're better, I'll help you back to your cabin." He turned to Pendry. "I have need of you. The peace officers say they'll join us against the King, but they want to hear from you about everything."

Pendry glanced at Jewel. He didn't want to leave, but he wanted to help.

She nodded to him as if she was telling him to go. She smiled and settled back into her pillows. She wasn't going anywhere yet. He could come back later.

He stood and nodded to her, then he and Ferga left. He glanced back and saw Jewel had closed her eyes. She looked so peaceful and beautiful; it was hard to believe that only the day before she was bleeding out from a stab wound. But there she was, safe and resting, and he'd kissed her. More importantly, she'd kissed him.

31

Jewel

Jewel woke to Lavender setting a tray of food on the table next to her bed. There were flowers in a vase of water on the table: beautiful gold and white flowers.

"How are you feeling?" Lavender asked, sitting on the bed.

"Ok. Probably as ok as I can feel after an injury like that," she said, sighing. Had she dreamed of Pendry kissing her? No, she didn't have dreams like that. Only nightmares or jumbles of random things. But that couldn't have happened. She felt that rush of emotions at the memory, making her heart flutter and her stomach twist.

The divider was pushed aside and Marina walked in.

"Oh good, I like seeing you awake. I like seeing you resting too, but awake means you can eat," she said, walking to the bed and setting down a bag of medical supplies on a nearby chair. "And Lav brought you food. Let me change your dressings, then you can eat more comfortably."

She pulled down the blankets gently, and unbuttoned the bottom of the large sickbay shirt that Jewel was wearing. Marina was so gentle with her hands; she'd always liked helping people so it had made sense to Jewel when she'd decided to be a medic.

She peeled off the bandage on Jewel's stomach and examined the stitches. "Looks good. It's fully healed closed, but you should stay in bed until tomorrow at least, that way it won't reopen." She applied some ointment that felt cold as ice, then she applied a new bandage. "Right, Lav can you help her roll over so I can check the one on her back?" It was a question but she said it like a command.

They rolled her onto her side and she felt Marina changing her dressing.

"It's a good thing the sword missed your spine, not that it wouldn't have healed but you had a rough time with that after the wall. This should heal much faster without any bone injury." She took a deep breath, "So," she said in a drawn out, singsong voice. "Was that Pendry I've heard so much about?"

Jewel looked at Lavender and saw her smirking. "When?" she asked Marina.

"When you were injured, he was the one holding you right?"

Jewel could hear the smirk in her sister's voice. "Um, I think so, I'm not sure." That wasn't true, she remembered him catching her, and he'd said he caught her.

Lavender nodded, "That was him. He's handsome isn't he?" she said giggling.

"Very, I can see why you like him." Marina finished the bandage and helped Jewel roll back and sit up against her pillows.

Both sisters sat on either side of her bed.

"So?" Marina asked, leaning forward.

Yes, Marina was gentle with her hands and caring of others, but she was also the one who was most ready to talk about guys and romance. It didn't help that she had no shame about any conversation.

Jewel could feel herself blushing. *Oh they're going to know.*

"I knew it," squeaked Lavender. "Ugh, he's been gazing at you like he, well, I don't know what, but I could tell just by how he looked at you that he's head over heels for you."

Jewel covered her face with her hands. Her face felt hot and she couldn't help but smile. He had been looking at her funny for the past few days.

Boy am I blind.

"So?" Marina asked again giggling. "You obviously like him. Have you told him?"

"Stop hiding your face." Lavender said, slapping playfully at her hands. "I want to see that love sick grin of yours."

"Oh." Marina gasped. "Did he kiss you?"

Lavender gasped, both sisters leaned in closer.

Jewel couldn't stop the laugh that bubbled out. There was no point in trying to hide anything from them, they knew her too well.

"Eek!" They both squealed. And leaned in even closer, practically laying on her lap at this point.

"Tell me everything," Marina said, pursing her lips, eyes dancing.

"Wait, she needs food." Lavender said, "And you have patients to attend to."

"Ugh. Fine," Marina said, standing and sulking. "But don't you tell her a thing without me. I'll be back to hear everything after I've tended to my other patients," she glared at them before turning and marching out.

Not much happened for Jewel that day. She had several people come and see how she was doing. Her mom stopped by and did her hair and told her how worried she was. But she had trouble paying attention to anything. She waited to see if Pendry would come back, but he must have been extra busy with the peace officers.

She rested in bed the whole day and got permission from Marina to leave sickbay the next day, on the condition that she use a wheelchair and not do any standing or walking. Marina had bribed her with leaving sick bay in exchange for her telling her everything.

They're having too much fun teasing me.

The next day Lavender pushed her wheelchair to the dining room. Jewel felt more comfortable now that she was dressed in her own skirt and sweater. She had a blanket bundled around her to help keep her warm. She'd suffered so much blood loss that she was struggling to keep warm.

"I made sure today we would have some of your favorites, and I want you to eat as much as you can stand," Lavender was saying as they neared the door.

Ferga was just opening the door when they turned the corner. He waited for them and held the door.

"Glad to see you up and about," he said beaming at her.

"Glad to be out," she replied smiling.

They entered the dining area and she saw Ferday and Pendry sitting at the table talking. Her chest grew tight when she saw Pendry. He was smiling and talking with Ferday about something, but she didn't catch what it was.

They turned, noticed them entering and jumped to their feet.

"Ouch, blasted ankle," Ferday said as he clutched at Pendry's shoulder. "You go give her my kiss would you?" Pendry blushed, but didn't move.

"Ferday sit down; I'm happy to see you, but there's no kiss needed," she said as Lavender pushed her up to the table.

They all sat down and looked like they'd relaxed a little.

"I see Marina is keeping you immobile," Ferday said grimacing as he rubbed his ankle. "She threatened to keep me in a wheelchair. Thankfully, I convinced her to go with the crutch."

"That wasn't how I heard it," Lavender retorted. "Marina told me you hammed up your ankle pain trying to get a wheelchair. You'll be fine in another day or so, you big baby."

Jewel was trying to listen to what they were saying but she felt someone looking at her. It was Pendry giving her that look again. *How did I not see it before?* She thought, feeling herself blush slightly.

"Right. Well, Ferday, we'll be having a meeting to plan the attack for the inner ring after you've eaten. And you two," Ferga said pointing at Pendry and Jewel, "you two are to rest. Pendry thank you again for helping get things situated with the peace officers. If you're up for it, I'd like you to fight in the attack for the inner ring, but Jewel, you're done fighting. I'm not pushing your luck any farther than we have."

Jewel smiled, she didn't feel like fighting anymore. She leaned back in her wheelchair feeling content to just be there for a while. *This is nice, resting and being near friends and family,* she was happy with this.

32

Jewel

Jewel sat in front of the fire with a cup of tea. She'd eaten and decided to stay in the dining room and watch the fire. She finally felt warm, and not like she might start shivering any second. She wasn't sure where everyone had left to, but it felt good to be alone with her thoughts and warm with her tea. She no longer had any thought of dying. In fact, for the first time, she was planning what life might look like with her actually living.

She thought about Greta and her boys, and about her cabin. She wondered if it was time to make it a little more permanent and plant a garden. She thought about the conversation she'd had with Pendry about someone living with her at the cabin. She liked the thought of that. She could picture life at the cabin with Pendry, sitting on the porch together or in the parlor. Yes, that sounded like a life she'd enjoy living.

She thought about the first time they'd talked. She really had been rude, although she hadn't trusted him. What had happened in the past week or so that had made her trust him entirely? Sometime on their journey in, they had become friends. And sometime after the mission, it had changed for her. She'd never trusted anyone so much, unless they were family. Everyone in her family had trusted Pendry the moment they saw him. What had they seen that she hadn't seen at first?

She heard the door open and saw Pendry walk in. He had on a pair of glasses that looked just right, and made it feel as if he'd been missing them this whole time rather than just having gotten them. There was something in his hands, but she couldn't quite tell what it was.

He walked over to her and stood a little awkwardly.

She smiled up at him. She'd always had to look up at him, but from the wheelchair she had to lean her head back to see him.

"Hello. I like the glasses. They look good."

He sat in one of the chairs and leaned forward. He looked nervous and like he was trying to focus. He didn't acknowledge that she'd said anything. "I— I wanted to talk to you earlier, but I wasn't sure what to say."

He was blushing; his glasses had slid down his nose a little. Jewel reached out and pushed them up gently. "That's ok, I think I understand."

"Well, I," he paused, "I have something for you." He held out his hand and in it was a delicate necklace. It had a slender silver chain with a green glittering stone wrapped in silver. There were two flowers made out of silver wrapping around the stone: a gardenia and a lilac.

"Oh," she said, touching it gently, "it's beautiful! Is that..."

"It's the rock I picked up in the woods." He smiled his crooked smile. "I would have been to see you again yesterday, but I asked Ferday if he knew anyone who could help me with this and it took the rest of the day. It wasn't done until a little while ago." He stood and helped her put it on.

"Thank you, I love it." She looked down at it around her neck. "How did you know my favorite flowers?"

He smiled as he knelt beside her. "Your grandmother told me after you left. I was going to get you some real ones, but they aren't in season."

"This is better," she said, gently caressing the smooth green stone. That had been the moment they became friends; when she'd teased him about the stone.

He took her hand in his and looked at it fondly. "I was wondering if you'd thought about what we'd talked about the other night? If you'd like to have someone at the cabin with you?"

"Is that your idea of asking me to be with you?" she said playfully.

He looked back up at her smiling. It was crooked, and probably her favorite smile. "Well, do you? Do you want me to be with you?" He had that same look he'd been giving her. A longing and wistful look.

"I think the more important question is do you? And if yes, why?" She said it playfully but she really wanted and needed to hear him say it. She could feel his pulse pounding through his hand. Hers was pounding just as hard.

"Jewel," his smile grew. "I love you and I want to be with you. Do you want to be with me?"

She leaned forward and kissed his forehead. "Yes," she whispered.

He cupped her face in his hands and kissed her, making her chest feel tight and breathless.

"Haha! Yes!" They turned to see Ferday teetering on his crutch and slapping Ferga on the shoulder. Ferga was grinning from ear to ear. She hadn't heard them come in. How long had they been there? Did she care? No, she decided, she didn't care.

Neither did Pendry; when she turned back to him, he kissed her again.

Pronunciation Guide

Names:
  Ferday (Fair-day)
  Ferga (Fur-guh)
  Pendry (Pen-dree)
  Gradiare (Grah-dee-air)
Things:
  katshme (Kat-shMee)
  crestym (Krest-yim)
Creatures:
  grawn wrathe (Gron) (raith)
  evnton wrathe (Ev-tun) (raith)
  waren cat (wAren) (Kat)
  faie (Fay)
  yaksme (yaK-shmee)
  lionton (Lyon-Ton)
Places:
  Leanna (Lee-ana)
  Hamndle (ham-nDel)
  Kevka (KevKah)
  Trenten (tren-Ten)

Hannah Baribeau was born in Astoria Oregon, grew up in Indonesia, and currently lives in Wisconsin. Writing has always been a passion, and crafting worlds and stories has been something she has always loved. Traveling around the world and learning different cultures and traditions from a young age cemented her love of telling and listening to stories. When not writing, she is the stay at home mom of 4 young boys. Needless to say, life is and has always been an adventure for Hannah. *Gradiare* is her first publication, with plans of many more to come. To follow along on her progress find her author page on instagram (@baribookly).